WARRIOR SAINTS - VICTOR
STONEHAVEN ACADEMY SAINTS BOOK 3

CARLA THORNE

CHAPTER 1

Shanar

Neutralized.

A beautiful word—especially where Mary was concerned.

Mary Antonia Hunter had been neutralized.

I couldn't stop saying it to myself as I followed my Agent's slick new car toward his home.

Neutralized... Neutralized...

I'd have preferred the word *dead*...

But we were getting there.

And that stupid angel, Sebastian, couldn't have done a better job of dropping the ball when those three kids were splattered against that mountainside.

What kind of being for the Creator leaves the scene?

Note to self: Find out why the being for the Creator left the scene... something may be up with that.

I slipped my dark, supernatural form into my Agent's—

Gavin's—car. I thought that little chunk of feces would be so scared he'd drive off the road.

He carefully pulled over and rolled to a stop in the grass instead.

He'd used his blinker.

"Nice ride," I said. "You're welcome."

"What took you so long? It's been months since the accident."

"Excuse me? I was doing a victory lap around the realm and letting the earthly dust settle. I do have other work, you know. You're not the only putrid sac of bile I have to boss around. Now, about Mary."

"Don't worry about Mary."

"Really? Because I am worried about her. I did come to congratulate you on your work with Jacob, but, I mean, it wasn't exactly what you were supposed to do. It was a start. Mary is completely paralyzed with guilt and grief. She should be dead, but there's still time for that."

"I'm taking care of it."

I laughed.

He turned in his seat as if he could somehow look into my eyes and stare me down. Everything about his threatening demeanor—while pleasantly refreshing—was lost on me. Who did he think he was talking to?

"I thought you were gone." He sneered. "I thou—"

"What did you think, you ridiculous scrap-pile of human cells? That I'd forget you didn't actually carry out the job I gave you?"

"Dealing with Mary is going to take time. I barely got away in Colorado. Someone could still find out. They haven't given up trying."

"Yeah, whatever. I'm helping to keep your crimes concealed."

"Well, stay out of my way. I'm taking care of it, and then you're going to leave me alone."

I fashioned my form into phantom arms and circled his chest.

I squeezed.

"Look, boy, are you going to sit here and act like you can tell me what to do? I rule everything in your immediate atmosphere. I decide what you have and don't have. I decide, you hear me?"

He struggled to get free.

I squeezed harder. "Did you really think you could buck up against me with your newfound confidence and somehow you'd be in charge of this situation? Because here's the thing. I still want Mary, and because you so completely failed to deliver her to me on the mountain, I'm going to make you keep trying until you do."

"I told you I'd take care of it."

"I don't want your promises. I want results."

"And I told you, you'll get what you want when you get it."

"Are you really this stupid, boy? Are you trying to just tell me what I want to hear, all the while harboring some fantasy you'll still end up with Mary? Things will never be right with you and Mary. We had a deal, and you have reached the point of no return with your collateral damage incident with the death of that other kid. The thing is, there's blood on your hands. I can smell it... I can taste it." I cracked his rib. "And I can expose you at any moment, and the whole world will know you ran your friends off the side of a ski slope."

He gasped for air. "You don't scare me. I know what I've done."

"And I know what *I've* done. You wanted sex, nice things, football success... I've taken care of it all, and you will take care of Mary for me."

He grunted. "Stonehaven Academy is barely standing. That has only made my work more difficult. And how am I supposed to accomplish anything or play ball if you keep causing me unexplained injuries? Haven't you read your *Villain Handbook*? Who's the stupid one here? I can't work if you keep slowing me down."

I almost pinched his ridiculous fat head off his ridiculous bag-of-bones body.

But he might have been on to something.

Nah... He only ticked me off. I squeezed until he came close to passing out.

"Don't ever think for one minute, boy, that you in any way have any power or persuasion over me. You understand? You'll be fine as long as you keep doing what I say."

He managed to squeak out a couple words as he neared passing out.

"What's that, boy? I didn't hear you."

"Go to hell."

The last bit of air left his lungs.

"See you there. And bring Mary."

CHAPTER 2

Ivy

My Aunt Connie had a ladder in her closet.

It was an actual ladder that moved from shelf-to-shelf, kinda like the ones in old, dusty libraries. Her badge of excess—the high-ceilinged, extra-tall, and extra-large closet—stopped me in my tracks every time I saw it.

Especially when I wasn't supposed to be there and was snooping for clues about my father. It was an overwhelming task, given I had to search in and under designer purse drawstring storage bags, and in sweater boxes, shoe boxes, and regular boxes for any sign of pictures or documents she might be holding that would explain my newly-discovered dad.

I'd walked right past the housekeeper when my aunt left the house, and rushed to the master bedroom. Despite the fact her knob of a husband had the place under the constant lens of security cameras, I knew there was no surveillance in the closet

—which was ironically ignorant because that's where the bulk of Aunt Connie's most valuable possessions resided.

Meanwhile, Scout played look-out in his car at the end of the long driveway and out of sight. He was supposed to text if Aunt Connie came back, and I was supposed to leave as nonchalantly as I'd come in, as if I just stopped by for a visit. I was there all the time. Who would care or notice?

I picked my way through several neatly stacked boxes and flipped through everything from clothing receipts to old term papers Aunt Connie and her husband wrote in college. For a couple who'd gone almost completely paperless, they had an awful lot of useless folders. One contained manuals for appliances that had died when I was in grade school.

The boxes of mementos were in full view. Faded ticket stubs from concerts and movies were scattered in the bottom like the puzzle pieces of some happy young college girl's social life. Barrettes and ponytail holders rested on photographs and school musical programs.

And there was my mom with Aunt Connie's protective arm around her shoulder.

Connie appeared to be having fun. My mom was not.

I hated that my mission to discover the truth about my father would likely derail my mother's stable existence. She'd come so far and accomplished so much. She worked, stayed on her meds, and moved forward. If she knew some stalker had cornered me on the stairs with a story about being my long-lost dad, she'd have torn him limb-from-limb and likely been triggered into some kind of mental health spiral.

I glanced at the picture of the sisters as Pink Ladies in *Grease* during high school. There was that and a whole box of ones like it from over the years, but not one picture was of my mom when she was pregnant or when I was born.

And there was no trace of anything related to my birth or the man on the stairs.

If it was that big of a secret, there had to be a reason.

My phone chimed as I moved the ladder.

Abort! Abort! Connie's home.

Dramatic much? I texted back. But thx. OMW.

I grabbed two apples from the fruit bowl as I slipped past the kitchen and out the back door. I smiled and waved at the camera. Aunt Connie didn't bother with the alerts on her phone, and her husband wouldn't blink because he'd seen me do that a thousand times. I ducked into the shrubs and headed to the road.

Scout's car was cool inside after my jog and brush-hurdling across the lawn.

Recent April showers had brought nothing but steamy humidity, and those mortifying cold days of winter and Jacob's death moved at a torturous snail's pace into the smothering, grief-stricken heat of spring and summer.

Scout took the apple I offered. "Nothing?"

"Nothing."

"You really didn't expect to find anything, did you?"

"No. They've kept this secret for years. They had to know I'd press for more info at some point. I'm sure they have a story ready."

"But you haven't pressed them for more info. You've only been snooping around for months. They have no idea your possible father reappeared."

I twisted in the seat and bit into my own apple. "You know that's because of my mom's mental illness. I don't want to get her riled up over nothing."

"This isn't nothing. We have zero answers about a possibly evil electrician who may or may not be your dad and may or may not have almost killed people in fires at Stonehaven." He slammed the car into drive and pulled onto the road in the direction Aunt Connie could least likely see from her house. "And he knows where you live!" His voice got louder. "He could be watching us right now."

"Hey, Scout?"

"Yes?"

"Don't drive angry."

The car slowed. "I'm not angry. I'm concerned. We've done all this research and I've hacked into everything I can hack in to and the guy's a ghost."

"That's because he's former military. Records are limited." I scrolled through the notes on my phone. "OK. One more time. He wasn't married to my mom, and he isn't on my birth certificate. He was active duty when I was born, so I have no idea whether he was there or not or what the status of their relationship was."

"But Aunt Connie would know all that and you could ask her without involving your mom, but *nooooo*, let's not do that."

"And." I ignored Scout's sarcasm. "His training as a US Marine more than lines up with his skills as an electrician and a person who could design and detonate whatever was in the scoreboard—*if* he had anything to do with that."

Scout glanced my way. "And your gut tells you he probably did."

I didn't answer either way.

I reached across the seat and pushed a curl of hair off of Scout's forehead. "The thing I keep coming back to is my stupid middle name. Why would a new mom who didn't have anything to do with her baby's father let him give me his mother's name? He made a point to tell me that. Like it was proof of something."

"Or maybe he saw the public record of your birth and made something up because he's a criminal and is stalking you."

I snapped my mouth closed. Scout had a point. He always had a point, and it was the same point and the same conversation we'd been having for weeks.

I'd always wanted to know about my father. What if he'd finally come for me?

"I don't want you to be disappointed, Ivy, and I sure as heck don't want you hurt. We've had enough pain for a lifetime. Just talk to your Aunt Connie."

"I'm not ready for that yet."

"What if he isn't your father, and we've wasted all this time investigating while he's a criminal and running around loose?"

"And what if he is my father and wants to have a relationship with me?"

"There's nothing I want more for you, but the unknowns far outweigh the knowns."

I pulled a small piece of paper out of my bag. "Then we need more knowns. You know what that means." I waved the paper in the air.

He pulled into the temporary student parking lot at the school and took the first space he saw.

He turned my way with a stern glare. "No."

"We have to, Scout. We've done everything else."

"Everything but talk to the two people who have answers."

"I can't do that! I don't want to get everyone worked up if it turns out to be nothing."

"And what if it turns out to be something? How are you going to explain it to your mom, your aunt, the police, your friends—besides Deacon and Mary who already know? How are you going to tell everyone this guy approached you in a stairwell and that you kept it all a secret? Especially if he turns out to be a liar? Have you considered what it means if he's not your father? Why would he tell you that? What's his end game?"

"I'm just going to text him and ask him to meet me in a public place so I can get more information."

Scout pinched the bridge of his nose. "I wish you wouldn't. Not without S.W.A.T. backup or something."

"Don't worry, Scout, you're my backup. And Deacon and Mary too. I'm not afraid. I have my Warriors."

"Oh, trust me, Deacon and I will be there, but I'm not sure

about Mary. She's still not herself, and I think she would tell you this is a bad idea."

I tugged my backpack out of the back seat and closed the door. "I don't see Mary's car. Do you think she'll come?"

"She has to check in at the S.A.I.N.T. Lab every Tuesday and Thursday like every other displaced student. Today's the day."

Sadness overwhelmed me every time I thought of Mary. The injuries, the loss...the total devastation that was her new normal.

Scout too. I often wondered how long it took him to be able to even stand up after the loss of his family. Didn't we all have a right to be well and find happiness? And I always had questions about my dad, even when my mom and Aunt Connie so completely and casually continued to sweep him under the rug my whole life.

But fathers existed—and I wanted mine.

"Ivy? You OK?"

Scout wasn't going to be happy.

"I'm fine." I glanced at the slip of paper and tapped out a text.

"Please don't do that yet," he pleaded.

I hit send. "Sorry, Scout, I have to. It's time I had a dad."

"But you—"

"Yes, I know. I don't even know if I have one now." I checked my phone. "But we're meeting former Marine, Reed Logan, at the smoothie place on Friday at four-thirty. And he's either going to be the real and wonderful dad I never had or—I'll admit it—an imposter and attempted murderer."

CHAPTER 3

Deacon

I spotted Scout and Ivy from the place my mom dropped me off. "This way," I called out. "They moved the sidewalk again."

Ivy stomped around the yellow netting. "When will this end?"

"When they have all the school back together, I guess."

"I hate this," she said.

I shrugged. "Except for the whole part about us having trauma from the first small fire in the Saints Café, and major trauma from the Stonehaven Gym Fire…"

"Not to mention the rest of the trauma from the ski trip and that half the upper school burned down," Scout added.

"Right. Except for all that, I like the idea of online classes."

"I do too," Scout said. "I have two tests in the testing center today. If I pass, I'll already be halfway through my junior year."

Ivy looked concerned. "I'm not as far ahead as Scout, but I'm catching up."

I shuffled along the dusty path. I didn't want to admit how far behind I was.

It wouldn't be impossible to gain ground, I just had to *apply myself*, according to my mom. I was the first to admit I hadn't been doing that.

The whole thing was a surreal joke the universe was playing on us. We wound our way through a curvy, broken sidewalk and stood in line to enter a freezing room with too many people and not enough computers. Our regular teachers marked us present, checked our work, and answered questions, while contractors worked outside at warp speed to rebuild what was left of our high school.

The good news was that I could sleep late and attend online class in my underwear three days a week. The bad news was that we were all fractured and couldn't heal because nothing was normal. We didn't put on a uniform and see the same people every day. We didn't interact at lunch and catch up. We didn't see our friends or avoid our enemies.

We weren't tight. We weren't Warriors. We weren't anything without Mary and a routine.

Ivy shielded her eyes from the sun and studied the plastic banner that was tied between the two columns in front of the library. "S.A.I.N.T. LAB. What does that stand for again?"

"Student Academic Individual Nurturing and Technology Lab," Scout said.

"That is so...*ridiculous*. Who was in charge of that acronym? Should be more like the *Stupidly Annoying Idiotic Not Teaching Lab*."

Scout laughed at her, then got serious. "Can I make an observation?"

"Speak your truth, bro," I said.

Ivy did a massive eyeroll, but she nodded.

"You're not mad because we have to come to this lab. You're mad because of *why* we have to come to this lab. If everything was back the way it was before the ski trip, you'd be loving this."

"No, I wouldn't."

"Yes, you would. Know why? Because we've been given an opportunity here. My grandparents went to the board meeting last night. All tuition has been greatly reduced or waived. All we have to do is pay the fees associated with the online curriculum—and even that's negotiable. Our teachers are available to chat online and answer questions every day. We come here and check in twice a week and take tests. All our extracurriculars still happen over at the lower school. And the best part? We can knock out these modules and level up at our own pace. We can graduate early. We can get jobs and work on our college essays and applications and we can move on."

Scout was right. I was gonna have to up my game. My parents already couldn't afford the tuition, and I was never going to get my own car with four brothers in the house who all needed to drive.

"He's right," I said. "Look around. This will never be the Stonehaven Academy where we spent our freshman year and half of our sophomore one together. This year's graduates are going to walk in the big Baptist church down the street because our auditorium is gone. Even if we stayed on a traditional schedule, everyone is fooling themselves if they think we'll be back in these halls as seniors and reap the benefits of a brand-new, state-of-the-art school. It's not going to happen."

Ivy's expression fell as she gazed across what used to be the peaceful brick path to the reflection garden. "I just didn't want to look back at my senior year and have it be this. Death, destruction, and devastation."

"No one wanted that," Scout said and put an arm around her. "But here we are, and we need to make the best of it."

"Let's do it," I said. "I'll get serious. We need to get it done before the board realizes they can't pay these teachers and counselors forever with no money coming in. The whole upper school will probably fold before they know what hit them."

Ivy still didn't look convinced. "What about Mary? She isn't even here at the required time. We can't do this without her. We need our team to stay together. It might help her."

Mary... Who knew what to do with Mary?

"We texted this morning," I said. "She'll be here. She's supposed to give me a ride home."

"I got you if she doesn't make it," Scout said.

"Nah. She'll make it, and I think she'll be on board with our plan of accelerated learning—if we can get her to sit still long enough and talk to us."

"That's the problem," Ivy said. "She's distancing herself from us and that's what scares me. She's so consumed with rage and grief that she has her inner Warrior all flipped around."

"She'll come around," Scout said. "It takes time."

Ivy rubbed her hand across his back. "I know you understand this, and I hope you're right."

Scout nodded.

"Do you think she's afraid she'll see Gavin?" Ivy asked.

I looked at the ground and kicked a misplaced landscaping rock off the sidewalk. "I don't know."

All my greatest fears for Mary were more about what she *wasn't* afraid of. She was out of control in her anger, and Gavin was her number one target. Why that piece of scum's parents dared to stay in town—let alone send him back to Stonehaven—was beyond my ability to make sense of it. Of course his parents believed every word he said, but they were the only ones. Rumors swirled about the timing of events on the day of the accident, and more than a few people questioned Gavin's participation.

I'd talked to Char for hours about how a Warrior in Mary's position was supposed to deal with her situation. No one had any answers, and no one wanted to sit by and watch Mary self-destruct into the very kind of being who'd caused her pain.

"I don't know," I said again. "But what about you and your uh... quest, Ivy? What's the latest?"

Scout smacked and then rubbed his forehead like he had a sudden migraine.

It felt like I'd stumbled into a fight between my mom and dad. "What's happening right now?"

"I'm moving my research to the next level," Ivy said.

"Oh yeah?"

"Yeah, and I need you."

"OK. What do you need?"

"I need you at the Smoothie Shack at four-thirty on Friday."

"Sure. What are we doing?"

"I'm meeting my dad, and you're my backup." She leaned in close. "*Warrior.*"

CHAPTER 4

Mary

It was three in the morning when he finally showed up.

I didn't really sleep a whole night anymore. Truth be told, between the occasional panic attacks from my childhood drowning trauma, and the torment from the evil resident in my personal spiritual realm, I hadn't slept a whole night in years.

Unless you counted the times I was injured or unconscious and medicated in the hospital.

I'd dozed off around one-thirty that night, and by three o'clock, Shanar's dark force had penetrated the protective shield the Creator and Sebastian provided for me.

I understood it all then.

Once I knew I was a Warrior, I knew my job was to complete assignments for the Creator. I knew he protected me, and I knew he sent Sebastian to help. I knew I had a team of dependable like-minded Warriors to fight by my side. I knew I exhibited supernatural gifts beyond what the average person comprehended. I knew all that and more. I knew I carried special, or magical, or enchanted-like particles in my body and in my spirit that had come from the angel, Sebastian, himself. And no, I didn't think it was the magic of casting spells and making potions.

It was the supernatural gifting of the Creator.

And yet...

Despite my efforts to do the right thing, live up to the demands of my gift, and acknowledge the Creator's presence in my life, I still had a fatal flaw.

I was human.

And in my ignorant, human anger, and with my weak human logic, I'd made a mistake.

One mistake.

And Jacob was dead.

Why hadn't I listened to him and Char on the mountain?

If only I had, and not let my egotistical and emotional self make the choice, he would still be alive.

So, there we were. Me half asleep, and Shanar showing up to torment me.

I was ready. I had to be, because there was only one way to make it right. I would use my gifts on the ones who took him from me.

There would be no justice in the world until Gavin and Shanar were gone.

I barely moved a muscle when Shanar shook my space. His dark, suffocating cloud pulsed around me in the opening steps of our usual dance. I declined his offer and steeled myself against the mounting pressure in the room.

Fight, flight, or freeze.

Usually, I came out swinging for my life and freedom like a cornered feral cat. No more.

"You don't seem surprised to see me," he said.

"Nothing you do surprises me anymore."

Shanar's presence shifted in the room. "Well, that's disappointing. Usually we're in an all-out battle by this time in my visit."

The stench of him reached my nostrils, and I would have gagged if my teeth hadn't been clenched so tight. At the same time, the comforting scent of frankincense wafted past my nose like a long-lost friend. I swept my gaze across the bottles on my nightstand. Scout's grandma kept me in essential oils as I healed both physically and emotionally, but not one bottle was open or had tipped over.

Sebastian was usually the source of the familiar scent, but he was definitely not in the room.

I sniffed the air. The scent came from…me?

I sat up against my headboard and reached for my cat, Paisley. Shanar sent curls of smoky darkness toward my face. They reached my space and drifted away, even as the cat hissed and scrambled under the bed.

"Awww, c'mon," he said. "You can't still be mad."

"You have no concept of my anger."

"But you're still scared, right?"

I got up and purposely turned my back on him to pick through the small bottles. "Not even a little bit." I dabbed a drop of frankincense and lavender on my wrists and then touched the angel charm on my bracelet.

Everything vibrated. Shanar wasn't happy, and I didn't care.

"You should go," I said. "I need sleep, and you're bothering my cat." I got in bed and patted the space beside me. "C'mon, Paisley, whatever this ugly thing is can't hurt us."

He attempted one more swelling show of force. His voice boomed so loud it rattled my chest and puffed my hair away from my face. For a dark supernatural being who could probably transform into anything, he had a hard time making his point in my dimly lit bedroom.

He tried, I assumed, to get in my face. The awful scent grew. "You've never truly been afraid of me. That's your weakness. You don't know when to back down. You don't know when you're really beat."

I examined each of my arms and touched my face. "Really? I'm alive and well, and you're about to be tossed from my realm —by me—so you should just concede this one. Like I said, I need my sleep."

He moved closer. "Something has changed."

I feigned surprise. "Ya think? You killed my Protector. My life-long mate. You and Gavin did that, and now you and Gavin will pay."

"Yeah, yeah, whatever, I look forward to that battle, but that's not what I mean. Something else is different."

There was a long pause as he seemed to contemplate the situation.

I crossed my arms. "You are profoundly stupid for a phony supreme being, you know that? I have no idea why I wasted so much time fighting with you when all I really needed to do was show you a math problem. My guess is you can't add two and two and make four. Is that right?"

Once again, his anger flared. "I have no use for human academics."

"And yet you responded to my question."

"What is with all you back-talking imbeciles this week?" He stilled. "I know what's happened. It's that angel of yours. Sebastian. He's gifted you with more power. Something happened on the mountain. That's why he left you there."

"The *something* that happened on that mountain is that you and Gavin killed Jacob."

"True... But what happened between you and Sebastian?

You're not supposed to possess any part of him, let alone gather more. What have you done, you feisty brat?"

"Leave my room," I commanded. I picked up my small mirror and checked on my new blue eye. Everyone thought it was a fluke and might change back. The doctors had no explanation, but everyone else had turned it into some sort of romantic urban legend. *She took on the color of her dead true love's eyes...* I dismissed the morbid thought, but had been waiting to see what would happen when I was once again in such close proximity of either Shanar or Sebastian.

I'd guessed right. It flashed brighter blue for a moment, and a surge of my own power grew until it physically pushed Shanar away.

That seemingly shocked the pee right out of him—if idiotic supernatural beings peed. He did seem quite surprised as his form inched toward my window.

I had gained strength from Sebastian and fueled it with my pain and anger. The combination had created a new and bigger force, and I knew in my heart Shanar would have to leave my realm.

I glared in his direction.

"This isn't over," he said.

"Sure it is. For now."

My farthest window shattered as his dark force left my room, and a gust of warm springtime air floated in.

As expected, my dad responded to the crash and the alarm within seconds.

"Mary!"

"I'm OK, Dad."

He flipped on the light and caught sight of the window. "What happened?"

He rushed to look, and paused only to search for glass at his bare feet. I knew there was none. It had flown outward.

"Branch or something?" he asked. "There's no wind." He

stepped away. "I'll go get something to cover that until I can fix it tomorrow."

"Thanks, Dad. You want some help?"

"No. Do you have any idea what it was?" He looked around. "I don't see anything."

I pulled my cat close and covered myself with my quilt. "I think an evil bird crashed through my window."

CHAPTER 5

Ivy

The day had finally come.

I tugged my jean shorts into place and adjusted my deep purple *Forever Jacob, Saints Football* in memoriam t-shirt. "I'll get a seat," I said to Scout.

"And I'll get your smoothie."

"I want the—"

"I got it, babe."

"You got what?"

"The strawberry-banana smoothie you want."

"You don't know everything about me, Scout White. Maybe I want something else today."

"Do you?"

My shoulders dropped. "No. Strawberry-banana, please. And stop smiling like that. You still don't know everything about me."

He paced like a nervous tiger at the zoo as he waited at the counter. He kept his eye on the door and didn't check if he got the right change back.

He put two drinks on the table.

"Did you try something new?" I asked.

"Nah." We sighed together as he sat down. "We're stuck in a rut. A smoothie rut. Next time let's try something new."

But then we both took a drink and smiled.

Scout laughed as he wiped his mouth. "Change is overrated."

Deacon stepped in the door like he was on a mission.

"He's loaded for bear," I said.

Scout snorted. "What? He's what?"

"It's an expression I picked up. It means he's spoilin' for a fight or something. I don't know."

The chair legs scraped the wood floor as Scout changed position to better face me. "I know what it means. Stop spending so much time with my grandpa while he's working in the garage. That old maniac scratches his ears with a rusty screwdriver and writes paper checks to pay bills. We have a landline."

"So? I like talking to him."

"He's messin with you, Ivy. He also likes to tell how morphine and heroin were available over-the-counter to his grandparents when he was a boy. That explains a lot right there."

"Stop it. And Deacon still looks like he's ready for a fight."

Deacon reached the table. "I am ready for a fight. I don't think this is a good idea."

"He might be my dad, Deacon."

"And he might not be. I only agreed to this because Warriors stick together, and I know he wasn't the one on the mountain with Jacob. But there's still a possibility he had everything to do with the chaos at Stonehaven. I don't trust him."

My heart sank. "Can you two give me some credit here? I'm keeping an open mind."

Scout flicked the paper from his straw across the table. "She's right. She knows better than anybody when something doesn't track."

Deacon grasped the back of an empty chair. "All right. Sorry, Ivy. Let's figure this guy out."

"Isn't Mary with you?"

"No. Haven't talked to her since our group text about school this morning. She'll be here. She said she had to drive herself."

"At least she's getting out and talking more." I nodded at the chair. "Sit down, Deacon."

"No, thanks. I'm going to sit over there by the front door and observe. If something goes down, I have some control from there."

My mouth dropped open. "You guys *really* don't like this."

Deacon leaned in against the chair. "Of course we don't like this. We're ten minutes away from an episode of some crime documentary. We're meeting a questionable adult who cornered you in a stairwell and may have tried to kill people."

"I only want to know my dad."

"I get that, but if I've learned anything from Char and this big supernatural war we're in, it's that nothing is normal or average or a coincidence. People have died because supernatural beings are trying to kill us—and they're using humans to do it, and we don't always see them coming." Deacon shut his mouth in a hurry and dipped his head. "Geez, Mary. Sorry you had to hear that."

"It's fine," she said in a calm tone. "I couldn't agree more."

I scanned the room. "Where'd you come from? I was watching the door. And why are you wearing a yellow Smoothie Shack…polo? Oh."

"Yeah. I came in the back."

"To report for work," Scout said.

She nodded.

"Good for you," I said.

"Well, I have to stay busy. Us not having a school is a blessing and a curse. On one hand, I don't think I could handle the routine of seeing everyone every day like nothing happened... Then I can't handle not having a routine place to go."

"I know what you mean," Scout said.

"And I'm totally on board with the study plan we made, so let's rock this thing and graduate and move on. Stonehaven's misfortune has propelled us into new possibilities."

I had to stand up and give her a hug. "I don't want to start myself crying or anything, but I'm proud of you, Mary. I like your good, positive attitude."

She shrugged. "I don't know if it's all that good, but...you know."

"We know," Deacon said.

"All right then. I'm going to clock in, and I'll be watching like a hawk from the counter. If that electrician steps out of line, or any one of my arm hairs stands up in alarm, I will totally end that guy with an industrial-sized blender."

Deacon looked like he wanted to laugh. I think we all did, but Mary kept her scowl in place.

"No," she said. "I'm not kidding. No one else is going to die—except for Gavin. He has to die for what he did to Jacob, and we're going to totally render Shanar incapable of hurting anyone, but I mean no more good guys are going to die. I'm going to do a better job of watching out for my team of Warriors."

I stared into her intense and sparkling blue and green eyes. "OK, Mary. We appreciate that. We're a team." I paused, but I had to get it out there. "Umm... I think we're completely within our rights to destroy Shanar. I think we're gifted to do that. But there's still a chance the investigators will prove Gavin was the cause of the accident. You're not a murderer, Mary."

She stepped back, stood straight, and crossed her arms.

Message received.

"OK," I said. "Too soon. I love you, Warrior. We're all in this together."

"Yes, we are." She nodded toward the door. "And I hope for that guy's sake—and for yours—he's a great guy and a wonderful father, because I meant what I said."

I dropped back into the chair as she walked away and didn't know who to look at first—Scout, Deacon, or the possible father coming my way. "She is not OK."

"Nope. She's filled with anger and vengeance right now," Scout said.

Deacon turned to head for his seat by the window. "And with all that emotion, her usual abilities, and the extra dose of angelic power and matter she's taken on… Well, we have ourselves one dangerous and ticked-off Warrior."

"What a combination," I said. "Head's up. This is happening."

Scout and I stood as Reed Logan approached the table.

Scout shook his hand. "Can I get you a smoothie?"

Man, I loved that boy. We were in the most awkward and perhaps dangerous of all positions—considering the possible commercial blender assault and all—and my guy was going to make sure a man he already disliked and distrusted was comfortable and had a smoothie if he wanted one.

For my sake.

"No, thank you," Reed said.

We all sat, and I looked into the same exact brown eyes as mine. Everyone said I looked like my mom, and they were right, but my eyes couldn't have been any more like Reed Logan's.

He smiled and scrubbed his hands across his jeans as if he were nervous.

I took a long drink of my smoothie and then pushed it aside with my cold fingertips.

I looked straight into my eye-twin's gaze. "Why did you run from me in Colorado?"

CHAPTER 6

Scout

Ivy nailed it.

I was so proud of her. She could have gone all mushy and gushy and let the long-awaited appearance of Reed Logan rattle her, but she didn't. She looked that likely imposter in the face and got right to business.

"Why did you run from me in Colorado?" she asked.

Former marine, Reed Logan, could have been any basic late-thirties-early-forties dad. Ivy's dark hair and eyes were right there in front of us in masculine form, clothed in a button-down shirt and any dad's jeans. His hair was longer and messier than when he stalked the halls of Stonehaven Academy as either a real or fake electrician. I'd hoped so much for a clear sign the guy was not related to Ivy, but there were no immediate feelings either way, and everything about his appearance screamed *DNA match*.

But what about his other activities?

He took a deep breath as if he was trying to form words, and kept his hands still by clasping them in front of himself on the table.

"I shouldn't have gone to Colorado," he said. "I'd only recently become certain you were the daughter I'd been looking for. After the trouble at your school, I went more out of curiosity and worry than anything. It was inappropriate. So, when you spotted me, I realized I had no real plan to reveal myself and certainly no reason to be there. I was worried I'd get locked up far from here and it would take a long time to clear myself. In the end, I was picked up anyway."

"What do you mean you'd been looking for me? You know my name and my birthplace. You know my mom. What took you so long? If you wanted to find me, you could have."

He dropped his gaze and looked genuinely contrite as he picked at his cuticles and fingernails—just like Ivy did when she was nervous.

"I'm aware of your mother's difficulties. She didn't want me there, and between her and her big sister, Constance, they made it a bit impossible to stick around."

"By difficulties, you mean mental illness."

"Yes."

"And you couldn't handle her mental illness. But you thought newborn Ivy Lynette and Aunt Connie could."

He pressed his lips into an uncomfortable and angry-looking line and shook his head as he looked away.

Ivy had hit her mark.

"All right. I know you're not going to let me off the hook here, and that's OK, but can we just keep talking?"

Ivy shrugged. "Talk."

"Your mom didn't want me as a partner, or a father to you. She was pretty far off the beam back then. I didn't realize it. It's not that I wouldn't have done my part, it's that she wouldn't let me. Now, factor in that I was concerned about her stability around you and that the Corps owned me at the time and sent me out of the country, and you'll see why it was better to give her room. Antagonizing her may have made her illness worse."

Ivy sank back into her chair as if she'd been pierced with a spear.

"Stick with me here," he said. "I decided to stay away until you were older and could make some decisions for yourself. I'm not afraid of mental illness. There's no shame in being sick. But Constance loved you more than she hated me, and I knew she would make sure your mom got well and would take care of you both. And didn't she?"

Ivy nodded, but I could see the wheels turning in her head. She was contemplating timelines and bloodlines and the between-the-lines meaning of everything he said. And she was never going to buy that someone stayed away from their kid for some greater cause, or at least the way he explained it. She loved people and family and friends too much to ever accept a *it was for your own good* excuse.

She sat forward again. "How did you end up at Stonehaven Academy? Did you already know I was there? And before you answer, you should know you cannot lie to me."

He cocked his head just a bit and studied her face as his lips parted—but it was ever so slight.

Boom. There it was, the look I'd been waiting for her to lead him in to. The guy had abilities, probably similar to Ivy's. The next answer we needed was about who he worked for.

"I had an idea you were at Stonehaven Academy because of my search for you," he said. "You moved around a lot, but Constance always sticks out like a beacon because of her social status. A simple social media search brought me to you. I got into the school through the company that was contracted to help with the system. I am an electrician. That place was a disaster waiting to happen."

"What do you do now?" I asked.

"I'm retired military, so I work when I want. Usually it's electrical, but right now I'm thinking of taking a job at a sporting goods store in the hunting and fishing department. I like those things and I know a lot about firearms. I also volunteer at a center for wounded veterans."

"Are you a wounded veteran?"

"Not that you can see from the outside, kid."

Ivy closed her eyes in a long, slow blink, and I wished I could have read her mind right then even better than I usually could.

"My mom doesn't know about this meeting," she said. "Don't get any ideas about showing back up around my apartment or my school or anywhere else without my permission."

"That's probably for the best."

"Yeah. I don't even know for sure you're my father."

He reached into the pocket of the windbreaker he'd carried to the table. "I can fix that." He set two unopened genetic test kits on the table. "Let's do it. Set up an account, spit in the thing. Our results will link us. I'll swear to it, and it'll be interesting to discover our heritage together."

Ivy studied the boxes. "You're a total stranger to me. I'm not going to spit in anything with you. Gross." She pushed the kit back. "And without seeing you do your test, I won't believe the results."

"You'd make a good soldier, you know that? But it's lost on me how I could possibly cheat on this. If I'm not your father—which I know I am—I'd have to know who your father is and somehow make him do the test... Whatever. There's no point in trying to get around this test."

Ivy's lip twitched. I knew she wanted to do it.

"Tell you what," he said and got out his phone. "Let's set up our accounts and put the reference numbers in. Then we'll go sit apart outside and Scout here will proctor the exam."

"Gross!" I said. "I don't want to watch you spit either."

"You don't have to watch," Reed answered. "Just stand

between us on the sidewalk and take the test to the postal pickup when we're done. Completely neutral."

Ivy smiled. I couldn't refuse her when she smiled like that.

"Sure," I said.

Reed and Ivy tapped their way through the instructions and checked the time constraints. "I have a few minutes to wait because of my smoothie," she said. "But don't throw it out. I'll need it after."

Reed leaned in. "Anything else you want to talk about?"

"I don't want to ask you any more direct questions at this time."

"You sound like we're in court."

"We are in court, aren't we? Kinda? The court to prove who you are and what you're about?"

"Asking more questions might get you more answers." Reed sat back and then his brows raised as it dawned on him. "Ahhh… You don't want any more answers right now because I can't lie to you, and you're not prepared for if you don't like what I say. You don't want to know."

"Something like that. Can I lie to you? *Reed?*"

"I don't think you can. I think we can see and feel a lot about each other. And about other things."

"Maybe."

"I may have done some questionable things in the past, Ivy, but I wish you no harm."

"Time will tell," she whispered.

"Speaking of time, the only way to get to the bottom of all this is to spend more of it together. Can we do this again soon? Or there's a concert benefitting the veterans I work with. If I send you tickets, will you come?"

"Only if you send four," I cut in. "She's not going anywhere alone with you."

"Fair enough. I'll text you four barcodes and the details when I get them."

"I'm not going to lie to my mother forever."

"I understand. We'll handle this however you want."

Ivy collected her test kit and sent a subtle nod to Deacon and Mary.

I grabbed her smoothie and prepared to monitor saliva collection.

Reed pushed the door open, and their quick, unguarded glance at each other showed a level of familiarity I hadn't expected so soon. I only wished we had the whole supernatural picture and not just the daddy-daughter one.

I looked back over my shoulder at Mary and Deacon.

Everyone knew.

Ivy was her father's daughter.

CHAPTER 7

Mary

A cold blast of air hit my skin before I ever saw his face.

I turned and set a large metal bowl into the deep sink as Gavin entered the Smoothie Shack.

The manager continued through her closing checklist. "We're shutting down," she called out. "Not sure I can make what you want."

"He's here for me," I said. "I'll lock the door."

"Thanks, darlin'. I'm taking the drawer to the back office."

Gavin stood with his hands in his pockets near the center of the room as I made my way to the glass door. I brushed past him with every nerve in my body pinging against the urge to gut him with the blades I'd just put to soak in sanitizing water.

I clicked the lock and stood in front of him. He'd gotten bigger, taller, stronger, even better looking, and had the nerve to appear confident as he looked me right in the eye. "Hi, Mary."

He studied my face and leaned in. "Wow. They told me about your eye, but I couldn't imagine you without your matching green eyes. Do the doctors know how that happened in the accide—"

"Stop." I stepped back. I could only keep my cool for so long. "Don't you dare mention the murder in my presence." I glanced at one of the many cameras above my head. "You should remember you're under surveillance, so if you make any attempt to touch me it's all recorded."

"C'mon, you know I—"

"And if my parents were to walk by and see you here, you wouldn't make it to your car alive."

The train cars inside me—the ones I tried so hard to keep connected and rolling along the track—threatened to tip over and pile up like the train wreck I was.

I thought of Jacob, the murder, the evil that had tried to kill me my whole life...

"You sound like a crazy person," he said.

"Do I? My dad still has the tape from the pool incident, and everyone expects it's only a matter of time before there is proof of your involvement in Jacob's death."

Fear washed across his face—but only for a second. When he stood straight beneath my accusation, I knew the grip I had on my control wouldn't last. He really thought he'd never pay for his crimes.

"You should go," I said.

"Please, Mary..."

The urge to toy with him returned full force. I mustered the courage not to rip his skin from his bones. Not right then, anyway.

I put on my pretend, sticky-sweet smile. "All right. I knew I'd have to see you eventually, but why are you really here?"

"I thought we should talk."

"Why would you think that?"

The smile must have caught him off guard. "My mom has yoga in this strip center, and she said she thought she saw you." He skimmed his fingers across the top of a scarred and dirty table. "We've been together our whole lives, Mary. We need to get past this. I was hoping we could spend some time together and.."

"And what exactly, Gavin? Pretend you didn't run me and my friends off a mountain?"

"That wasn't my fault."

I sucked in a breath so sharp I had to hold my chest. "Wow. Not your fault." I braced myself against a table. "And you know you just admitted what everyone already knows. You were there. You should tell the authorities. Turn yourself in. You'll feel better."

"Listen," he pleaded. "If you would just hear me out. There are things you don't know, and if you'll only let me explain, you'll see it's best if we are together. We make a great team. There are things happening you know nothing about, but together we can make a plan to change things. We can work together."

"Now who sounds like a crazy person?"

"I'm serious, Mary. There are things you don't know. You are in danger, and I can help you."

I snapped.

I snapped like an over-tightened guitar string, and the only thing—*the only thing*—that kept my hands from his throat were the very same cameras I'd warned him about.

I crossed my arms to keep them still and got in his face. He backed up.

"Do you really think I don't know what's happening here?"

"Wh... What do you mean?"

"You know exactly what I mean. I know all about Shanar. I know you work for him. You reek of his evil, and the only thing

I can't understand is how you could be so stupid as to believe he will take care of you. He. Will. Not."

Storm clouds brewed in his deep brown eyes as fear edged in. "I don't know who or what you're talking about."

"Save it, Gavin. I've been fighting this battle my whole life, and you can't imagine my disappointment when I realized you were on the other side. I only wish I'd understood it all in time to save Jacob. God, how I wish I'd known more!"

"You need to calm down, Mary."

"I will never calm down again, and you should know that I already know how this all ends. Do you want to hear it?"

He looked away.

"Look me in the eye, murderer. Do you want to hear it?"

He pressed in harder against the wall near the door. "Please, Mary, can we talk like we used to?"

"I know you work for Shanar. I know he sent you for me. I know you think you can give him what he wants and he'll leave you alone after he rewards you. And I even believe you think somewhere in your twisted imagination that if you can get me over on your side that we'll both be all right. That is a lie. Now, listen carefully, Gavin. It's going to come down to you and me—and I am not going to die."

He froze in his spot and seemed to put his thoughts in order before his gaze met mine.

I had pushed him to the edge of his lingering humanity. The Gavin I knew was gone. Every last choice had been made. An odd sense of release and relief blanketed my soul.

"I'm not going to die either," he said in a clearer tone than he'd managed before.

"Oh Gavin... I'm sorry you can't see the truth."

"I see it. More than you know." He pressed his hands against the wall as if to steady himself. "You should chill. That blue eye of yours looks brighter or something. Maybe it's because you're so angry."

"I'm beyond angry, Gavin. I'm dangerous. Particularly to the likes of you and Shanar."

"You should probably have that checked out. It's practically glowing."

"Take a good look at it. The next time you're close enough to see it, you'll be dead before you hit the ground."

CHAPTER 8

D^{eacon}

Gavin scrambled to his car like a dog who'd been chased out of a trash can in the kitchen.

The look on Mary's face through the Smoothie Shack's window left no doubt she'd spooked him. He'd tried to stand up against her, but he was no match for her anger, and whatever she said to him made him cower like a whipped animal.

Once in his car, he pounded the steering wheel with his hands, and then rested his forehead there a while before he started the engine and checked his phone.

As for Mary, she grabbed chairs to flip on tables and pushed a broom as if the confrontation hadn't affected her at all.

And that was the problem.

Our half-Warrior-half-angel was stuck between two realms. I knew for a fact she leaned into Sebastian for help and comfort in her grief, though she remained angry he did not miraculously save Jacob, and freely admitted she didn't speak with him much when he tried to contact her. She still trusted the Creator and believed in all that was good, but the depths of her pain kept her from acknowledging it was not her place to avenge his death by her own hand. That meant, as Warriors, our bare backsides were exposed to Shanar and every bit of crap he could throw at us while Mary healed to full strength. No one else had the experience she had. No one else had the confidence. And with Ivy and Scout dealing with her dad and trying to decide exactly what he was, I knew I had to keep an eye on Mary until she was able to let go of her vigilante quest to terminate Gavin—even if the guy deserved it—because the journey into vengeance could destroy her.

I ditched my beat-up bicycle in the bushes and headed for Gavin's fancy new car. When I pounded on his roof, he jumped and dropped his phone.

The window slid down and the scent of leather and new-car drifted out.

"What do you want, Deacon?"

"Just checking in."

"What's your point?"

"No point in particular." I leaned against the car and made myself comfortable. "I was looking in on Mary. What are you doing here?"

"That's none of your business. Get off my car."

I didn't move. "Were you spying on Mary? Or stalking her maybe?"

"I have no interest in Mary. Besides, she's off-the-hook crazy right now."

"Really? I hadn't noticed. Then again, I'm her real friend, and seeing how her ex-boyfriend—that would be you—recently killed her current boyfriend, yeah, I can see how she wouldn't be super friendly toward you."

The hum of the engine changed tones as he shifted into reverse. He didn't bother to acknowledge my jab.

I pushed away from the car and leaned down. "Stay away from Mary, Gavin. You're not safe."

"I'm not afraid of Mary *or* you."

I rested my hand on the frame of the window. "That's too bad. You should be afraid of something because you have one comin'." I stepped away then turned back. "And I didn't say anything about me or Mary." I shrugged and crossed my arms. "I just don't want her caught in the crossfire when you get what you deserve."

He peeled out of the lot so fast, I was concerned for landscaping planters and street signs.

"What was that about?"

I spun as my heart thumped and my hands pulsed heat. "You scared the crap out of me, Mr. P. Where did you come from?"

"Here to pick up a pizza. What are you doing out here so late?"

"Checking on Mary. She's working at the Smoothie Shack."

He looked past my shoulder. "That was Gavin? Was he bothering Mary?"

"I'm pretty sure Mary was bothering him."

"Oh. She's not any better?"

"Nah. I personally heard her threaten at least three people today. One was pretty graphic. She won't last behind the counter in there."

"Let's hope she does. She needs the distraction."

"She seems to hold it together most of the time, then she snaps and says something scary. I don't know what she said to Gavin. I got here at the end of it, but he was pretty rattled."

"He has reason to be rattled, but you were on standby to make sure he got the message to stay away."

"I tried."

"You looked pretty cool over there when I drove up."

"I think we both know I'm about as smooth as a tornado in a trailer park. Mary can drop someone to their knees with one sentence and a pointed glare. I shook the whole time on my way to Gavin's car. I left my busted bike over there in the trees so he wouldn't start laughing when I tried to sound tough."

"The important thing is you understand your job. You're standing in the gap for your fellow Warrior. You're filling in and covering the team. No one told you to do that. You're doing it because you inherently felt the importance. Don't sell yourself short. Everyone knows who poured on the power at the Stonehaven Gym Fire."

"But that was during an assignment. I knew what I had to do."

"How is this not an assignment? Gavin started a war in your realm. It has to play out, and you are doing your job by watching out for Mary until she sorts it all out and feels like herself again."

"Right..."

Everything seemed so wild and out of control. I still couldn't believe what life I'd stumbled in to.

"Listen, Deacon, this small community is your training ground. You'll be out in the big, bad world soon. You'll need to keep your eyes open and learn to hear your instructions and not be taken in by imposters. This is your time to hone your skills."

"Speaking of imposters, any more official word on the electrician?"

"Between you and me, no. The insurance company is pressing for answers from the police, and the police can't pinpoint any criminal reason for any of the three fire incidents, so it's a mess. Why? You know something?"

I searched my mind for the correct response. Mr. Parrington didn't know about the whole Ivy-dad-electrician connection—that I knew of—and I couldn't betray Ivy. "He's still around. He has a connection to us, but we don't know how much, if any, is about the fire."

"Am I supposed to be reading between the lines here and pressing for more information?"

"No. I'll let you know if any real information comes out of it as it pertains to the Stonehaven fires."

"OK. Good talk. Glad we're aware we're on the same side and can trust each other, Deacon."

"Yes, sir." I scanned the brush for where I tossed my bike. "Uh, Mr. P?"

"Yes?"

"How do you do it? Being a Guardian and all. How do you keep it straight in your head between what's normal life and what's supernatural?"

"Years of practice. And focus. You're learning all that now."

I nodded and searched for my bike.

Focus.

Right. I was standing in a parking lot discussing the supernatural realm with my principal, who was also a gifted human. My supernatural Warrior team leader was mired in grief and threatening to dismember other humans with sharp objects in a quest for justice, and the rest of my team danced with danger over a newfound human father who may or may not be an evil being. Meanwhile, I'd just confronted an actual murderer who no one seemed to understand was truly responsible for another gifted human's death. Jacob *actually died*, and we couldn't prove Gavin's part in it. And did I mention I had supernatural powers and had been visited by the evil being, Shanar? Except that was no big thing because I also had an angel talking to me when I needed him.

Focus?

How?

I also had to dig in on my studies and catch up to my friends and graduate—all the while knowing it was my turn to be responsible for our core team of Warriors.

I swatted mosquitos away from my legs and set my bike on the path.

"Deacon?"

I jumped for the second time. How was I supposed to protect Warriors? I couldn't even hear someone coming toward me in a public parking lot and not act like I was a nervous wreck. I made a mental note to start remembering to check my surroundings at all times.

Claire Cannon?

Epic. I couldn't have been more sweaty, awkward, or dumbfounded.

Plus, I was straddling a bike that was too small for me and had a bent wheel and no kickstand. The loose chain swiped grease on my leg with every turn of the pedal. At least the wind kept the mosquitos off.

Unless I was sitting still as they swarmed me.

Which they were when the beautiful Claire Cannon, the object of my dreams and affection for more than two years, finally spoke to me.

Was there any way to look cool in that situation?

No. No, there was not.

"I thought that was you," she said.

"Hi, Claire."

"What are you doing?"

There was no way to fix it, so I had to play it. "I'm trying to get home on this pile-of-crap bike that me and my four brothers all have to share when someone else has the pile-of-crap car we also all share. I have two miles to ride. What would you say my chances are of getting home in one piece?"

She laughed in the flicker of the tall streetlamp. "There are five of you?"

"Yes."

"And one bike."

"Yes. Its name is Combo because it's a combination of all the parts in the garage. Sometimes it's one bike, sometimes we can get two if someone finds parts on the curb on trash day. Once, we accidentally created a scooter."

She laughed again and pushed a long piece of shiny, dark hair over her shoulder.

I think she batted her light brown eyes at me, but she stood in the shadow of the building and I couldn't be sure.

I chose to believe it was flirting.

"I saw Mary is working at the smoothie place and I'm sure she's having a hard time," she said. "How are you doing? I know Jacob was your friend."

People didn't usually ask how I was doing with Jacob's death. I was lumped in with Mary and the others because we travelled as a pack. I felt guilty most days because I hadn't trusted him as easily as the others did, and didn't always give him a fair shake. I could never give him that now.

I also could never go back and help Char or be there for Mary on the mountain and save his life.

I had to live with that.

"It all sucks, Claire. It all just sucks. Every day."

She nodded. "Sorry."

I looked around the lot. "Where's your ride?"

"I have my mom's car. I had to pick her up something at the drugstore. I thought I saw you and wanted to say hi." She waved. "Hi."

She *was* flirting—and she was as corny as I was at it. Who knew completely-put-together Claire Cannon was as awkward as me?

I propped the bike on a tree. "C'mon," I said. "It's late and it's dark. I'll walk you back to your car."

"That's sweet. But you live in the subdivision before mine, right? Slide Combo in the back and I'll drop you off."

"Uh... No. Greasy Combo is not allowed to ride in the back of your mom's car. That would be a disaster for us both."

"That's probably wise, but I would be happy to give you a ride and talk some more."

I looked at Combo.

Then I looked at Claire Cannon's purple tank top and long arms.

Her keys dangled at her fingertips.

I knocked the bike over and shoved it behind a shrub. "Later, Combo. I'll be back for you in the morning."

CHAPTER 9

Ivy

I stood in line outside the concert venue and watched my phone.

Scout kept an eye out for Mary, Deacon, and his unnamed date while I waited for the additional ticket to come in. While I was over the moon Deacon finally got his poop in a group and asked someone to hang out, it was uncomfortable to ask Reed Logan to send another ticket. It was, after all, a fundraiser for injured veterans, and we were going to take up seats and eat food without paying.

But if Reed Logan wanted me, he had to take us all and treat us all. I didn't trust the situation, and I was doing it behind my mother and Aunt Connie's back. I constantly searched the crowd for people who might know us. True, no one knew the connection to Reed Logan, but still... I was neck-deep in a lie by omission. My mother knew exactly where I was with my friends. She just didn't know why we chose that concert, or who invited us.

I elbowed Scout when I saw Deacon's date. "Hey! It's Claire Cannon, everybody."

"Welcome, Claire Cannon," Scout said.

Deacon stepped back and looked up as Mary approached. "This is a barn," he said. "Please tell me I'm not really standing in line to go inside a barn."

"Oh, zip it, Deac," Mary said. "It's a fancy barn."

"It's still a barn. And now I have this terrible feeling we're about to see a country band."

We all stepped forward in line. "We're in Texas at a benefit concert for veterans," I said. "What kind of concert did you think it would be?"

Claire laughed. "I knew it was a country band. Unlike some people, I actually looked up where we were going."

Scout raised his brows. "See? Claire Cannon's on the ball. Should we break the news to him it's a bar-b-que plate dinner?"

Deacon scoffed. "It's brisket, right? Sliced beef?"

"What else would it be?"

"Then we're good."

A shrill whistle pierced the air. We all turned to see Reed Logan with his cowboy hat poking out the door. "This way."

We stepped in the side entrance. Reed was all cowboy, from his pearl-snap, red and gray plaid shirt to his dark, worn, western-style boots.

There was a large buckle involved.

Deacon nudged me. "Can we send this new dad back and get a cooler one?"

"Stop. Some people think this *is* the cool dad."

"Here," Reed said. "Wristbands. The blue one is for your plate, and the bright yellow one is for no alcohol." He pointed toward the front corner. "There's a table right there for you guys. Someone will come by and scan your tickets. We're about to open the doors and I didn't want to lose track of you." He

47

swept his arm toward the table. "Welcome y'all. I'll be back around in a bit."

Mary hooked her arm in mine as we walked. "He's trying too hard, right?"

I sighed. "I think so. I don't know what's supposed to happen in this situation. I don't know that guy."

"Well, that guy is your biological father. That much we know."

"Yes. I don't need a DNA test to tell me that. I feel it. We all do."

Mary tossed her small wallet and keys on the table. "Do you have any feelings at all about the other stuff?" She glanced at Claire and lowered her voice. "The guy was every place that something bad happened to us."

"Yes, but I don't feel threatened when we're around him—like here or at the smoothie place the other day. Do you think it's possible for someone to be your blood relative but be on the opposite side of your feelings about good and bad choices?"

"It has to be possible. Not everyone in the same family makes the same decisions. And you weren't raised by him. You were raised by your mom and Aunt Connie. He could work for the Destroyer and still love you and want to be in your life."

"Or he could work for the Destroyer and be trying to lure us into a trap."

"Or that." Mary shivered. "Would anything surprise us anymore? I think we've seen the best and worst of what our supernatural realm has to offer in the fight between good and evil."

"You don't like Reed very much, do you Mary?"

"It's not about whether I like him or not. It's about whether I can trust him."

"I understand. And we have to be better at figuring it out before terrible things happen." I paused as Mary closed her eyes and blew out a breath. It had to be all she could handle to try and make it through a social event. "I'm glad you're here, Mary, but I'm sorry it's so hard for you."

"I couldn't miss this. I have to be present with you all to watch and wait. Always on guard, always prepared. I'm not afraid, and we need to know if Reed Logan is for us or against us."

"We do. But speaking of that, don't you think it's weird he came out of nowhere? Like where's he been? Where does he live? He said he volunteers with this organization and he got us the tickets and seems to know these people. That would suggest he's been in this area a while."

"Maybe just as long as you have. Is that what you mean? Maybe he's been following you and your mom?"

"Yeah. It's suspicious. Or maybe he stayed in this area because he knew we'd end up back near Aunt Connie eventually."

"I agree," Mary said. "But that's what these get-togethers are all about. You're going to get to know him and then decide what he's about and when to tell your mom. If he's a good guy, you need him in your life. He's your dad."

"And if he's a bad guy?"

"We'll deal with it. In the meantime, let's keep getting to know him. He'll show his true colors one way or the other."

"What if my signals are jumbled because he's my dad? And what if Scout can't tell because he's only worried about me? And maybe you can't see it because you have so many other things on your mind..."

"Deacon seems more in tune these days."

"How?"

Mary nodded his way as Deacon led his date to the food. "Look at him. He's gained confidence since Colorado. He's embraced his Warrior life, and he knows he has work to do."

"He does seem different. And look at him go with Claire Cannon. He's been working on that forever."

"I'm happy for him," Mary whispered.

I let the subject drop and took her hand. "Want to get a plate? This place is starting to fill up."

Scout perked up. "Hey, I want a plate."

"How about I bring you back one? You might have to wave your wristband."

Deacon and Claire returned to the table.

"Sure," Scout said. "I'll wait here with Claire Cannon and Deacon."

Claire smiled wide as she set down her plastic utensils. "All right, wait a minute. Why do you guys always refer to me with my first and last name. *Hey, Claire Cannon... I'll wait with Claire Cannon.*" She laughed. "I feel like there's a joke here I don't know about. You can just call me Claire. My name is Claire."

"*Wellll...,*" I said. And then I couldn't finish, because I had no reason. Claire Cannon had always been this huge subject on Deacon's radar. We all knew where she sat, what she wore, and what she ate for lunch because Deacon usually had something to say about Claire Cannon's status, though he never had the nerve to actually do anything about her. Claire Cannon had become a big, full-name kind of deal in our minds.

"Never mind," I said. "And sorry. We'll call you Claire from now on." I patted Deacon on the shoulder. "And Deacon here can explain to you how we got in that habit in the first place."

CHAPTER 10

Ivy

Everything was too loud and too crowded.

The music pulsed and the bass line thumped harder as the night wore on. People drank too much and edged in too close and the voices rose.

The guys wouldn't be caught dead in a country line dance, but me and Claire and Mary tried. Claire nailed it, and I wasn't bad. I'd always participated in drama and choir and retained most basic dance steps and choreographed routines.

My only real problem was that I had on the wrong kind of boots.

Reed Logan kept a close eye on us and talked when he could. It was clear he was a big deal on the committee for the benefit, which answered the question about where he'd been.

He'd been somewhere near me and had been for years.

He worked the room and buddied up to sponsors and contributors, but then he took time to sit with some of the disabled veterans who benefitted from the services of the foundation he volunteered for. His smile was sincere, and he appeared to offer genuine concern. He knew the men and women—the soldiers—who'd come to hear the band, and he danced with a woman who had only one arm and half a leg. He held her steady, and she laughed and hung on when he turned her too fast. Did they know each other that well? Or did he just know exactly how to make her feel good about herself when she wasn't confident, but wanted to dance?

Everything about Reed Logan looked too sweet and too pleasant and too...perfect.

I could see him as a young and handsome Marine. My mom was always beautiful, and any woman would have fallen for his charismatic air. What a pair they must have made. He oozed good ol' boy country charm, and tipped his hat when any woman wandered by him.

And then it was too much for me.

The meltdown started in my mind as bomb blasts and cries echoed in my head. I made the mistake of zeroing in on a woman at a table with a man who used a wheelchair. She clutched his hand, and her love for him was clear. And he loved her too, but she wanted to dance and he could never give that to her again. The pain and disappointment on them both detonated an explosion of emotion inside me. I glanced at the able-bodied men who waved their dates away when they tried to pull them to the floor.

Get up and dance, you lazy grumps! I screamed to them in my head. *Don't you realize there are people who can't?*

Everyone's pain crept in on me. There was so much noise, so many voices, so much despair. I had always been told by the Creator's voice that I was not part of the chaos. But chaos reigned in that room and it got louder and stronger and I could not fight my way out or hear any clear instruction as to how I should help. My *move child* instructor's voice wasn't there. Was our realm trying to send a warning message, or was it only my usual human empathy?

I covered my ears.

Scout put his arm around me and leaned in. "What's happening?"

"Everything in this room is alive in my head and trying to get my attention. I need to get out of here."

He tugged on my hand. "We're going out for air."

Mary pushed her chair back. "We'll all come," she said.

"No, wait," I said. "Give us a few minutes." I nodded toward Reed. "Let's see what he does. Watch him and then come on out. I think we're all about to be finished with this night."

My control returned, even as I pulled Scout across the crowded room and slipped out the side exit. Thank the stars, I'd learned to recognize the struggles in my head before they crippled me. The more I understood my abilities, the more I knew the Creator's voice when I heard it. Everything else was only noise or some poor soul's cry for help. If I could help as a human I did. If the Creator used the customary *move child* command, I was all over it.

But it was different that night. It was too much, and the signals were crossed and teeming with activity. Was it simply that I usually avoided such large public events for that very reason? Or was Reed Logan messing with me?

I took a deep breath of fresh, but humid air.

Scout leaned against the splintered, wooden wall. "Better?"

"Yes. Thanks."

"What happened?"

"The usual absorption of everyone's emo stuff, but there were no clear Warrior signs, and Deacon and Mary don't seem to be bothered by anything."

"It's probably the size of the crowd then. You can't help what you pick up from hurting people."

"No, but if someone is messing with me…"

Reed Logan popped out of the door right on cue.

"Are you OK?" He looked around the darkened area. "Don't go too far out here. This is a family-style event, but people are starting to get rowdy."

"Ah, yes, they are," I said. "That room is jam-packed with some strong emotional baggage. But you know that, don't you, Reed?"

He stepped on the cinderblock, hopped to the ground, and let the door close behind him. "I'm not sure I follow."

"Yes, you do, but we'll get to that." I crossed my arms. "How long have you been in this area?"

"I never completely left the Houston area except when I was deployed. My parents, they're gone now, but they had a house out in Katy. I still have it and lived there a while."

"Until you looked for me again and found Aunt Connie on this end of town."

"Yes."

"But you've been a part of this organization a long time."

"Yes."

"So, you've never really been that far away from me."

"Only when I was overseas."

"And you've always known where I was."

"Not exactly. Your mother did move a lot." He paused to remove his hat and scrape his hand through his hair before he set it back on his head. "But I had a general idea most of the time. I wasn't lying the other day. I wasn't always sure, but again, general idea, and I did pin it down on social media."

"Yeah, like I'm not exactly lying to my mother about tonight. She knows I'm here, but not about you."

"I only want to get to know you, Ivy, and figure out how to approach your mom. I thought you were having a good time with your friends tonight. I saw you can dance." He held out his hand. "C'mon. Will you dance with me?"

I wanted to take it. Somewhere in my stupid little girl heart, I wanted to take my daddy's hand and dance.

Scout knew better.

"She's not Texas two-steppin' with you in there. Are you delusional? You're a grown man and she's a teenaged girl. You'll look like a pervert. No one in there knows you're her dad. Wait. Do they?"

I panicked. "Please don't tell me you've gone and told a bunch of people you've found your not-so-long-lost daughter."

"No." The hat came off again. He used it to tap the side of his leg. "No. And he's right about the dance. That was inappropriate. I'm sorry. Look, I don't know what I'm doing here."

"Wrong," I said. "This is where you lose me. You say you don't know what you're doing, but that's not true, is it? You know exactly what you're doing."

"How do you figure that?"

"We share abilities, don't we, Reed? You were working against me in there. I picked up what every wounded veteran was carrying around in that room—everyone but you. You know your way around the supernatural realm of cognitive abilities, don't you? How are you trying to play me? You can't read my mind. The Creator has promised me that much. My assignments are mine and you can't interfere, but you sure were trying to crack my cerebral code, weren't you?"

Scout's eyes widened in the dim light of the lone bulb that lit the side entrance. "We should go, Ivy. This is out of hand."

"I wasn't trying to do that, Ivy. I told you, I only want to get to know you."

"By sneaking up on my brain? By trying to crack my head open in that room? I got news for you, cowboy, I don't crack so easy."

"Anything extra you felt in there was involuntary if it came from me. I can't help it if we're connected. You're my kid. It's only reasonable we share certain traits."

"I consider mine gifts from the Creator. Where did yours come from?"

"I—"

"Wait. Did you mess with my mother's mind? Did you scramble her brain and then leave us behind?"

"I didn't do anything to your mother, Ivy. She has mental health issues. You can't give someone a bi-polar or schizophrenic disorder."

"I'm thinking maybe doing that'd be right up the Destroyer's alley."

Scout grabbed my hand. "We're done here."

Mary and Deacon tumbled out the side door like two people who no longer believed there was nothing going on. Claire came out behind them.

Scout and I immediately knew something was different.

"What is it?" Scout asked. "Where is it?"

"Unclear," Deacon said and glanced at Claire. "Hey, Claire do you mind running around the front right quick and finding the cop who's on duty? Something's up out here. Maybe someone's breaking into cars or something."

"Sure." She sprinted along the side of the building, and Deacon showed visible relief that he'd managed to send her away.

Mary stepped front and center. "There."

Deacon joined her. "Where?"

We all glanced out across the darkness. In the daylight, when the event began, cars had parked in the grass wherever they could find a spot. Now, in the darkness, it was hard to make out anything in the open field near the barn.

Headlights flicked on and trapped us in the glare.

"I guess that would be it," Scout said. "What's the threat?"

My mind was slow to settle after the mental fiasco in the barn, but I saw him with total clarity in my head.

Move child...

Ah… There was the voice. The only one I trusted.

"It's Gavin," I said.

"Yep," Deacon agreed. "That's his new car. What is he going to do? Shoot at us? Run us over?"

"I don't know," Mary said. "But I won't let him crash into a barn full of people."

We all moved forward.

"Alrighty then," Scout said.

And no one cared or remembered that Reed Logan stood nearby.

Mary sped up. "I'm going to pull that punk out right through his window."

The engine revved and we kept walking.

Mary stopped not five feet from the front of his car. He grasped the wheel and glared at us as his face became clear through the windshield.

"We're not afraid of you, Gavin," Mary yelled. "What are you doing here?"

He didn't answer or move.

"Do something," she taunted him further. "Come at me."

I braced as Gavin hit the gas. Mary and Deacon's arms flew out in a defensive move I'd never seen them make before. It looked like instinct, and sounded like crackling fire when they moved together as one. The scent of frankincense lingered in the air.

Sebastian was there.

Gavin made a sudden, sharp turn to speed right past us and onto the pavement toward the exit.

We all exhaled.

"What the heck was that?" Scout asked.

"I don't know," Mary said. "He's playing games and messing with us. It won't end well for him."

I turned to find Reed Logan right behind me. "What are you doing?"

"Uh... My daughter and her friends just walked straight toward an apparent dangerous kid in a fast car." He shook his head. "I didn't see everything you did at the fire, but I know people called you heroes. And you really do it, don't you? You faced that kid head-on."

"Save it, Reed. I don't know what this little act you have going on here is about, but know this: I don't trust you." I pushed into his solid chest. "Am I going to keep trying to figure it out in case you're really a good guy and can be a father to me? Yes, I am, because I deserve that, and I'm just naïve enough to believe I could have it, even though you left me. But will I let my guard down? No. Because here's the thing, and it's very simple. Gavin had to have a reason to drive off because we know for a fact he wants Mary dead. So, what was the reason he drove off?"

Scout came to my side. "Was it because he knew our backup showed up and there was no way he'd be able to overcome us? Even with a car aimed straight for us?"

"Or," Mary added. "Was it because this whole thing was orchestrated by you as some kind of contained threat to expose something?"

"Yeah, *Dad*. Was Gavin only here on orders from you?"

CHAPTER 11

Mary

I slipped into my bedroom and put lavender and cedarwood in my diffuser. It helped me sleep, and I could take all the help I could get.

"I know you're here," I said. "What do you want?"

The comfort, warmth, and shield of Sebastian's protection filled the room. "I'm always close by. What do *you* want? We haven't exactly been on speaking terms. You spoke first."

I sprawled on my bed and punched a pillow into submission under my head. "What was all that about tonight?"

"Which part?"

"All the parts. And why don't you visit in human form anymore?"

"It is not necessary. Your Warriors know who I am and have learned to hear me and feel my presence."

"But somehow you came up short for me."

"One day, you will stop blaming me for the Destroyer's work."

"Whatever you say," I said. "What was that new thing that happened when Deacon and I raised our hands against Gavin's car?"

"Deacon has always been more gifted than he realizes. He has amazing power he can use when necessary. You, too, are powerful, and you carry my energy with you. Surely, you can't be surprised when a car is headed for you and the realm unites and reacts to protect you."

"But that was a powerful and almost electrical reaction."

"It was."

I closed my eyes. Was it big because Sebastian showed up? Or did Sebastian show up because it was big?

"Why didn't Gavin do something with the car? He had us right there. He could have tried to wipe us out. He wouldn't have succeeded, but he could have tried."

"Even the Destroyer chooses his battles wisely."

"Gavin is gone to me, I know that. Is he also completely gone from the Creator?"

"That is between Gavin and the Creator."

"I feel he's made his choice."

"You can't possibly know Gavin's deepest truth."

But I did. I knew, and it made me sick. Jacob was gone because of Gavin. He could never come back from that, and he needed to pay for his crimes.

"What about Ivy's dad?" I asked. "I feel like I need a whiteboard in here to make a chart and keep up with all the good people and the bad ones. Where do I put him on the chart? I won't allow him to hurt Ivy."

"You've taken a lot upon yourself. Your compassion as a human and a friend is fighting with your Warrior heart. It may surprise you to know it's not your call to decide who pays for their crimes and how. It's not even your place to have a whiteboard to sort them out."

"Says you. It only makes sense to know my enemies and the enemies of my friends."

"But it doesn't make sense to handle their judgement."

Easy for him to say. He didn't have to live my life without Jacob, and walk in my shoes filled with anger, guilt, and regret. He didn't have to look at human Gavin and know what he'd done, and he didn't have to fear for the lives of my family, my friends, and my fellow Warriors.

"Mary... I see your struggle. I feel the deep sorrow, but you cannot be effective in your role if you hold on to vengeful thoughts."

"I don't think of vengeance. I think of justice."

"Don't fool yourself, and neither one of those things is a Warrior's job. Warriors are ambassadors of the Creator, gifted for good things and protection. You are problem solvers, critical thinkers, and physically powerful humans in the face of earthly assault by the Destroyer."

"And we get physically wounded and lose people we love, so forgive me if I want to be way ahead of Ivy's biological father situation before it's too late." I sat straight up and used my hands like a scale to represent the choice. "Good guy or bad guy?"

"Stop trying to sort humans. It's not your call. But... Reed Logan has a choice like everyone else."

"Maybe. But something tells me he's been working for Shanar and the Destroyer for a while."

"And something tells me, a human man with a strong Warrior daughter may have yet to make up his mind—or perhaps the new relationship will change him."

"So, you're saying I'm right. He is not on our side. That makes him a threat to Ivy. He must be stopped. That also means he was behind Gavin's production tonight. He wanted to draw us out and see what would happen. He was in control of Gavin the whole time. Wait. How close is he to Shanar? Can Shanar…? Does Shanar use Reed Logan's body when he wants to be in human form? Is that a thing? Because I need to know."

"Oh, but listen to how your human mind spins. It turns and turns in business that is not yours. It is no wonder you can't sleep. You have taken on burdens that are not yours to bear."

"Says the supernatural being who does not have to live with my pain, and who left me alone on the side of a mountain."

"Someday, we will come to an understanding about that."

"Will we though? I cannot and will not forget what happened."

"I didn't say forget. I said understand."

"Whatever. What do I do about Reed Logan?"

"Reed Logan is Ivy's father. She has to work it out."

"But she's excited and vulnerable. I don't want her to get hurt."

"I know you're feeling protective of your friends, but Ivy is strong. And remember, you have everything you need inside you to defeat whatever threat is assigned to you. Don't go looking for trouble. You're angry and you want to fight, but not every fight is yours."

"Jacob and I weren't looking for trouble when it found us on the mountain, Sebastian. I won't be caught by surprise again."

"At some point, you have to let go of your thirst for revenge, Mary. A Warrior with a chip on her shoulder is a Warrior with divided attention."

"Oh. So now I'm not a good Warrior."

"You're the best Warrior, Mary. But even the best Warrior's judgement can be marred by misplaced anger. You are not a vigilante. You represent the Creator."

"And Gavin represents the Destroyer. We're natural enemies. He's fair game."

CHAPTER 12

Scout

I was so sick of having a stupid pool.

My grandparents rarely got in it. It had sat empty and deteriorating before I came to live with them. Then, all of a sudden, they decided it had to be repaired and full of water. I had to keep it clean and invite my friends. I had to pretend to enjoy myself while other people flopped in the water, oblivious to my fear.

I had to sit on the side and watch my girlfriend and my other friends have fun while I clung to the edge like a complete coward.

I couldn't do it anymore, I just couldn't. So, all I *did* do was study and follow the curriculum to graduate from high school as soon as possible. That was the only good thing about Stonehaven Academy nearly burning down. It had set us all on a different kind of path to our futures.

And nobody needed something new and different more than me.

At least that's what I thought.

"Hey, Scout, you ready?"

I jerked as Deacon's too upbeat voice startled me. "Somebody sounds like they had another good date last night with Claire Cannon."

"You know it." Deacon puffed out his chest.

I took another swipe at a bunch of twigs that had dropped in the water during the quick thunderstorm the night before. "Anything you're going to share?"

"Not at this time, but she is amazing. And beautiful. And she likes to kiss. A lot."

"I thought you weren't going to share."

"Why wouldn't I share about how much an amazing girl likes to kiss me? And, speaking of that, aren't we going to go looking for pressure-washing work today? I need to make some money. I need to go on more dates and push my parents harder about finding another cash car. They're looking, and they know we need another car around the house, but making insurance money would help my cause."

"Yeah, we're going, but I have to finish this first. You could help, you know."

"How?"

"Hose off that patio furniture I got out of the shed. My grandparents want me to prepare for pool season. There's a broom there to dust off the cobwebs first."

Deacon froze with his hand out toward the broom. "No spiders are going to jump off there are they?"

"C'mon, dude, knock off the dust and hose everything down. I gotta get all these leaves and crap out of the water before I can go."

"I hate spiders, Scout, you know that. What if one is hiding under the arm of the chair or something and flies out and lands on my face?"

"Spiders don't fly, Deacon. Sometimes they jump, but that's a different thing."

He stepped back. "How far do they jump?"

"*Duuuuddde...* No spider is going to jump on you. Start sweeping."

"*All right.* I'll stop worrying about flying and jumping spiders when you stop worrying about stepping in the shallow end of the pool to grab a stick."

Everything got quiet, and I hated myself because he was right.

"Scout, look, I'm sorry. That was too far. You have every reason to struggle with your fear of water and I'm just a big chicken about bugs. It's not the same."

I shrugged. "Except you're right. Nothing about this chemically-balanced, clean water in a big concrete hole in any way compares to the nightmare of being washed away by flood waters in a car. Yet, I can't separate the two and realize the girl I love just wants to mess around in the hot tub with me and I can't bring myself to put a stupid big toe in there."

Deacon dropped the broom. "Wait. Ivy wants to mess around in the hot tub?" He headed my way. "No. Sorry. That wasn't your point. How can I help? You need to be in that hot tub."

"Yes, I know, but don't let your imagination go nuts on my account. Ivy and I are not..."

"Yeah, I get it," Deacon said. "But what I hear is that you're just about ready to really try and overcome your fear. Let's go with that. Let's start slow. We'll be miserably hot when we get done with our work. We can take one step at a time. Literally. We'll sit on the top step and get our feet wet. Maybe tomorrow we get two steps in. The next day—"

"I get it, Deacon. I'll think about it."

"You need to be ready when Ivy comes over to swim."

"I know."

He stepped back and raised his hands before he picked up the broom. "I'm jus' sayin'. I got you, bro. This is important."

"You've made your point." I moved to the other side of the pool. "About Claire... How did that happen? Did you finally get up the nerve to ask her out?"

"No, man, she found me in the parking lot the other night after Mary had her big confrontation with Gavin at the Smoothie Shack."

"You stuck around after me and Ivy left?"

"Yeah. I felt the need to check in on her, and sure enough, Gavin showed up. We had a little talk."

"Nice. You set him straight?"

"Yeah, apparently so straight he still showed up at the barn."

"Guess you can't effectively threaten a murderer who works for a supernatural evil being. Imagine that."

"Yeah, imagine."

"And Claire just found you in the parking lot? Like Char just found you at the ski slope? Do you think she's...? You know."

"No. I don't think Claire is anything but an exquisite regular girl."

"Wow. You're seriously bustin' out the real words for her. Exquisite?"

"I'm trying to broaden my vocabulary. You guys have me all stressed out over graduating early and going to college. I'm reading books and dictionaries... And doing stuff with numbers."

"That's terrible, Deacon. It must be horrible to have to actually use the amount of intelligence you have. I saw your PSAT scores, remember? You totally have what it takes."

"Shut it, braniac." Deacon set the broom on the side of the house and went for the hose. "Anyway, how's it going with Ivy's dad?"

"Who knows? She now texts him more than she texts me. I worry any day her mom or Aunt Connie is going to catch on and check her phone. He wants to meet again in neutral territory and talk. Ivy's determined to pick him apart until she knows what he really is. We'll be at the Smoothie Shack again Friday. You in? We need you."

"Of course. I'll bring Claire."

"Cool with me as long as you have a plan to handle her if a sudden assignment comes up. I saw how worried you were at the barn. She's an innocent in all this and would not understand if she got caught in something."

Deacon wiped sweat away from his forehead with his t-shirt. "I know."

"I almost forgot," I said. "I have other news."

"You have bigger news than Ivy wanting to do stuff with you in the hot tub?"

"Nah, nothing's bigger than that, but it was unexpected news."

"Well, what is it? Don't leave me hanging here."

I pulled the trash can full of debris to the shed. "My grandparents are buying a lake house north of Houston."

"Really? I thought they loved it here."

"Turns out, they had intended to sell and move a while ago. Grandpa likes to fish and always wanted a small boat to ride around in. They would have been gone by now, except…"

"Except that you came to live with them and they didn't want to move you again."

"Yeah. They raised my dad here. Anyway, they were going to wait until I went to college, but then thought, what the heck? Buy a place now so they can go any time they want. They'll sell this place someday, I guess. And they had no idea when they started looking that I might be going to college earlier than expected."

"Funny. All I'm hearing is how you'll have the place to yourself when your grandparents are fishing on the lake."

I grabbed two bottles of water out of the garage fridge and tossed one to Deacon. "Yeah, I hear that too, but now that we've put all this pressure on ourselves to make money and graduate early, we don't have much time left to party."

"There is always time left to party, dude. Not only that, now there's a lake house involved. Is there a dock to jump off of? Oh! A rope swing! Can we use your grandpa's boat?"

"Take it easy. They're still working out the...details. What the heck?" I grabbed the net and headed back to poolside. "Aww, man, don't make me chase you all over the place."

Deacon came to my side. "What is— Whoa! Snake in the pool! Snake in the pool!"

Deacon stomped, pointed, and yelled out the news as if expecting the snake police or someone would show up and help. He yanked his phone out of his pocket. "Who do I call for this?"

"Stop it, Deacon, I'll have him out in a minute if you'll stop shaking the whole pool."

"That snake is three feet long. We need help."

"That snake is only eleven inches long and we don't need help."

"How do you figure that?"

"It's a harmless Texas brown snake. See those little flecks on its brown skin?"

"I'm not looking at that thing. I don't want to die."

"It couldn't kill you if it wanted to. It's non-venomous and its mouth is small. And you are not its food source."

"What does it eat then?"

"Stuff out of and on the ground. It probably lives over there in the flower garden."

I snuck up behind the snake where it had slithered against the side, and scooped it into the net. Deacon ran the other way as I carried it to the grass and flipped it out of the net.

"You can come out now, Deacon."

"Funny. I wasn't hiding."

"No?" I put the net away for the second time. "We're really a mess, aren't we?"

"How's that?"

"You're all excited to go to the lake, but you can't handle one small, innocent snake in a clearwater pool. What do you think is in brownish-green lake water with a muddy bottom? You can't see anything."

"I expected we'd have the music cranked up and make enough noise to scare things away."

"OK. Sure."

"And why are you a mess?" Deacon asked as he inched toward the pool to double check.

"Well, duh. I have a pool *and* my grandparents' lake house and I can't get in the water."

"Oh, yeah… And by the way, that whole thing I said about getting in the pool when we get back—"

"You're not backing out, Deacon. If you expect me to get in the pool, you're getting in that pool."

"Not if there's a snake in it."

CHAPTER 13

Deacon

Claire Cannon was the best kisser.

I'd had fun with Char and our short, ski-trip romance, and we were still friends, but Claire had always been who I wanted for an actual girlfriend.

Not that I called her that or anything. Didn't want to scare her into not kissing me.

But what else did you call someone who wanted to spend time with you? And who wanted to kiss you…a *lot*?

I held the Smoothie Shack door open for her.

"Over here!" Ivy waved from a corner near the counter and pulled out a chair.

I didn't mind sitting with Scout and Ivy and even Reed Logan if I thought it would help, but I considered my job there was more about backup and lookout.

"Sure," I said. "But I thought it would be better if we sat near the front where we can study and..." I tilted my head away from Claire. "And take watch."

Ivy yanked on my t-shirt and pulled me toward her. "Deacon, look at me."

"Yes?"

"You and Claire Cannon need to be over here with us."

I'd learned not to argue with Ivy's intuition. I took a couple more chairs from nearby. "Have a seat, Claire." I glanced at the new bulky brick panel on the far, side wall. "What is that? That wasn't here last week, was it?"

"No," Scout said. "It's a piece of the old gym wall from the original Stonehaven Academy gym. Apparently, they found it in renovation and noted the old school logo hadn't been damaged. They rescued it."

"Yeah," Ivy said. "The Smoothie Shack owners' kids are in the lower school. He put that monstrosity there to raise money. Make a donation, sign the wall. Stonehaven is rising from the ashes and all that."

"It's ugly," I said. "And takes up too much space."

"I think he intends to send it back to Stonehaven," Scout said. "He's going to have a sculptor add to it when the new construction is complete and make it an artistic piece or something."

"After everyone has written on it and little kids have smeared smoothies all over it?"

"I don't know, Deacon, but they're trying to preserve the painted logo in the middle. It's covered with a clear, plastic panel, see? Mary said it took them two days to find a way to safely mount it to the wall. They had to call out an engineer to make sure it was properly anchored 'cause it's so heavy."

"No doubt. What can I get you, Claire?"

At the counter, Mary did several things at once. She started and stopped blenders and poured one drink while taking an order for another. Incredible efficiency and multitasking abilities aside, it was the fact that she seemed to do everything with such anger that concerned us all. She slapped a napkin on the bar like she was trying to put out a fire, and then smiled straight at her customer as she ripped a receipt off so hard the little card-swiping thingy almost bounced off the edge.

"Brutal much?"

"Hey, Deac. What do you and Claire want?"

"Claire wants her blueberry thing, but you can surprise me. Nothing from the vegetable side of the list though."

"Wouldn't dream of it."

"What's up in here this afternoon?"

"I don't know, but Ivy's got something going."

"I feel that. Do you think it's because she's still lying to her mom? She doesn't like to upset her, and I think it's wearing on her that she's keeping secrets."

Mary shrugged and took my money. "Yeah, well, if Reed's a decent guy they'll get through it. And if he's not…"

"How are you, Mary? Really."

"I'm busy, that's what I am."

I followed her down the length of the counter as she scrambled to get change and snatch two straws out of the basket for me. "Maybe we can talk later."

"Sure."

Mary's *sure* was about as solid as my love affair with snakes and spiders. She didn't want to talk—at least about anything important. I knew she was working through everything, but she'd lost a piece of her rational edge, and she was in no mood to talk about it.

We hadn't fully discussed the car incident with Gavin either. There were some additional sparks of energy and power as we joined together, without fear, to stop that car. I'd never felt that much strength pulse through my body. It was even stronger than the surges that helped me push through the gym doors at the pep rally. I glanced at my hands. No heat pulsed as I picked up our drinks, and nothing tingled in my muscles as I returned to the table to find Reed Logan.

But Sebastian's protective buffer was all over the place that afternoon.

We didn't know why.

Reed Logan extended his hand. "Nice to see you again, Deacon."

It couldn't have been more awkward. Tension squeezed us like a vise, and the problem was, we couldn't pinpoint Reed's intentions. Scout didn't trust him, Mary didn't like him, Ivy wanted a dad, and I wanted to be ready to throttle the guy if Shanar used him to threaten one hair on any of our heads. It was a tall order while I tried to pay attention to Claire and make sure she didn't know anything that could hurt her—while still being my charming self and not losing all the kissing stuff.

How was being a Warrior and dating a non-Warrior supposed to work? And if she had another role in the realm, what was the shortcut to find out what it was?

Two kids ran by our table and crashed into Claire's chair as they raced to put dollar bills in the giant empty pickle jar.

"Sorry," they called out.

Claire smiled and scooted in.

"Here you go," Mary said, and handed them each a different colored marker. "Sign your name or draw a small picture and bring these back, OK?"

They nodded and ran toward the large brick wall.

"Ivy tells me you all are trying to accelerate your studies," Reed said. "She also says how much she hates that S.A.I.N.T. Lab."

"I like the idea of graduating early," I said. "But I don't like the idea of the extra work." I glanced at Claire. "It takes my time from other things."

"That makes sense," Reed said, like he was trying to be some parental guide all of a sudden. "And this is the time when you should be attending regular classes and participating in school activities."

"And we would be," I shot back. "If the school was still there."

"I promise you, Deacon, that school was an electrical nightmare. I'm glad it burned down while you were out for the winter break. Otherwise, you all could have been in there when it finally caught fire—and it would have caught fire." He leaned back in his chair as Ivy studied his every move and twitch. "I'm just sorry you all aren't going to get your final few semesters in your school. You've all had more going on than you should. This is the best time of your life."

Scout raised a brow. "Is it though? Everything looks pretty complicated from here."

"If you have something to say, Scout, you should say it. I told you I would answer your questions."

"It's more of an observation."

Reed raised his hands. "Let's hear it."

Ivy looked worried. "What's the matter, Scout?"

"The problem here is the position you've put Ivy in—put all of us in. It's unlikely, but her mom or Aunt Connie could come by here at any time. She was caught up in the excitement of meeting you, but this has gone on too long. You're the adult, and you cornered her in a stairwell and dropped a bomb in her life. You should have taken the responsibility for approaching this the right way—by talking to her mom and hashing out the details."

"I agreed to this," Ivy said.

Scout touched Ivy's hand. "I know, and I understand." Then he turned his suspicious gaze back on Reed. "But you're her dad, Reed. If you cared about her like you say, you wouldn't have put it on her to orchestrate these meetings. You would have handled it like a grown-up and approached her mother. Biological fathers have rights, and Ivy has a voice. There was a better way to do this."

"You're absolutely right," Reed answered.

"And that's another thing. You're always happy to admit you're wrong, but rarely do you do the right thing in the first place. Why?"

"I don't know. My life is complicated."

"Too complicated to do the right thing the first time? That doesn't make sense. You've got her lying to her mom."

Claire cleared her throat and scooted her chair away from the table. "I'll be back."

"Sorry, Claire," Scout said. "Didn't mean to make you uncomfortable."

"Nah, just have to go to the restroom. We all have our family stuff."

Reed looked apologetic. Or was he just trying to *look* apologetic?

"Look, kid, I'm not lying about having a complicated past. Right now, I care only about my daughter, my country, and my work with the injured veterans." He stood. "But when you're right, you're right. I'll make arrangements to see your mom, Ivy, and I'll explain this was not your fault."

Ivy grabbed Scout's arm. "He's leaving! You're making him leave!"

"He's right, Ivy. Don't worry. We'll talk soon." Reed extended his hand toward Scout. "Thank you for watching out for my daughter."

If the guy was playing us all, he sure made it look easy.

A slight sound of thunder rumbled overhead. Those who heard, turned to look at afternoon sun as it flowed through the front window.

I shrugged. "Another storm?"

Ivy smacked her hand on the table. "No! Hold on!"

"It'll be fine," Reed said.

"No, it's not that." Ivy glanced over her shoulder at Mary.

"Call 911," Mary yelled.

And then she vaulted over the counter.

CHAPTER 14

Mary

Someone let out a roar. A deep, guttural growl that blossomed into a roar.

It was me.

Wait. It was me?

All I knew was, I felt a warning shock in my body, and then I realized the ridiculous load of bricks that was attached to the wall was not going to hold. I knew those two, innocent little boys were about to be flattened on the floor and smashed into bloody pancakes because someone had a not-so-bright idea to attach an old collage of bricks to a flimsy strip-center wall.

It just made me angry.

The place wasn't that busy, and the energy had buzzed of something sinister and wrong since I'd come to work. The presence of Reed Logan didn't help. I was already on guard because of him, but I thought the appearance of the rest of my team of

Warriors would help. It did, but yet, there we were—about to be elbows deep in catastrophe.

Again.

I rushed for the crumbling wall. Most of it had torn away in one sheet and fell on the boys, while other dangling bricks dropped one by one with sickening thuds. There was a fair amount of dust as their mother screamed into the gaping hole in the wall and dove for them. Red and dark blue markers rolled away as an afterthought in the destruction.

I was aware of Ivy phoning for help.

I was aware of Scout controlling the small crowd.

I was aware of Deacon at my side as the simple task of lifting the wall and pulling out the boys seemed so logical and possible.

I knew basic first aid—Scout made sure we all took a course from his troop after one of our first assignments. I knew not to move a victim if at all possible, but I also knew the boys couldn't breathe for long under a pile of rubble. I caught glimpses of dusty hair and clothes, and I heard their little boy moans.

We had to lift the wall, protect them from additional tumbling bricks, and have Scout and Ivy gently drag them straight out to safety.

Mine and Deacon's combined abilities could certainly get that done quickly, and if we needed help, it was already there or would arrive in moments.

Deacon took a position beside me and planted his feet firmly apart on the ground. "Scout! Ivy! Be ready to pull them out when we lift."

"Right. It's not stable enough to just try to move the wall of bricks. We have to pull them clear."

"Exactly." Deacon glanced my way. "You ready?"

Rage bubbled inside me. I nodded and took a breath.

And nothing happened.

Nothing.

I expected the crackling energy that had shown up between us when we faced Gavin in his car. I expected the scent of frankincense and the nudge of Sebastian in our realm to push us through.

I expected power.

Doubt suffocated me as I looked at Deacon and heard more soft whimpers from below. "What's wrong?"

"I don't know. Concentrate!"

"I am concentrating."

"It doesn't feel like you're focusing with me!" he shot back.

Energy wafted off him in waves of pulsing currents. The sudden appearance of green-hued stripes with golden borders flashed around his head, then colors came and went like circling butterflies around his body.

I blinked and lost all connection to the scene. Had my new blue eye turned my vision into a kaleidoscope of sunbursts and color? Or was Deacon actually emanating his very own light show? For all I knew, I was stroking out.

I stumbled and caught Ivy's gaze.

"Mary!" she yelled as she studied Deacon's body and then mine. It was clear she saw it too. Did everybody?

"You have to step away," she ordered. "Now. Deacon's got this."

"What?"

But the command had already reverberated in my head like a bouncy ball in an empty gymnasium. It was loose and out of control and I could only remember the last time someone gave me a direct order to stand down and I hadn't listened.

The focus I so desperately needed slipped through my fingers, and Ivy's stern command took hold.

I had to let go.

Not only was I unable to unite my abilities with Deacon—I was actively blocking him.

Why?

I stepped away as a surge of energy blasted past me and bolstered Deacon.

"Get ready!" he shouted.

Ivy and Scout dove for the floor as Deacon summoned everything in himself and everything from his supernatural forces.

The chunk of wall lifted to expose enough room for Scout and Ivy to grab for clothing, hair, or whatever they could reach, and gently tug the boys outward.

Others tried to get close and Deacon warned them to stay away.

Help converged on the scene in a circus of lights and sirens.

Deacon held on and screamed over the noise as his face grew more tense by the second.

"Are they clear?"

"Another second," Scout yelled. "Mine is stuck."

I helped Ivy and caught a glimpse of clothes and flesh tearing from the smallest kid's arm as Scout finished his work and pulled him through.

First responders froze in the near-buried doorway as Deacon held the massive and heavy piece of assorted building materials level and secure near his chest.

"Is everyone clear?" he cried out again.

"Yes," Scout yelled back.

"I'm dropping this."

It hit the ground in a thunderous cloud of dusty smoke.

And Deacon stumbled away with nothing more than a rip in his jeans and one missing shoe.

I raced to prop him up. "Where are you hurt?"

He looked at a trickle of blood that ran from a nick in his forearm. "I'm fine."

"I'm not sure you are. That amount of weight... You could have hurt your back or have internal injuries."

"I don't."

"But you might."

He jerked away. "Believe me. I've been hurt enough doing Warrior business to know when I'm hurt. I'm not hurt. It might be a miracle, but I'm not hurt."

"Let me get you outside to an ambulance just in case."

"No! All that matters is the boys."

I turned him toward what was left of the wall. "They're both awake and being cared for."

He spun back my way as Ivy and Scout approached. "What happened back there?"

"I don't know," I blurted. "There were colors all over you, and my mind was crowded... I don't know."

"Not here," Ivy said.

"No. I want to know what happened. We had nearly electrical energy at the barn and absolutely nothing today. I was a lone Warrior on the heavy-lifting end. And I mean the literal heavy lifting."

"I'm sorry, Deac..."

"Not here," Ivy pressed. "There was something new today. We'll talk away from here."

He seemed to listen to her. "Fine. Keep an eye out for my shoe."

Claire Cannon stood at the side of the counter, likely in shock.

Deacon rushed to hold her. "Sorry," he kept repeating. "Sorry you had to see that."

Her wide eyes met his as the corners of her mouth curled upward into a slight and likely forced smile. "That was...amazing. What you did. That's not possible, is it?"

Scout tried to help. "He's stronger than he looks. We should go. Right, Deacon? We should get Claire out of here."

"Use the back," I said. "I don't think I can leave. I'm technically still at work. I'll manage the fallout..." I continued to mumble as I searched for the reasons behind my failure.

Ivy scanned the room as noise grew, and I stood dumbfounded in my tracks.

"I'll be right there," Ivy said. "I need to find Reed. I forgot about him."

Reed!

That had to be it. That likely evil Agent of the Destroyer had messed with my abilities and crowded my brain. Shanar had used him to distract and distance me from my assignment.

But if that were true, how had Deacon managed to break through with what appeared to be a new multi-colored sign of his powers?

Ivy rushed to the table and knocked a chair out of the way. "Reed? What's the matter?"

The man sat hunched in the corner with his hands pushed tight against his face.

"Reed!" Ivy shouted and tugged at his wrists.

He jerked and almost knocked her back.

"Reed," she said again. "It's me, Ivy."

"Ivy."

"Yes. Are you hurt?"

"No." He scrambled to get up. "Sorry. I have to go."

"Wait. The door's blocked. Just sit a minute."

"There's a back door. Are you all right?"

"Yes."

"I have to go. Sorry."

He grabbed the edge of the counter and used it to steady himself as he walked its length and disappeared through the hallway to the back exit.

I grabbed the sides of my head and surveyed the mess. I couldn't think. "What is happening? Why couldn't I help, and what's wrong with Reed?"

"I don't know what happened to you." Ivy picked up the chair. "But Reed's a soldier, and this looks like a war zone."

CHAPTER 15

Deacon

Claire knocked pieces of sheetrock out of my hair, brushed dust off my eyebrows, and pointed to the passenger seat of her mother's car.

I pulled off my one shoe and peeled off my grubby socks to shake them before I complied.

She got in beside me and stared ahead as she gripped the steering wheel. She didn't say much, she just started the car and let the fan blow air on our faces.

"Do you need to go to the hospital or something? You seem fine, but you'd think something like that would hurt you. Sometimes people don't realize they're hurt until later."

"I'm good." My hands still pulsed heat. I was sorry I hadn't gotten to try to help the boys more. I didn't know if I still had any healing power in my hot fingers, or if I'd moved on in my abilities. I couldn't exactly lift walls with supernatural strength and pull victims to safety at the same time, and then concentrate on tapping in to healing energy... Could I?

Claire frowned. "What happened in there?"

I knew it was Warrior business, but other than that, I didn't know what to tell her besides the obvious. "That wall of bricks they tried to put up didn't hold. Stupid idea. Those boys could have died. They still might. They were awake, but what do I know?"

"Timing is everything," she said with a hopeful tilt of her head. "And you were there. I caught the tail end of it. That thing must have weighed a ton."

"It wasn't as heavy as it looked," I lied. "I need to go by the house and get cleaned up, but do you want to go eat or see a movie or something?"

"Sure." She put the car in reverse. "You're pretty calm for a hero, Deacon. The place wasn't busy today, but there were phones out. It's going to hit social media like the fire videos did."

"Then the sooner we duck into a theater, the better."

When Scout's grandma answered the door days later, I handed her a bouquet of flowers, six muffins in a paper bag, and a colorful mylar balloon.

"What's this, darlin'?"

I put my hands on my hips. "I have four brothers at my house and we still have muffins to spare."

She smiled. "Thank you. Everyone is upstairs."

"I have more stuff in the car."

She nudged the door with her backside to let me back out. "I'm going to go put these daisies in water. Love them. Thanks."

Once upstairs, I put the two large wicker baskets on the ottoman. "We have a cheese assortment and a muffin assortment." I swept my hand in the air across the display. "My house is full of baskets like this and some came with flowers and balloons."

"Nice," Scout said. He tugged the plastic from around a container of fancy cheese spread and went back in for the crackers.

"I'll get drinks," Ivy said.

But Mary didn't say anything.

"No, it's not nice," I said. "It's unnecessary. And embarrassing. People are coming to my house."

"Yeah," Scout said. "I saw a teaser on a Houston news app that they're doing an interview with the boys."

"They came to my house, Scout," I said again.

"I know, Deacon, just like they came to all our houses over the fire. The second one. Not the first or third one."

"My mom got a call about that interview. They wanted us too."

"And everyone agreed we weren't going to talk." He dropped the crackers back in the basket. "Look, it's always like this after an assignment. The public responds."

"No." I raised my hands in protest. "There's something wrong about that. We're supposed to be helpers. Fighters. Warriors. Not public figures. How are we supposed to work and keep the rest of our families safe? They have no idea this is not just a series of coincidental events. Are you all not thinking the same thing? If the Agents of the Destroyer can get to us, they can easily get to everyone we love. I don't understand this. Why is this happening?"

Ivy offered me a can of Dr Pepper and I couldn't even take it. "No, thanks."

"I've thought about it," she said. "I thought we were supposed to be inconspicuous and help people. Almost everything we've done has turned into a spectacle."

"That's exactly my point," I said. "I talked to Char about this. There's no fanfare when she does something. She gets things done and moves on. She's not even spotted sometimes. She saved a guy when he and his girlfriend tried to take a selfie on a ledge and he lost his footing. She walked away before they could stand up and thank her."

"She's been doing this longer than us," Ivy said. "Maybe it's practice. She's learned to hear things sooner. She works with more stealth."

Scout went back for the crackers. "Or maybe her assignments are not as big as ours or involve as many people. Even Char couldn't have hidden from the gym fire or the wall in the Smoothie Shack."

"She also seems to work alone," I said. "Maybe we're this close just long enough to get better at our jobs. Then we'll be able to handle some assignments on our own."

"Not when they involve so much physical strength," Scout said. "You picked up a brick wall, dude. I think we work as a team." He glanced at Ivy. "Except for Corey. Ivy's cognitive abilities seem to allow her to help one-on-one."

"Yeah," she said. "But I agree. If it were a massive physical undertaking, I'm not sure I could do it."

I laced my fingers behind my head and walked around the room. "Maybe you won't know until you're faced with that circumstance. I never do."

Mary still had not said a thing. We were a team. She was our leader—at least so far. But something had gone horribly out of balance when the wall fell. She knew about it first and sounded the warning bells, but she hadn't been able to deliver.

I pushed it. "We can't go on like this. I want my normal life back. I don't mind helping the Creator, but I can't get anything done while dodging well-wishers and media in my own driveway. I'm too full of muffins. I'm never too full of anything. My parents said they're going to talk to everyone else's parents. Do we really want our parents talking to each other about this?"

"Calm down," Scout said. "Let's back up and think. We always figure it out."

"Is Claire OK?" Ivy asked. "Or is she freaked out?"

"She doesn't seem to be, but we spent the rest of that afternoon huddled in a movie theater trying to wait for word on the kids and hoping no one saw us when we came out. She doesn't know what to make of all this." I crossed my arms and again studied Mary. My patience was running thin. "Are you going to say something?"

"I don't know what to say. It was a weird day."

"You must be thinking something."

She tossed the pillows off her lap and stood in a huff. "Reed Logan. That's what I'm thinking. Reed Logan."

"What about Reed Logan?" Ivy's tone was defensive.

"I know he's your father," Mary said. "But he's still an unknown. I think his presence there interfered with my ability to work."

"It didn't bother Deacon," Ivy shot back. "In fact, he got stronger when he had to pick up your slack."

"So now I'm slacking?"

"Don't pretend you don't know what I mean."

Mary sagged against the couch. "I know something went wrong."

"And you think it was Reed?" Ivy went on. "In case you don't remember, he was balled up and catatonic in the corner. I don't think he's working for the Destroyer. I think he has PTSD. I haven't been able to get a hold of him since then."

"Hold on," I said. "We need to talk about all this."

Tears rimmed Ivy's eyes as she stood and quickly regained control. "He's my dad. I've never known my dad. You get that, right? It would be nice to have him in my life. And now it looks like he's messed up from the war. And he won't answer me…"

Scout tugged on her hand until she sat back down.

"We do get it," I said. "But I also get that he's done some questionable things."

"Well, can we at least get the facts before we decide he's a bad guy? None of us have been ourselves since Jacob..."

"Yes, I know," Mary snapped. "I'm a walking, talking, blue-and-green-eyed vengeance machine. I can't help it. I want Gavin dead."

I stepped toward her. "But don't you see all that anger is interfering with your assignme—?"

"I have a right to be angry." Her eyes got wide, wild, and scary. "I'm gonna be angry for a while. Get used to it. And how do you know my anger was to blame? Do you have any idea what was happening around you while we were working together to lift that wall?"

Uh... I guess I'd missed something. "Wait. You said there was something new. What do you mean?"

Ivy slumped. "You have no idea? We thought you knew and we just haven't had a chance to talk about it."

I looked at Scout's blank stare.

"Don't look at me," he said. "I didn't see it. You know I'm only good for logic and analytics."

"That's not true. You're also the snake and oil person—not to be confused with a snake-oil person—but I wouldn't admit to that. And you're our pool person. We need you."

"Gee, thanks. I'll go down in Warrior history as the one who had a pool."

"And now a lake house," I added.

Mary's head snapped up. "You have a lake house?"

"It's not official, but yes. We're about to have a lake house to visit, but can we settle something here first? We're off track and everyone is antsy."

Mary dropped her head in her hands and pulled her hair tight in her fingers on the sides. Pain and rage still hovered around her like a black halo of despair. She didn't look up.

"Ivy," she said. "I'm sorry. I didn't mean to imply my meltdown was all Reed's fault. He's just still an unknown."

"And I'm sorry I got so defensive," Ivy replied. "That's my dad." She smiled at Scout. "I have a dad."

"*And?*"

Ivy looked back at me. "Oh. And you lit up like a whole herd of My Little Ponies, a box of Lucky Charms, *and* an entire fleet of retired Care Bears all had babies and exploded in an aura around your body. It was quite the show."

CHAPTER 16

Mary

Everyone was on my last nerve.

Ivy couldn't help but to defend her father—a guy who quite possibly was the human body Shanar used to complete heinous acts against us. He was the obvious person to believe was behind all the moving parts of the Stonehaven Gym Fire. He'd followed us to Colorado, and I didn't buy his reason. And yes, he looked like every depiction and description of a traumatized veteran, but if he were truly evil, it could have been an act. I knew more and less every day about my job as a Warrior. I thought I'd had it figured out. And then Jacob... I never expected so great a loss. I knew then that everything was much bigger, stronger, more costly—more important than I ever imagined. It wasn't a game, and the dark forces continued to grow. And that, I guess, was the secret I continued to uncover. I'd been trained my whole life to fight my enemy. I was the only one in our group who knew so early about the war. And then I had my team, but I'd been crushed and wounded, and ground into the dirt under immeasurable pain.

And when I came up to breathe, it was the fire of rage that fed my soul, and not the loving, compassionate drive I needed to be a Warrior and hear my true leader's voice.

The voice of the Creator.

And, all the time, I flirted with the sharp, black edge of revenge and still tried to help when I knew the Creator needed me. Something got in my way, but hey. It was one assignment, and it was probably Reed Logan who dampened my performance. It wouldn't happen again. I knew I was strong, and I knew I wasn't finished. Somehow, Gavin would pay for his crimes, and all I had to do was combine my anger and my job and regain my focus.

And back to Reed Logan.

I was never going to trust that he hadn't infiltrated our group to fracture and destroy us, and that he wasn't truly there to ultimately harm Ivy. I was going to expose him. I knew my fellow Warriors were concerned that I wasn't on my game, but I would get better. It just still hurt.

It hurt.

All the time.

It hurt.

Reed had Ivy completely under his spell and I felt for her, but could do nothing more as I tried to maintain my last strands of stability as I grieved and moved through the motions of everyday activities.

The big showdown was coming. Reed fit in there somewhere.

Deacon held out his hands in an exaggerated gesture. "I'm waiting... What happened at the wall?"

"I felt everything before it happened," I said. "I knew that wall was coming down when I jumped across the counter. I thought maybe I had the speed to swoop them out of the way.

But I didn't." I reached for a bottle of water. "And then I knew you would be there with your strength, Deacon, and it would be so simple. Lift the wall, pull them out."

"But then you couldn't. I didn't feel you in there with me like I did in front of the car that night. And I almost lost my nerve because I thought I couldn't do it without you."

"That's it," Ivy broke in. "That's why the additional, uh, whatever it was came to help."

"I'd call it a manifestation," Scout said. "What you described and the way you said you saw it sounds like a new manifestation of an ability to me."

"Right," she agreed. "But I knew as soon as I saw it only on Deacon that the answer was you two had to split up. If you stopped trying to do it together when you couldn't, the new ability could land squarely on Deacon—who was apparently open to it—and it carried him through the assignment."

I fought an eyeroll.

"Sorry, Mary," she continued. "I didn't mean to imply you weren't open to the extra help."

"I know what you mean," I tried to say nicely. I knew she meant no harm, but, like I said, everyone was on my last nerve that day.

"What did you guys actually see?" Deacon wanted to know. "Because I didn't feel any different. My hands got hot, but that's normal for me now and expected. And I didn't feel the extra energy like when we pushed open the gym doors."

"I saw green ribbon-like things with gold borders," I said.

"Yeah," Ivy agreed. "Then more stuff came and went. There were sparkles and all kinds of colors. They all kinda converged inside a bubble all around you."

"Wait," I said. "I didn't see a bubble. I only saw colors. Then again, your optical abilities far outweigh the rest of ours."

Ivy snorted. "Yay me. I get to hallucinate."

"Visions," Scout corrected for the millionth time. "Visions."

"Whatever, but Deacon, you had colors around you. I have no idea what it means. There's no manual for *Warriors 101: Abilities with Color.* So we'll have to wait it out and see if it happens again. If I had to guess, I'd say it was just the way Sebastian looked when he came to help. Or maybe he had other Enforcers with him to support you, and together, the light came out."

I glanced at them all and smacked my hands on my thighs as I stood. "And I'll be the one to say it since you're all thinking it. He needed extra help from somewhere because I wasn't present."

"We didn't say that," Deacon said.

"But you're thinking it. I let something—or someone—pull me out of the fight. I was caught off guard. It won't happen again. I have to go to work."

"The Smoothie Shack is back open?"

"No. Tomorrow. But we're still cleaning and receiving supplies for the re-opening. It actually didn't take that long to clean it up, and the property owner got someone in there right away to slap up a new wall."

Ivy smiled as if she had a bright idea. "We'll come tomorrow to show our support."

"Well, can you leave Reed Logan behind? I'm still trying to figure out if he's working against me."

I knew the words were too harsh the minute they flew out of my mouth. I hated the hurt look on Ivy's face, and I hated instantly that I'd lost control of my words.

"I didn't mean that the way it came out, Ivy. It's not Reed I'm really mad at."

"Yes, it is, Mary, and it's fine. He's not around, so don't worry. I won't be bothering you at work with my dad."

"It's not your *dad* I'm worried about, Ivy. It's the fact we still don't know enough about him. Doesn't anyone else remember he was actively working against us in the hallways at the fire? And that he had a cell phone pointed at a scoreboard? And that he is the guy who followed us to Colorado? Come. On. We need to be sure what his intentions are because I, for one, don't believe he's an all innocent and cuddly papa bear. Where's he been all this time? Please tell me you don't all think this guy isn't dirty in this!"

"I want him to be OK for Ivy's sake," Deacon said.

"I do too," I said a little too loud. "But I'm worried that's not the case."

"I'm right here," Ivy said. "I can hear you bashing my dad. But you don't have to worry. We won't be at the Smoothie Shack ever again."

"Stop!" Scout shouted. "Stop right there and listen to me."

I wanted to punch the wall like some angry drunk, and Ivy's cheeks had pinkened to bright red as she either tried not to cry or tried not to tackle me.

Nevertheless, we all turned Scout's way.

He stood. "Raise your hand if you know what's happening here."

He was the only one who raised his hand.

"Really, you guys? You don't know?"

I stopped short of actually snarling at him. I'd turned into a nasty rabid racoon who didn't want to be cornered under the porch with any truth.

"This is exactly what the Destroyer wants," Scout said. "We're agitated in general and we're turning it on each other. We're still grieving. We lost our school. The elusive electrician turning out to be Ivy's dad is unbelievable, and the timing alone raises suspicion. Our stress is up and our defenses are down. We're crumbling."

"No, we're not," Deacon said. "We're not. We had another assignment. We saved two boys."

"*You* saved two boys," I said. "I was on the outside looking in."

"But it's not supposed to be that way," Deacon said. "We'll get it back. You were the first to know."

"But I'm the one who couldn't help and isn't sure what blocked me."

"But it isn't one of us," Scout said. "That's the point. We have to figure this stuff out together. We can't argue and point fingers. We have to stick together. Shanar would like nothing more than to split us up and destroy us."

"He can't do that," Deacon said. "No way, no how. I won't let him. Not after everything we've been through. Not after Jacob. We're going to pull it together and get back on track."

"Scout's right," Ivy said. "He's totally right. The Destroyer is attacking from the inside out. Classic bully move. I'm not playing this game." She stood and came my way. "Look, Mary, I know my dad is the big unanswered question, but he's my dad. Even if he's guilty of something, I want to hear the truth from him and really know if he's sorry or not. I don't know if it'll make any difference, but I need to know too."

I nodded. "You're right. You're all right. And no, we're not giving an inch. We're a team." I glanced at my phone. "I'm sorry about all this. I'm just…sorry. I have to go to work."

Ivy stole a hug as I tried to leave.

I tried my best to stop and hug her back, but it was half-hearted.

Why couldn't they see how dangerous Reed Logan really was?

I contemplated my moment of weakness.

It wouldn't happen again.

Gavin, and everyone else responsible for Jacob's death, had to pay.

And Shanar had to be banished from our realm forever.

CHAPTER 17

Mary

I dimmed the lights in the seating area and headed for the counter to finish cleaning.

I knew the moment someone slipped in the yet-to-be-locked door behind me, but I didn't care.

"We're closed," I called over my shoulder.

"Then you should lock the door and turn off the sign."

Mr. Parrington's sweet and comforting voice caused a wash of moisture to hit my eyes and nose. I held it back as I turned to smile.

I pulled out my keys. "Help yourself." I tossed them his way. "I'm not making any more smoothies tonight."

He laughed. "This reminds me of my Pizza Hut days."

"That doesn't sound *too* sad," I said. "I can manage with the fresh fruit and vegetables and the powdered mix, but ovens and crust and all the toppings…gross."

"It was pretty bad. I burned myself a lot."

I pointed to the last blender in use. "I know I said no smoothies, but it's no trouble. Watcha want?"

"What's your favorite?"

"Tell you what. I'll mix up a house special from what I've got left here."

"Why not?"

He wandered around to look at the new wall while I whirled a bunch of fruit into...something.

I set a concoction in front of him as he settled onto a stool. "Here's a spoon too," I said. "I left some chunks of fruit in there for you." I prepared to clean up my last mess and caught his questioning gaze. "Are you looking at my weird eyes, or checking for a limp, or trying to get a glimpse of the crazy girl who kicked down a barrier today at the S.A.I.N.T. Lab? Which is it?"

"I only want to talk, Mary."

"Right. You and I haven't really spoken much since the ski trip. You've been busy with the fire..."

"Yes, and you can't imagine how hard it is to keep up with everyone when the school is a war zone and no one is ever in the same place."

"Are you talking as a principal or as a Guardian?"

"Both, but right now I'm here as your Guardian. Someone who knows your realm."

"C'mon. Are you sure it's not because I sent a whole ream of paper flying in the wind when the printer in the lab wouldn't work? Because anyone would have done that. As soon as I got it unjammed and back online, it had the nerve to inform me it was out of black ink. Ask anybody. That ream of paper I ran outside and released into the wild was the least that printer deserved. And that paper flyover caused all the construction noise to stop for one glorious moment so we could think."

He ignored my dramatic reenactment and dipped the long

spoon into the tall cup. "This is good. You should write down what leftovers you put in here and sell it every day."

I dropped a wet rag in the sink and collapsed onto the stool the owner kept hidden by the cash register. We weren't supposed to sit behind the bar, but by the end of most days we were so tired we sat to clean and put things in the dishwasher. "Why are you here, Mr. Parrington?"

"I'm worried about you, and I wanted to see how you're doing. Can we have an honest conversation about that? Guardian to Warrior?"

"Every conversation I have is honest. I hate lies."

"I know that about you. I actually appreciate it, but I also think you're a little out of control here and there. I'm not saying I don't understand it, I'm just saying I'm concerned."

"No need to be concerned. I can take care of myself."

"Oh, I know that. Nothing scares you, Warrior Mary Hunter. You're not afraid of anything. In fact, I think you're looking for a fight everywhere you go."

"Did the others send you?"

"Not at all."

"Then what's the point of this visit?"

"Have you been seeing your counselor?"

"My parents make me go, but there's a lot of sitting and staring at each other. I dozed off once. She did not appreciate that, but I reminded her my parents' insurance paid for the fifty-minute hour, and that day I felt like a nap."

He switched to the straw and took a long drink. "I bet counseling is hard for you." He chuckled and balled up the wrapper and tossed it passed my head and hit the can. "I mean, what are you going to tell her? The truth?"

"Yeah," I said and crossed my arms. "That'd be a riot."

"There are many of us working in this realm, Mary, but we're not always easy to spot. You can talk to me, or I can find others you can talk to."

"I have my people."

"Your people are teenagers. There are adults who've been at this a lot longer than you. They understand."

"Yeah. So many others, but I'm alone because my Protector was taken from me."

"And that has you so angry you can't see straight."

"Despite my sudden eye-color change, I see fine."

He leaned in. "It is startling at first. I've never seen that happen before. I assume you have an Enforcer... A guide. What does he or she say about that?"

"We're not speaking much at the moment."

"You have to lean on the only people who can help you, Mary."

"No one can help me."

"I know no one can truly ease your pain, but you can't keep that chip on your shoulder forever. You have to keep your wits about you."

"We're back to my behavior in the S.A.I.N.T. Lab, aren't we? People are complaining? They think I've lost it?"

"Everyone is worried about you."

"There's no need to worry. That barrier partition I kicked was already falling down—or at least was on the demolition list. I saved them some work. And all this other anger I carry is for one person. You know who that is."

"It's not your job to punish Gavin, Mary. You could put yourself in a very vulnerable place if you take matters into your own hands. Your abilities are a gift and serve a purpose. It's not your place to seek revenge, no matter how much you feel it's deserved."

"So I've been told."

"You don't want to be in the middle of a fight for your life and discover your enemy has the upper hand because you've fallen to their level of depravity. You need to understand there are more battles coming. You have to be in the right frame of mind to handle and win them."

"I'm doing the best I can to hold on here, Mr. Parrington. Gavin can't get away with what he's done. He just can't."

"He won't. I promise. But you have to power through. That means leaning into the pain and walking through it. There's no way around, no easy way out. It just has to hurt and hurt until it hurts a little less each day and you can move forward."

"Is this counseling session over? Because I have some sanitizing to do."

"You need to hear me, Mary. Your gifts and your purpose are so far beyond what we've seen that the realm knows it's special. Others know about you, but we don't know all your significance. Deacon, Ivy, and Scout are only beginning to understand the true depths of their gifts, and it's your job to lead them. You can't hold a grudge and risk leading them astray. You have to be in charge. You have to be the example."

"Maybe the Creator should call someone else. Maybe it's not in me after Jacob to be the leader."

"You're the *only* one who can be the leader. Don't you see that? That's what your whole existence has been about."

"I can't let go," I whispered. "I can't stop seeing Jacob die on that mountain."

"I know."

"Gavin did that."

"I know."

"He has to pay."

"He does. That battle, that death, and that healing process is probably the hardest thing you'll ever do, but you can't be the one to collect on what he owes for Jacob's life. You have to pull it together and lead your Warriors."

"What if I can't?"

CHAPTER 18

Reed

Of all the stupid mistakes I'd made in my life—and there'd been too many to count—I'd made the most of them in that last year. And that was saying a lot considering there'd been some doozies before that.

I'd partied my way through high school because I couldn't concentrate. My thoughts were way too scattered to focus on any one thing. I couldn't control the constant parade of technicolor ideas that flew through my mind. I couldn't stop hearing the silent waves of distress coming from the people around me.

I was in kindergarten when I thought the devil lived under the sandbox on the school playground. At least I thought it was the devil when the feeling passed over me and I thought I heard my name.

I never told anyone.

If you're quiet and polite and smile a lot, people never know what's penned up in your mind. You just suffer alone and get to be the oddball who pushes it too far once in a while and takes too many chances.

Sometimes that makes you the hero.

Sometimes it makes you a jerk.

College obviously slipped through my fingers, and the love of my life might have saved me if the odds weren't so catastrophically stacked against us.

We were fine, the two of us. All she needed was to find her stability, and all I had to do was find a job and accept that the mechanics of my mind were not a curse, but rather a gift. My aunt had told me so straight up when she died. Explained the whole thing. I had a gift. I was supposed to ask the Creator for help.

I was so angry with her. She died before I could take back the mean things I said, but for the love of anything that was ever holy, why hadn't she helped me sooner?

Still, I neglected to latch on to that lifeline, and instead, found myself in the horrors of war, making bargains with the Destroyer.

That was the biggest mistake I still planned to undo.

Among my other big, idiotic blunders: Leaving my little family.

The worst one yet: Thinking I could come back for them.

I must have circled the apartment complex twenty times before I decided to park and try to breathe. I'd gotten myself into that mess, and I had to get myself out. I'd done everything backward. That was the story of my life. Even if I had a snowball's chance, I'd never be forgiven for seeing Ivy behind her mother's back. I looked exactly like the devious and dangerous person she thought I was, the terrible man who took off when she needed me most.

I guess I was all of that and worse.

Much worse.

I waited until dusk.

Ivy's mom would be in for the evening, and Ivy would be strolling with four dogs at a time all around the apartment buildings.

I hated that Scout was right about everything. Nothing got by that kid, and that group of Warriors was as tight as any band of brothers I ever fought beside. Yeah, they had their struggles because they were young and naïve, but who was the not-so-savvy one then?

I should have done it differently from the start.

Instead, I was there, hat in hand, about to take the biggest gamble and make a fool of myself.

The door swung open and it was clear she thought Ivy had forgotten her key or something.

"Maddie." I tugged the felt rim of my best Stetson through my fingers until it spun too fast in my nervous grip.

She was exactly the same.

"No one calls me Maddie anymore."

"Sorry I—"

"And you don't get to call me anything at all."

CHAPTER 19

Ivy

I handed Muffin's leash to her owner as the door slammed on the floor above me.

That was my door. Had something happened to my mother?

I paused on the landing below to see Reed Logan setting his hat on his head as he cursed under his breath and took one last look at the door before stomping down the stairs toward me. I rushed to the ground floor way ahead of him to wait.

My mom blew up my phone. *Where are you?*

4 more dogs to walk.

I'll come find you. Watch for strangers.

She was scared I would run into Reed, and was probably reeling from his sudden appearance. I was torn. I knew I should check on her.

I pounded on a door—a mean-looking but harmless shepherd-mix's door—as I waited.

I'm grabbing Buster. I'm fine. I'm inside the complex with a lot of people.

All true.

Reed hit the last step and headed down the walk as I dragged Buster out of his apartment.

"Reed?" I'd startled him. "Walk with me this way."

"Oh. Ivy." He looked all around. "I took your boyfriend's advice and tried to fix this, but turns out I'm not good at that kind of thing."

"Don't move," I warned. "Stay under the awning."

As I suspected, my mom came out in her yellow, floral-print, comfy pajamas, and peered over the rail, three floors down.

I stepped out on the grass and smiled and waved. "Right here. I'm fine." I tugged on Buster's leash and moved on as she scanned the whole area.

"This way," I said to Reed.

"No, Ivy. I don't want to deceive your mother anymore. I'm sorry. I should have never approached you and put any of this on you."

"Give me a minute, will you? You haven't answered my texts since the wall thing."

"Your mom won't talk to me."

"I'm sure she's in shock," I argued. "We'll try again. C'mon, let's go back up."

"No!"

His stern and irritated command caused me to stumble and shrink like a cowering puppy. Buster gave him a stink-eye like I couldn't believe. I hated I was so sensitive. All the feelings, all the time. Scout called me a *human emotion sponge*. It wasn't an insult. He was right. I couldn't control how easily my feelings got hurt, and it was a constant battle to not tear up over my stuff and everyone else's. I was trying to get better. I wanted to kick more butt like Mary.

"Look, Ivy, this is not the time." His tone softened. "Maddie doesn't want to see me."

"Maddie?" The name was foreign to me.

"Yeah... I guess no one calls her that."

"No," I whispered. "They don't. Did you know my pretentious grandma?"

He attempted a smile and dipped his head. "Briefly. She wasn't a fan of cowboys."

"I guess, but how could she not be a fan of a Marine?"

"She was a fan of education, money, and business suits. I had none of that at the time."

"Maddie..." I kept repeating the name. "It suits my mom, but all I ever heard growing up was Constance and Madeline, Constance and Madeline... I get by with calling my Aunt Constance *Aunt Connie*, but just barely, and not in public."

"I can't stay here any longer, Ivy. It's not a good idea. Your mom could come down. I don't want to derail her. She looks great and she's taking good care of you. That's all I ever wanted. Maybe someday—"

"You have PTSD, right? That's what happened at the Smoothie Shack. You froze up."

He stalled as Buster snorted and rubbed his snout into the ground.

"You can't lie to me, Reed, remember? It's nothing to be ashamed of."

"I'm not ashamed—of that. I'm ashamed of other things. I was triggered in there because of the sounds. It took me a minute to gain control. It's a work in progress."

"And that's why you hang out and volunteer so much with that group of injured veterans. You get support there too."

"That day with the wall wasn't that bad, but it did surprise me because it hadn't happened in a long time. I've been other places with sounds and smells and it didn't bother me. I think it bothered me there because I was worried about you and I couldn't help."

"I didn't need your help. Mary, Deacon, Scout, and I look out for each other."

"I'm aware of your frequent episodes of heroism. Your team is strong. You need to stick together. Strategize together. Work together. Don't let anyone defeat you."

"You're not on active duty. Why do you sound like a soldier talking to a fellow soldier?" My skin pebbled as a shiver chased another shiver around my body. "And why do I feel like we're not on the same side of the battle all of a sudden?"

Buster's ears perked as he stood still and scanned the area. The side of his mouth curled to reveal a row of teeth before he licked his chops and plopped to his bottom, nearly on my foot, still watching and looking up to check on me every few seconds.

"I'm not the man you think I am, Ivy."

"I don't know for sure what kind of man I think you are, Reed. *Yet.* I'm still figuring it out. I know you're my dad. I know we share abilities. Care to let me in on any secrets?"

"I haven't made the right choices for a while now. That's why I should have never let you know I was here. And because of those choices, and because I need to straighten some things out, you won't be seeing me."

I tightened my grip on Buster's leash as my heart fell into my shoes. "That's convenient. For you."

"You don't understand everything—"

"Don't I? There's a trail of deceit all over your mind right now. There's fear too." I stepped closer. "You have raging water rushing behind those eyes. You're drowning. You don't know how to save yourself."

"But I know how to save you."

"I don't trust you to save anything right now."

"You can trust me, Ivy. I won't let anything happen to you."

"I don't need saving. I'm the one who helps with the saving of others. What are you in to, Reed? Is it all PTSD that has you wrapped up in darkness and confusion? Or are you actively working against me and people like me? I know you know who I work for. I see it now."

Alice from Wonderland herself couldn't have fallen down a more confusing or tragic rabbit hole. Our hopeful conversation had turned harsh and ominous in half a heartbeat. I didn't know who I was looking at, but he stunk of danger and reeked of a pitiful and futile need to be OK with me, while turning his back at the same time.

He tried to walk away. "I have to go."

"You still love my mother. Maddie. Your Maddie. And now I see she still loves you. She never moved on and she could have. You can't handle the way she looked at you or what you felt when you saw her, so you're going to run. You're running from the fight."

"No, Ivy, I'm running to the fight."

"I guess I'll see you there then."

And that's when my dad left me.

For the second time.

CHAPTER 20

Scout

Ivy came rushing around the house as night fell on my efforts to do my weekly clean up on the pool. Bloodthirsty mosquitoes took what they wanted from my lower legs as I hurried to finish and get in the house.

"He's gone again." She crashed into my arms. "It was awful."

"Whoa. Are you all right?" After a moment, I held her at arm's length. "What was awful, who's gone, and how did you get here?"

She looked at the starry sky and ticked off the answer to my questions on her fingers in the glow of the pool lights. "The conversation with Reed was awful, he's gone, and my mom dropped me off. Long story."

"What happened?"

"My mom was unsettled, so we headed out to hit a drive-thru for milkshakes and I asked her to stop here. I need to talk to you."

"Where is she?"

"She's in the car out front, eyebrows-deep in a strawberry shake."

"Is she OK? Let me ask her to come in. My grandma will visit with her and slap some essential oils on her or something."

"She won't come in. She's in her pajamas."

She tried to snake both arms around me in one of her vise-grip hugs. "Wait. What happened at your place tonight?"

"It's not good, Scout."

"Well, we can't leave your mom on the street."

She shoved away from me. "I know! But I don't know what to do. I'm stuck in the middle of something. There are things I can't tell my mom, and something happened to her tonight that I'm sure she'd never discuss with me, but I already know and I can't talk to her about it."

Agitation raced across my skin with the ugly scrape of a dull razor blade. "Reed Logan left you in the middle of a mess, didn't he?"

She twisted her fingers together and tried not to look directly at me. "Yes?"

"Dang it, Ivy, is your mom OK? I mean really OK? Did Reed mess with her mental state? Does she need help?"

"Oddly, I don't think she does. She's the steadiest she's ever been. Her support system keeps growing, and she's well. She's regulated. But..."

I let out a long sigh. "But she's sitting on the curb in her pajamas with a milkshake."

"I don't think it's that weird. I asked her to bring me here."

I swatted skeeters away from my legs and reached for a can of insect repellant by a lounge chair. "I actually kinda agree with you. Hold still. Let me spray your legs."

"I don't know what to do. I need to talk to you."

"All right. Stay here. You know my grandma's good with everyone. I'll have her go out and say hello and buy us some time to talk. If Reed Logan, a guy she hasn't seen for years and wasn't expecting to ever see again has approached her, she might have an issue."

"But you're the one who said he needed to do the right thing!"

"Yes, but I hope he didn't just show up at her door or something. What part of taking it slow does that selfish guy not get? He could have started with a note or a text or something! You have to ease in to something like this."

Ivy dropped her gaze to the ground and turned away.

"Oh, don't tell me. He did it, didn't he? He showed up at her doorstep and shocked her?"

"He apparently didn't get the memo on how to proceed in this situation. But right now, that's the least of our issues."

"Stay here," I said again.

She kicked at the slate walkway around the pool. "I'm not going anywhere."

Once I put my grandma in charge of Ivy's mom, I headed back out and coaxed Ivy onto the creaky old swing my grandpa dragged home from a yard sale and put by the pool. I'd never seen my grandma so enraged over one of his *finds*.

But Ivy's cuddling sent that image right outta my mind. The closer she snuggled, the better I felt about everything. Except Reed. I'd begun to have even more serious doubts about that guy.

"All right," I said. "Start at the beginning."

"Oh, Scout, you should have seen him. It was so weird."

"Weird how?"

She curled her legs under herself, and I sent the used contraption into a gentle swing with a push of my toe—and hoped we didn't crash and burn.

"Weird like he was split in two. One minute he was Reed. Then he wasn't. His whole demeanor changed right before my eyes. Then I got the worst vibe from him."

"But when did he see your mom? Were you there?"

"I was out walking dogs, then the next thing I knew there were doors slamming, and texts from my mom... And there was Reed. I don't know what happened and I can't ask her because then she'll know I know about him..." She shuddered with an inhale and grabbed my shirt and pulled closer on the exhale. "Anyway, he saw her and then I saw him as he tried to leave."

Sneaky.

The guy was sneaky. He had to know he was about to open Pandora's box when he went to that door. He should have had a better plan to take it slow, one that wouldn't shock Ivy's mom. The woman wasn't as fragile as Ivy still tended to believe. I knew she'd grown in confidence and control since I'd known Ivy, but Ivy still had the mama-bear-protection thing going because she'd taken care of her mom for so long.

But Reed Logan knew. He knew what kind of chilly reception he'd get, and he had to know Ivy was somewhere close at that time in the evening.

He was a sneaky one.

"What kind of vibe?" I asked.

"Like remember when we first met him, he was charming and friendly. He appeared to be genuine. We always questioned his motives, but he didn't alarm us."

"He's always alarmed Mary."

"Mary is looking for a fight everywhere she goes. Did Reed really concern her? Or was she just needing someone to take her anger out on?"

"Good question." I rubbed her arm and then played with the dangling hair that lay on her cheek. "But obviously, she's on to something if you saw through his good-guy appearance. What do you make of what you felt?"

"My dad left me, Scout. I don't know what I felt because now I feel numb."

"No. You can't be numb right now. You have to get the whole story out and we have to dissect it and see what to do next."

"Everything changed when he saw my mom. He was different when he came down those stairs. He admitted he had PTSD, but he was trying to apologize or explain something the whole time, but he never really did. He just said he had to take care of some things, that he didn't want to upset my mom, and that I wouldn't be seeing him. It was like a very frustrating and surreal chess game. I know he can't completely get into my head without my permission, but we can read each other's uh... Like we can see between the lines of each other's thoughts. I can't explain it. He let his guard down and I could see. I felt he was struggling. He's made some bad choices. He said as much."

"How bad?"

"I think we were right all along," she whispered. "I think he was working with Gavin and Shanar on the Stonehaven Gym Fire."

I stopped the swing hard and twisted to face her. Words failed me as I met that desperate, deep-brown gaze. "I'm sorry, Ivy. This is when I wish your gifts weren't as strong as they are."

"I know." She squeezed her eyes shut as two large teardrops rolled straight down and splashed on her dog-walking t-shirt. "Sometimes I wish I had more physical strength like Mary and Deacon, or had the kind of computer brain you do. I hate it when I look at someone I care about and have to admit they are not what they seem. Do you know how hard that is, Scout? I've wanted my dad my whole life."

I wanted to hold her till sunup and let her cry it out. I wanted to take the pain and make her understand it would be OK. But would it? Now all I knew was that our soft underbellies were completely exposed to the one force we were fighting to avoid and defeat. I needed more facts.

"Listen, I need your absolute and total intuitive answer on a couple of questions, OK?"

"Of course."

"And don't be offended. I have to ask. You realize Reed slipped up and you saw a part of him he probably didn't mean for you to see."

"What I saw was a man who still loves my mother and who suffers from PTSD."

"I know." My shoulders slumped and I dropped my gaze to the ground as I thought of my own dad. "I know you want your dad, but that may not be possible in the way you want, and we need to be completely sure of what we're dealing with."

She nodded.

"Do you think he had anything to do with the big fire? The one that ended our school year as we knew it?"

"No. Just the Stonehaven Gym Fire."

"All right." I paused to gather my courage. The next question was going to paralyze us both. "Do you think he was in Colorado to help Gavin kill Mary and Jacob?"

"No."

"And you're sure that's your true abilities talking and not your hopeful heart?"

"I'm sure."

"How are you sure?"

"What lived behind his eyes—in his soul—was trying to warn me. He was trying to tell me he'd changed. He said out loud for us to stick together and be strong. He knows it isn't over, but he's trying to break free of what he's done. Don't you get it? The only reason I was able to see through to his real nature is because whatever shield Shanar has around him isn't holding. He's fighting to get out. Finding me and seeing my mother started a shift in his realm loyalty."

I wanted that to be true, but I had my doubts. Not about Ivy's assessment of his crimes and his allegiance to Shanar when he invaded our lives and school, but of her conclusion of a white-knight-on-a-stallion whose love for her and her mother was so powerful that he would choose to break free and be a better man for their sakes.

Proverbial leopards didn't change their proverbial spots.

I wrapped my arms around her. "Ivy, you know I want you to be right, but he has to man up and admit his part in that fire. People could have died, and if he admits to helping Gavin set that whole thing up, it might lead to revealing Gavin as Jacob's killer."

"I need some time to wrap my head around this."

"Mary is gonna... We can't tell Mary this right now. She already wants to kill Gavin on sight. I'm afraid she might actually do it. Reed's right up there on her hit list. She won't be able to rationally process this."

She twisted out of my embrace and sent me into wobbly acrobatics on the swing as she paced in front of me.

"Don't you think I know that? It's what scares me the most. Even if the man has changed, he's not off the hook for everything else he did. That's why I need time."

"Time for what? Time to let him keep hurting you and your mom and others?"

"No! Time to see what happens. He won't hurt me and my mom. He wouldn't do that. He said I wouldn't be seeing him. I think he's trying to make it all right."

"How? Don't you see he's just giving himself time to get away? I know you want him to come back and redeem himself and be what you need. I know you have this new fantasy that he'll come home and you'll have your dad and he and your mom will reunite and live happily ever after. I don't think that's going to happen. I'm sorry, but I don't see it. He left, Ivy. I'm sorry, but he left because he's guilty, and I don't know how he can come back."

The girl I loved had collapsed into a weepy, inconsolable

heap on the hot concrete. I hated the position Reed had put her in. I hated more what was about to come. There was no way it would end well for any of us.

And Ivy's tender heart would be trampled the most, while her dad—the criminal—would forever be an *if only* in her genuinely forgiving heart and mind.

I knelt by her side. "We'll keep this to ourselves for a couple of days, but Mary and Deacon deserve to know. We can't keep it from them. It puts them in danger, and rocks our already unsteady hold on what's currently happening in our lives."

She nodded as wet splotches dotted the ground in a steady rhythm. "I know what we have to do." She crawled into my lap. "But Scout, you have to believe me. I know what I saw."

"And I believe you." I cradled her head against my chest.

"He cracked right before my eyes. He cracked. And he's picking a new side."

CHAPTER 21

Shanar

Humans.

Tedious, irritating, and completely useless.

I found the two I wanted to meet—Reed and Gavin. They were lounging in the bright morning sunlight at a park not far from what used to be Stonehaven Academy's high school buildings.

They drank coffee from tiny holes in plastic lids on the tops of white paper cups like it was the most important thing they'd do all day. Why did I bother with them?

I slipped past joggers and moms with toddlers as I moved in my supernatural form to the bench where they sat in their miserable, exhausted flesh-and-bone sacks.

I didn't really do the whole cheerful morning thing, but I tried. "It's nice to see two of my favorite Agents in the same place."

Longtime friend, Reed Logan, didn't seem all that happy to

feel my cuddly force between them on the seat. He stood and spiked his cup into the trash can more like an angry football player than a responsible citizen.

"Why did you summon us here? It's dangerous."

"It's a pleasure to see you too." I shifted enough for him to catch a glimpse of the dark and slimy truth of mine and his existence just below the surface of my disguise. With one turn of my swirling mass, I could peel back a curtain and reveal atrocities only he could see. Fields of corpses, sights of rotting flesh, and curling tendrils of smoke, ash, and blowing sand usually shut down whiny Agents on the spot and reminded them of the death and destruction I carried from the Destroyer's own private collection of misery. And oh, it was misery. The metallic scent of battlefield blood, and the suffering cries of dying comrades, designed especially for the soldier's torment.

My form was not all light and airy fluff, even in the daytime. I always carried the consequences of the particular human I was targeting. I held their darkest crimes and most secret failures.

How else could I torture them but to show them exactly what they were capable of—or what they didn't prevent?

What others saw as horror movie special effects were, in fact, the truest depths of the depravity the humans were capable of when they wanted something and lived in moral ambiguity. Just because they didn't participate didn't mean they weren't responsible. Turning blind eyes to heinous acts didn't necessarily bathe their hands in dirt and blood, but careless and spiteful words and actions always wounded someone somewhere.

And actions, once set in motion, always continued churning through space and time, crashing into and destroying things far into the future.

I turned my attention to the juvenile pile of turds on the other end of the bench. I knocked him off the edge.

He knew better than to respond as hot liquid splattered onto his face.

"Anyway," I turned my attention back to Reed. "You've managed to gain the trust of the little band of Warriors. The protection around them is so strong, I can hardly keep up with them anymore to thwart their efforts, though they do seem to be in a bit of trouble since Colorado. A little disjointed maybe? You must stay close to your daughter and report back what's happen—"

"No. I'm finished with all this. Our partnership ended when I left the military."

"That's hilarious, because wasn't it you who helped the pool of vomit over here orchestrate and carry out that exploding scoreboard fiasco?"

"That was a mistake that won't happen again. I didn't know that was exactly where my daughter was working for the other side."

"Stop. You're embarrassing yourself. You've known all about your girl-brat since the day she was born. Don't be stupid, soldier. You thought you were going to be clever and play both sides of the fence. You know it doesn't work that way."

Reed turned to leave. "Nevertheless, I'm done with you. I fulfilled our agreement and made you look good to the Destroyer. I'm leaving this area forever."

"You're going to leave the girl-brat on her own? Where I can get to her?" I laughed out loud. "You make it too easy."

"You're not touching my daughter or her mother. You can't. That group of Warriors is the one we've always heard about. They are stronger than your threats. They mean something to the world and to the Creator. They've defeated you so far, and they will only get stronger."

"What defeat? They've barely escaped with their lives. And I snatched their human, Jacob, right out of their grasp. Well, the chunk of poo over here did that with my help, but still... They're not that strong."

Reed spun back. "You've seen how powerful they are, and they're just getting started. They could end you."

My anger thundered out of control. The ground shook as I spiraled into a tunnel of wind and sprayed dirt and trash across the nearby play area. Stunned runners and frightened park visitors gazed high into the thrashing branches and plumes of dust. Then they ran.

"I am a powerful supernatural being. I cannot be ended."

Reed didn't seem impressed with my show of supremacy as he waited for the disturbance to pass. "And you find it necessary to show this power in a public family park on a lazy weekend morning?" he asked. "You've lost more than a touch of your smooth and persuasive sales pitch for the dark side."

"I could finish you on this spot."

"No, you can't, remember? I'm the one who knows the trouble you got in to with the Destroyer. I'm the one you broke the rules with. You can't kill me, and you can't make me do anything."

"But I can get to your girl-brat and her mother. Or do you really think that bumbling band of Warriors can protect them? Are you willing to take the chance? The Creator doesn't hear you anymore. You've burned your bridges there."

"And you've burned yours with the Destroyer as it pertains to me. You remember the wartime desert, right? You had evil to control and play with on both sides, yet it wasn't enough to pull the strings. You wanted to be in the fight."

"And you wanted to live. It was a win-win for both of us. You couldn't run into fire and be the hero with your pathetic human form, and I couldn't settle old scores in my realm. So what if I used your body to get some things done? We both came out heroes. You got scores of medals for what you did—or rather what my power allowed you to do."

"But you broke your realm's rules. You're not allowed to enter a physical human body on Earth."

"You allowed it. You practically begged me to help you, and we were both better off for it in the end."

I never tired of tormenting humans, but I was getting weary of my going-nowhere conversation with my old war buddy.

Reed dropped to the bench. "I'll say this one more time. I'm leaving this area. We are finished, and my daughter and her mother are off limits."

"I can't do that. You're too valuable."

"I can be valuable anywhere in the world. It doesn't have to be here, and it doesn't have to put my daughter and her mother in danger. You can't touch them."

"Are you saying you'll still be available—just not here?"

It was clear the weak human struggled with the decision, though his evil streak would surely outweigh any good intentions he ever thought he could maintain. He'd made his choice years ago, and it wasn't like he could be free of me anyway. I could do what I wanted with his girl-brat and her mother.

"I'll be around. Far from here. And you can't touch my daughter or her mother."

I switched my focus to the younger Agent. For everyone who hadn't run from the disturbance or who had wandered back, it looked like nothing more than a couple of guys on a bench.

I took the opportunity to get close to his ear as he continued to clean coffee from his face and shirt. I startled him with a loud slurping noise. In his haste to twist away, he again fell off the bench.

So entertaining.

He stood. "Don't bother messing with me. You don't impress me either. Everything is under control on my end."

"Is that a joke? Mary is still alive and well and making

smoothies. I need to finish her off in order to set everything back to normal in my realm. I need her life."

The insolent boy snickered. "You make a lot of noise for someone who seems to have a lot of groveling to do to get back in the Destroyer's good graces. You lost a battle to Mary when she was only three, and you apparently couldn't follow the rules with the girl-brat's dad here. We have no reason to even listen to you. You are the joke."

I bashed his face into the wooden slats of the seat.

"Hey!" Reed yelled. "Knock it off. He can't accomplish anything with a caved-in face."

"And why do you care?" I shot back. "You were just leaving."

Reed stepped over to the boy. "Listen kid, you don't—"

"Enough!" I roared.

Gavin spit blood on the ground and pulled his phone out of his pocket. "See?" he said and waved it wildly in the air as if I was going to read it. "I told you I had it under control."

I wasn't standing there like a useless human. I could comprehend a text.

Gavin, in case you deleted my number, it's Mary. Please meet me at the testing center after S.A.I.N.T. Lab time. I need to talk to you.

CHAPTER 22

Mary

I pressed my back against the late afternoon sun-warmed bricks of one of the few remaining exterior walls of Stonehaven Academy. My body still ached from time to time when I slept wrong or sat too long in a chair at the lab. I needed to get back on the track and run. I knew I needed to. But the focus I once held for building muscle and staying fit for soccer disappeared in the pain of rehab for multiple injuries. Looping that track seemed like a monumental effort for my tired and broken body.

Especially when all I wanted to spend my energy on was justice.

Weeks and months had ticked by since Jacob's murder, and Gavin still ran the streets in his new car like nothing had happened. Like he wasn't a killer, and like he'd never be caught and pay for his crimes.

He stared at me all the time in the S.A.I.N.T. Lab. I avoided him, but he was always there. I knew I'd rattled him that night at the Smoothie Shack, but he still skulked around as if he wanted—no, *craved*—my attention. And all the cards were on the table. I'd made it clear I knew his intentions, and I was certain of his guilt. I wasn't going to let him kill me. What did he think he could possibly gain from me? How disturbed was he that he thought anything would ever go back to the way it was?

That's what I intended to find out, because his mere presence was messing with my ability to do my Warrior work, and it was twisting my mind into more confusion and despair. I couldn't let distraction hinder me again. I couldn't have a repeat of what happened at the wall.

It was time to regain the upper hand.

Gavin came around the corner and let his backpack slide from his shoulder until it dangled at his side. His eye twitched. "I didn't think you'd really be here."

"Why not? I texted you."

He rushed toward me. "And I'm so glad you did. We can work this out, Mar—"

"Stop talking." I pushed away from the wall. "Where's your car?"

"My car?"

"Yes, your car, Gavin. That shiny new toy your parents could miraculously afford after the ski trip."

"What's going on here, Mary?"

"Are we going for a ride or not?"

A glimpse of typical and tiresome primal maleness crossed his face.

Such a stupid guy response. He thought it was about a hookup? A chance at romance again?

He stepped closer. It wasn't intimidation so much as it looked like desperation.

Curiosity and a bit of hesitancy burned bright in his own eyes as he stared first at my green one and then at the blue.

"Your car?"

He nodded. "This way."

I'd taken back a sliver of the control he'd rattled loose in me. If he wanted to play cat and mouse, he was in for the game of a lifetime.

He should have never doubted I was the cat.

It didn't really hit me until Gavin took us through our favorite chicken nugget drive-thru place and passed me a large sweet tea. There were so many memories attached to that, I thought I might puke.

I swallowed the sour taste in my throat with a big gulp of the tea and focused on my mission.

Weaken Gavin.

Torture Gavin.

Destroy Gavin.

I squeezed on the door handle. I could still get out, but the squeak and scent of the new leather seats in Gavin's car reminded me he was alive and Jacob was not. I should have been in Jacob's new car, not Gavin's, and that thought held me in place like a pierced butterfly on a science project's foam board. I needed to settle the score or at least start the process. It's not like I could be in any more agony.

Me and that butterfly had a lot in common.

Gavin pulled to the stop sign at the intersection. "Uh... Where did you want to go?"

"Somewhere quiet where we can talk."

"We could go to the park—"

"Where no one will see us."

He made a left. "Have you seen the new parking garage by the movie theater?"

"No."

"It's under construction, but you can drive around the levels when everyone leaves. Sometimes it's roped off, but it's easy to get around."

Trespassing, wet concrete, and loose materials to puncture tires.

Right up my alley. "Sounds fun."

"We can take our food up there and..."

"I said it sounds fun."

Gavin scanned the area as he drove around the barrier and entered the near-finished structure. Scattered construction trash and fast-food cups and bags blew around in swirls as wind passed through the garage.

He looked smug and confident as he maneuvered around a pile of rebar and hit the gas to take one of the tight curves to the next level. I wanted to grab his head and bash his face into the steering wheel like I'd seen people do in the movies.

I managed a fake smile instead. One that looked like I was having fun. One that made him think he took my breath away with excitement.

He grinned wide and accelerated more at each turn until the sky appeared again and we skidded to a stop on the top level.

A glimpse of the old Gavin emerged as he grabbed what he could carry and quickly came around the car to catch my door and help me out. I wanted it to be those innocent days when he smelled good and tried hard to please me, but there was no mistake. I was in the presence of pure evil. No amount of gentlemanly behavior could erase our past or his crimes.

I walked along the edge and peered at treetops and orange caution tape around the newly-designed walkway below. "That's quite a drop," I said.

He set his drink on a stack of concrete parking bumpers and shrugged. "I guess. I'm not afraid of heights, are you?"

I ran my finger along the top of the hot, smooth wall. "Not in the least." I glanced at all sides to sort out the direction. "The theater is that way... The new strip center is over there... And this side hasn't even been cleared."

He shrugged again and looked for a way to sit on the awkward pile. "I hadn't noticed."

I tested the seat he found for us.

"They're not going to move," he said.

"Right. Don't you worry about surveillance? Parking garages have cameras."

We settled on top and he handed me a bag of food. "We're not doing anything. All they can do is tell us to leave. They don't have a gate across the entrance yet."

I nodded to neon orange, spray-painted arrows and other symbols that marked certain places. "What do you think all that is for?"

He took a passing glance and opened a ketchup packet. "I don't know, Mary, it's probably where they need to fix or redo something. It's a parking garage. You said you wanted to be alone to talk and we're here. Is this what you want to talk about?"

Our hands touched as we both reached to grab one of our wrappers that threatened to blow away. I expected him to jerk it back, and I think he almost did.

But then he paused to gauge my reaction and did everything but look me in the eye.

And I paused to take a breath and will myself not to strangle him and take a satisfying long walk home.

His fingers, cool and damp from the sides of his cup, lingered over mine until he finally took hold in a wary attempt to stay connected.

"I don't know what you want, Mary. The last time I saw you, you threatened to kill me."

My insides shriveled, and it took a lot to get a breath without gasping for air. "Did I?"

"I know you hate me, but we can fix this. I tried to tell you... We can work together—"

"Just stop." I pulled my hand away and tried not to react too quickly, or too harshly—or too willingly. "It will take time," I choked out.

"I understand."

He still couldn't look me in the eye.

It was a mind-numbing exercise in control, borderline insanity, and contempt as he quietly dipped waffle fries into ketchup like we'd done together all our lives. But we were sitting together on a pile of concrete knowing full well who we each were and what he'd done. And he still...*still* thought he could charm his way back into my heart. Whatever dark force from the Destroyer lived inside him had convinced him he was more powerful, even smarter than us both. The fact he could even stand up under the weight of his certain guilt convinced me he was too far gone to be saved. I almost pitied him.

Almost.

And I almost couldn't recognize myself as I sat there with a murderer and plotted to end him.

Again, almost.

When he finally had the nerve to look at me, the shards of evil in his gaze reminded me why I was there. He was going to put on his best show to pull me in, deceive me, and deliver me to Shanar.

And I was going to put on mine to draw him out, hear his confession...

And find justice.

CHAPTER 23

Scout

I looked around the yard to make sure no one had come in.

I dipped my toes into the pool on the end with the steps, and then carefully made my way in.

Three days in a row.

It had been three days that I'd been able to submerge my butt in the water on the second step.

Deacon had gotten me to the first one as promised, and that was more of a battle of wills than anything. He said he would help, and I said I would let him. No way could I not get to that first step after all the commotion when I found the snake in the pool. He agreed to touch the next garter snake I caught in the garden if I agreed to sit on that first step. I plopped my butt down before he had a chance to back out. From there, my feet were under water no matter how hard I tried to keep them out.

I shook like a leaf and thought of all the places I would find Deacon's perfect snake in a hurry.

And Deacon laughed like a hyena—which surprisingly helped. Like when the airplane flies through so much turbulence it must be going to crash, but the flight attendant stands in the aisle with a smile and a bag of twisty pretzels. If they're not worried, I'm not worried. If they're smiling and handing out pretzels, they're not concerned about falling from the sky. And somehow it equated in my mind that if Deacon was laughing and splashing in the water, it was all OK and we weren't going to drown.

It made perfect sense, except that nothing made any sense when your family had drowned.

Nothing except for the PTSD and anxiety. That part I could understand.

It wasn't as if I didn't want to get in the water. I was tired of being the embarrassingly obvious person on the outside. My friends tolerated me, but I was about to have a lake house to use. There would be a boat and likely a jet ski in my future. Deacon made it perfectly clear what an idiot I was for missing all the hot tub time with Ivy.

Still…

It was a hard road to get into waist-deep water, let alone allow it to cover my head.

But I had to take the steps. I had to be ready. I couldn't be the one left behind on the dock.

And I totally had to see Deacon pet a snake.

Anyway… I wasn't doin' the Deacon the Dolphin thing, but I had my body in the pool.

I had about two hours to get one more step farther before the rest of the Warriors arrived for our much-needed meeting to catch up. I was not looking forward to the fallout of Mary and Deacon finding out Ivy's dad was every bit as rotten as we thought he might be.

My grandpa walked by with a shovel. "Get all the way in that pool, boy."

"Trying. And what are you doing? Are you going to whack me with that thing?"

"Would it help?"

"Probably not."

"I could try," he offered. "Knock that hydrophobia right outta you."

"I don't have hydrophobia."

"No?"

"No." I eased to the next step on my bottom, and then stood and went one more for good measure. "I have aquaphobia."

Grandpa tilted his head as sweat glistened on his scalp through thinning hair. "You're afraid of Aquaman?" Then he busted out laughing.

"You're hilarious." Water rippled as I moved and I froze for a second and thought about that ripple. "Aquaphobia is fear of water. Hydrophobia is like rabies."

"OK. You should hurry up. I think your little girlfriend would like to be in the hot tub with you." He made a giddyap click with his mouth and wiggled his fuzzy brows. "Go on. Dive in." He jabbed the shovel in the air and then laughed again.

"Do you really think you're helping me right now? Isn't there anyone else you can annoy?"

He headed into the shed.

I gathered some water in my hand and splashed it on my shoulders. That was a big step, and one my grief therapist said would help. *Touch the water... Splash the water... Don't try to do it all at once...*

Yeah, well, I hadn't done anything in the water for a while. It was time I did.

"Scout?"

"Ivy!"

Water splashed in my face as I turned and inadvertently took two steps more away from the stairs. Droplets landed in my hair and dripped on my back. The sickening feeling made me want to bolt from the water, but I wasn't going to scramble out of there like an angry wet cat in front of her. I tried to steady my breaths and will the water to stop sloshing around my body.

"I'm sorry I startled you."

"You're early," I said with an unwelcoming bite.

"Well, excuse me. I'm not here for you. I'm here for your grandparents. Your grandpa is gathering tools and we're supposed to—"

"I thought I told you to stay away from him and his crazy stories. I know you miss your dad and stuff, but trust me, that old coot will get you killed around power tools."

The way she looked at me... Let's just say I knew I had done it then.

She narrowed her gaze. "Do you mean to insult me and your grandparents—who love you very much, by the way—because I caught you in your own pool?"

"I didn't—"

"Because you're embarrassed?"

"Yes. Sorry. I didn't mean to snap, and I sure didn't mean to hurt your feelings by mentioning your dad."

She planted her hands on her hips and looked everywhere but at me in the pool. "All right, then. I'm willing to forget any of this happened if you are."

"Done."

"Fine."

"Fine."

She headed for the door to the kitchen.

"Ivy, wait."

"Yes?"

"What are you doing with my grandparents? If you don't mind my asking since I really shouldn't be talking right now..."

"Service hours. I'm keeping up with my extracurriculars even though our school is virtually flattened. Your grandparents' church is helping one of my clubs do work in the community garden. It's our day to pull weeds and stuff."

"Right. You were talking about gardening tools."

"Yes. Your bad-influence grandpa and I are not taking a circular saw to the tomatoes." She rolled her eyes. "And I like his stories," she mumbled as she walked away.

It was only a couple of seconds before my grandpa headed back out of the shed—laughing his saggy old butt off. "Bet you'd like me to hit you upside the head with that shovel now."

"Would you?"

He shook his head and walked on with a bunch of gardening gloves and a rake.

That's when I realized it. I was standing in waist-deep water. And I was almost OK with it.

CHAPTER 24

Ivy

When I got in the kitchen, I closed the door and pressed my back against it and tried not to squeal too loud.

Scout's grandma came around the corner. "What's going on?"

"Scout's in the pool."

"Ah... Yes. He's been doing that for three days."

"He didn't tell me."

"He probably wanted to surprise you."

We pivoted and peeked through the blinds as if it were suddenly a matter of international importance and we had to spy on a target.

"He's still standing there," I whispered.

"That's the farthest he's been." She grinned wide and cuffed me on the arm. "Won't be long now."

"You think?"

"Sure, hon, he's actually in the water."

I dropped the slat. "He's not moving."

"He will. He has to work this out."

"Should I go back out? I was shocked when I saw him and wasn't going to make a big deal about it, then he was a butt... Should I go back out? To encourage him?"

I was surprised when she wrapped her arms around me. "Thank you, Ivy."

Her body shuddered with what I guessed was a burst of tears. I snuggled against her warmth and took in all the comforting, motherly feels.

Words felt heavy in my mouth when I wanted to speak. I didn't know I'd done anything to be thanked for, but the loving hug went on. It danced on the edge of a painful abyss until emotions spilled over between us in a spiritual-like space confined to our embrace.

She'd released a spasm of intense pain. I caught it in gentle hands and held it for her. It fluttered on my fingertips in its dark beauty, and when I could, I let it go—because she couldn't.

I saw it leave in my mind's eye, floating away like a thousand blue-black-winged butterflies.

In its place, I accepted her nurturing gift of touch.

It was my first real hug.

My first real hug?

How could that be?

I held her tighter. "You're welcome, but why are you thanking me?"

She stepped back. "For everything. You have no idea how special you are, do you?"

"Special?"

She ran her hands down my arms. "Ivy. You've brought joy and healing to our family. Scout is conquering that pool because of you."

"But I don't want it to be because of me. He has to do that for himself. So he'll feel better."

She wandered into the kitchen and grabbed her wide-brimmed garden hat from the counter. "See? That's why your special. You're not thinking of yourself. You rarely do. You absorb everyone else's pain. You can't help it."

"You make it sound like a bad thing."

"No, it's an extraordinary thing. You just have to be careful to practice self-care. You can't take the weight of everything you sense and feel. You have to allow quiet time for yourself."

Right. I was a Warrior. My empathetic skills were hardwired to work with my intuition and sensitivity to the events around me, and likely were connected with my assignments.

I could barely separate my real life from my Warrior one anyway, let alone find the basic human buried under all the extra voices in my head.

She paused and stepped close again. She pressed her thumb on my forehead and smoothed it across my skin. "Stop."

"Stop what?"

"Stop frowning like that. You'll thank me in about forty years. You're a deep thinker like Scout. I know you have a million things going on in that brain, but you're going to have to slow it down and not miss all the good things as you pass through your journey."

"I don't mean to sound rude, but what do you know about my journey?"

She smiled. "Everyone has a journey. Yours is just much more interesting than most."

"What else do you know?"

"I can't honestly say. I know there's something going on between the four of you. I know it's bigger than the rest of us can understand, and I think it's important and you need to be careful."

Well, she had that right. She'd been there in Colorado to scrape us all off the floor when Jacob died. She knew something, even if she didn't understand it.

She patted the hat onto her head and handed me a small cooler full of bottled water. "We need to get to the garden." She opened the door for me. "Thank you for being so good to Scout."

"Scout means a lot to me. It's not hard to be good to him."

"And thank you for the hug. It was a gift."

I nodded.

I could say the same about hers.

CHAPTER 25

Ivy

I stretched out on the ratty old swing Scout's grandpa had dragged out of someone's scrap pile. All I knew was his grandma was fit to be tied about it. But I liked the creaky old thing with the torn, flapping awning and the rusty squeak. The gentle, swaying seat was the perfect place to wait for the others.

I'd only closed my eyes for what I thought was a second when the swaying stopped. Scout looked down on me with those changing hazel eyes of his. Man, those eyes were beautiful. He stood there in his khaki cargo shorts and a balled-up Stonehaven Saints shirt in his hand and not on his body. I was way too interested in how much he'd filled out since we'd met. That skinny freshman had turned into a real live man somewhere along the way. It's not like I didn't know it was happening. We were always together, and a long time had passed since we met in that garden. Sometimes it took my breath away to know the way someone I loved looked at me when he wasn't sure I knew he was looking. How did it keep getting more intense every day?

I scrambled to sit up.

He started to pull on the shirt. "You OK?

"Yeah," I said and patted the dry-rotted cushion beside me. "Trying to wake up."

"Sorry I woke you. Couldn't tell if you were sleeping or just thinking with your eyes closed."

"Both. I think." I couldn't turn away from the sight of him stretching the too-small shirt across his abs. "You know my sleep is weird. And I think you've outgrown that shirt."

He sat and glanced down. "I guess. Me and Deacon have been working a lot outside. According to my grandma, hard labor gives you muscles."

He flexed.

I blushed.

The best thing about my embarrassing thoughts and reaction was that Scout remained typically and obviously oblivious.

I looked away. "Hey, have you ever had a really interesting hug? Like you didn't expect it to feel the way it did, and it could have been awkward, but it turned out to be the best hug you ever had? And you realize it's what a hug is supposed to be?"

He'd already moved on to the other arm and had a hand over a very promising bulging bicep. He turned a stern gaze on me. "What did my grandpa get you in to at the community garden?"

"What? Nothing. Why?"

"Who hugged you?"

My usually laid-back and cuddly man-boy was about to get worked up.

"Oh no! No. No. Nothing happened. It's not that kind of thing."

"What are you talking about then?"

I stood and pulled my sticky t-shirt away from my body to fan about a hundred degrees of heat away from my torso. "It's really getting hot out here." I wiped sweat from the back of my neck. I laughed. "Might have to jump in the pool."

"Who hugged you, Ivy?"

I sat again. "Let me back up, because I'm having a revelation here…"

"Vision, premonition, intuition," he corrected.

"No. Not Warrior stuff. This is a plain old revelation. A discovery."

"OK."

"You're my best friend, Scout. I tell you everything. We talk about…*everything*. And I'm realizing as our relationship gets more mature…" I tried to choose the right words to not sound like a…

I don't know what I was trying to do.

"Spit it out, Ivy."

"All right. We're not children. Everything isn't as innocent as it used to be. We've crossed some barriers about how we feel about each other. We're growing up."

"And this is a surprise to you?"

"No, of course not. I'm just seeing that I have to be careful what I say and how I say it."

"You can say anything to me. We only have each other to talk about some of the crazy stuff we have to talk about."

"I know. And I trust you completely. But right then when I said that about someone hugging me you got all like…jealous. Like angry-eyes jealous."

"Yeah. I'm your boyfriend. I don't want some other guy hugging you."

"I know. But that's the conclusion you jumped to, and it couldn't be further from what I wanted to discuss. And between that and the way you were looking at me and the way I was looking at you, well, I realize I have to be careful what I say because I don't want you to be uncomfortable or get the wrong idea about anything."

"Hold up a minute. What do you mean the way you were looking at me?"

Ooops.

I tried to look away.

"Don't you look away. This isn't about me being uncomfortable, this is about *you* being uncomfortable."

"I'm not uncomfortable."

"Yes, you are. I saw you checking out my pecs. You're the one who brought up my shrinking shirt. You're embarrassed because you like what you see."

"I'm not embarrassed! I've always said I was attracted to your brain and kind behavior. The fact you're such a good kisser is a bonus."

"And now that my chest has expanded, you're attracted to that and my biceps."

"No. Yes. No."

He laughed out loud. "This is good. You're afraid you can't keep your hands off me, and I think you liked it when I got jealous." He pulled out his collar and dipped his head into his shirt. "Watch out. She might try to touch you."

"I can control myself. Your chest muscles have no hold on me."

He laughed even louder. "Well, good for you, because, in case you forgot, you also have chest muscles and they stick out farther and I'm sure they are much nicer than mine. And it is extremely difficult for me to keep my mind and hands off them when they're pressed up against me during all that great kissing we do."

I was shocked at first.

And a little mortified.

Then I snorted. "I'm sorry, Scout. You're always a perfect gentleman."

"Yeah. Do you know how hard it is to be a perfect gentleman all the time?"

"Every guy should be like you. You make me feel so safe."

"Well, according to this conversation, I'm the one who needs protection. Guess I need to keep my biceps and my triceps and whatever other fancy ceps I have under wraps."

"This is getting ridiculous." I gave him a quick kiss on the cheek. "And we're off track."

"Sure. Let's get back on track. Who were you hugging?"

CHAPTER 26

Ivy

Scout bounced his knee against mine. "You were telling me about a hug."

"Yes. Your grandma hugged me."

"Well, that certainly takes the spark out of our discussion."

"I know. It was weird. And so magical."

He shot me a sideways smirk. "Now you're just making things up."

"No, listen. She hugged me because, well, never mind why, but it was a special hug. And it got me to thinking."

"About…?"

"A hug has powers. I did not know that until today."

His cheeks flashed red. "Duh. I have hugged you enough to know your hugs have special powers."

I elbowed him. "Stop. I'm being serious."

"All right. What do you mean?"

I stared at two ants as they traveled across the ground in

front of us. I avoided smashing them when I set the swing in motion. "I was completely shocked to realize today that I've never really been hugged."

Scout stretched his arm across the back of the swing. "Not to go back to our kind of hugs or anything, but I can assure you, the way I feel when I hug you... There's nothing more powerful than..."

I touched his leg. "Please, Scout, I promise this is not about us. I know how we are together. Your affection for me and your complete and total dedication to my happiness is not in question here. Do you understand?"

"Yes. I think."

"I'm talking about when other people hug me. Like people I don't know too well, or people I don't know at all." I struggled to find the words for what I meant. "When your grandma hugged me today it was like we connected. Something passed between us. I know my mother loves me. She hugs me, but I never felt the comfort when my mom hugged me like I did when your grandma hugged me."

"And that makes you feel bad."

"Yes! Shouldn't my own mother's hugs be the best kind?"

Scout met my gaze and brushed the pad of his thumb across my cheek. "Not if her hugs only take from you and not give you anything in return."

"What does that mean?"

"You're an empath, Ivy. You're an emotional healer. Whatever's inside you finds whatever's inside other hurting people. When you physically connect with them, you give them something they need."

It sunk in. "And if I need something, the right person can give it to me."

"Exactly."

I paused the swing with my toe. "My mother loves me, but

she can't give me anything. She's been sick her whole life so she can't help me. She can only take what she needs from me."

"That's probably true. She can't help it. She survives from your energy and the way you actively help take care of her."

"No wonder I'm so tired all the time."

A laugh rumbled in his chest when I rested my head on it. "No wonder at all."

"And you know my Aunt Connie isn't the warm and fuzzy kind."

"Right."

"And my dad... I missed all the dad hugs. He's like me, you know? With the abilities? I bet if he'd been around his hugs would have helped me, and maybe he wouldn't have gotten himself in trouble if he'd stayed with my mom. I can tell he still loves her. Something's going on there."

"You're probably right about all that. You're right about most things."

"How does it take a person until they're a teenager to understand a real hug?"

"You're not a typical teenager, Ivy."

"I know, but I didn't know I was missing good hugs. I should hug more people."

"Watch it now."

"You know what I mean."

"Yes, I do. And what I mean is that you should listen more to your intuition. If you feel like someone needs a hug from you, they probably do."

"Your grandma's an empath, Scout. Why didn't you tell me?"

"Well, I wasn't sure where this conversation was going. I thought she had those kinds of gifts, but I figured she was in there putting essential oils on you and brewing some stinky tea. I didn't know you were exchanging emo hugs. What exactly happened?"

"She put her arms around me and I was immediately comforted. I wanted to hang on for as long as she'd hold me."

"There's the difference then, isn't it? When most people hug you, they take something from you. They need something and they take it, but they don't give you anything in return. My grandma was giving you motherly unconditional love and support and it made you feel good."

"That's exactly right. She gave me something beautiful—but she also gave me something else."

"What'd she give you?"

"She gave me a piece of her grief. She needed to let it go. She did it with gratitude."

"You're losing me. I thought what she gave you was good."

"It was. But it was also an honor to take her grief."

"What uh… What did you do with that?"

"I let it go for her."

"So, you both felt better because it was a good exchange. You helped each other."

"Yes. It was my first real hug."

CHAPTER 27

Ivy

Mary rounded the corner toward the pool with her usual scowl in place.

My heart ached for her.

She spotted me and Scout cuddled on the swing and looked elsewhere. I moved away from him. It was hard to be happy and content when her heart was still so shattered. My comfort with Scout, and Deacon's growing relationship with Claire Cannon, left her on the outside—just when she needed us most.

I looked past her shoulder. "Isn't Deacon with you?"

"No. I think he's afraid to come because he owes Scout a snake-petting session."

Scout laughed. "I have to find the snake first. Plus, I want it to be a little bit of a surprise so he doesn't completely chicken out, but I don't want to scare him."

I pulled a chair into the shade and moved so she could sit on the swing if she wanted. "Have you been at the Smoothie Shack more since they reopened? I feel like I haven't seen you for days."

"Just working. And studying. And working on a special project."

"A project for school?" Scout asked.

One of her shoulders jerked up in a half-hearted shrug. "No. Let's say it's more for the universe."

"Are you on an assignment?"

There went that shoulder again, but she added nothing. Everything about her demeanor caused alarm bells to ring in my ears. We'd been saying for weeks we had a rogue warrior on our hands, but we understood her gruff speech and verbal threats against Gavin. We all wanted justice, but we didn't think she'd actually act on it. It would make her no different than him.

Didn't she know that?

We heard Deacon before we saw him.

"Y'all have any snakes?"

"No snakes," Scout called back. "You'll know when it's time to settle your debt."

Mary leaned Scout's way. "Please tell me you have a snake."

"No way. I said I don't want him to be scared. He's already afraid. I want him to have a positive experience so maybe I don't have to listen to him complain all the time about harmless wildlife."

That little exchange was proof of my greatest concern. Our fearless, moral-high-ground leader, and fair and gifted Warrior, had been reduced to a prankster of the universe. We already knew she'd become a bit of an avenger. We just didn't know how bad it was.

And it was going to get a whole lot worse when she heard about Reed Logan's true motives.

Deacon peeled off his shirt and shoes and slid into the pool. He did a few of what Scout called his Deacon the Dolphin moves and then swam to the side. "Did you all hear the news?"

In our circle, that could mean anything.

"What news?" Scout asked.

"The school. The official school year is coming to a close early, so everything is shutting down for the summer. The construction is going to be more extensive than first thought, and they settled with the insurance company."

My ears perked. "Does that mean they've closed the investigation to the fire?"

"Well, the Stonehaven Gym Fire is forever going to be a mystery, but the last fire was definitely ruled electrical."

"No one's asking any more questions?"

"There will always be questions," Deacon said. "But for now, everyone is in rebuilding mode. There's been a settlement, and an anonymous benefactor has donated a lot of money for construction, so they're finishing out what's left of the school year and moving the S.A.I.N.T. Lab to the lower school."

Mary stood and paced. "What about us? We're in the middle of our grand scheme to graduate early."

"Well, we're not the only ones who had that idea. Now everyone is either going to accelerate, or move to a different school. Some of the parents are hot about it and want their students to have a full four-year experience so they're changing schools. Others are going to keep distance learning and going to the testing lab until we're just...done."

Visions of a senior prom, a purple Saints cap and gown, and my mother and Aunt Connie making a scene with large signs in the audience flashed through my mind. "Wait a minute. What about a graduation? All the sports and clubs and senior activities?"

"That's the thing," Scout said. "Most students want all that and are going to jump ship."

"But," Deacon said and pointed his finger in the air before he did a dive and came back up. "For those of us who stay and do the accelerated thing, there will be a graduation in December. Like a group thing at a nice place."

"Oh Mary, you're a soccer player. And a good one," I said. "Will you have to move so you can play soccer?"

"I don't care about soccer anymore."

"But you might not feel that way forever. You don't want to miss an opportunity to play."

"Honestly, Ivy, I don't care. I was never good enough for a scholarship or anything and I didn't intend to go to college to play soccer."

"And I planned on living at home and being in community college a couple of years anyway," Deacon said. "It makes no difference to me."

"Wait," I said. "What about letters of recommendation, college counseling, and all that stuff?"

Scout pulled out his phone. "It will all be offered and taken care of." He scrolled. "It's all right here. The guidance people will still be there and all the certified teachers take turns in the lab. We just keep doing what we're doing and going to the S.A.I.N.T. Lab twice a week throughout the summer and we'll graduate—in a cap and gown—in December."

"I don't know how I feel about that," I said. "It was one thing when we thought they were actively working on the school and we could see progress. It was like if we just hung on a bit, maybe we'd get back to some kind of normal before we actually graduated, but this way..."

"This way," Scout said. "This way we know the school as we knew it is gone. They're going to rebuild and we're not really a part of it."

Mary rubbed her forehead as if she had a headache. "I thought we already settled this. I thought we were going to speed it up and get out of here so we could get on with our lives."

"We did," I said. "But it's sad to know it's all so final."

"Everything is already final," Mary cried out. "It's over for us here. We can't have a normal four-year experience after what's happened to us. It's already lost. We need to move on."

Deacon hopped out and grabbed a towel. Since he spent more time in Scout's pool than Scout did, he had his very own hook and towel on the wooden bar Scout's grandpa constructed along the wall. "We are moving on," he said. "There will probably only be a handful of us who choose to stay and do it this way in December, but I don't care either. I agree with Mary."

"I'm in." I sighed. "It's a lot of pressure to take care of my mom and constantly make nice with my Aunt Connie. It will be good to get it done so I'm out from under feeling like I need to do things for my aunt because she's paying my tuition. I'll be in community college with Deacon until I can figure out how to pay my way through the rest."

Scout rubbed a hand across my back. "You'll get into a good college, Ivy. You'll find scholarships."

"Easy for you to say. You just finished up your junior year. On a computer from your own apartment upstairs. And you tested out of some other things, and are already scheduled for all your college entrance exams. I don't think the rest of us are that far ahead."

"Again," Mary said with a stern and impatient glare. "We can do this. We will do this. We need to move on."

"All right," I said. "But first I need to talk to you all about Reed Logan."

Deacon plopped on a nearby chaise. "Where's he been, anyway? It's like he disappeared. First, he wanted to be in all your business, and now he's gone."

"I don't know where he is," I admitted. "He tried to see my mom, and it didn't go well. Next thing I know I'm learning things about him I'd rather not know—"

"What things?" Mary demanded.

"Look, Mary, I have to get this out in my own sweet time. All your stomping around isn't helping me. We know you're angry. It's old news. And when I do tell you what I know, you have to stay calm and think."

"That doesn't really help me calm down."

"It's gonna have to," I snapped back.

She twisted her fingers together and tried to hold her hands still.

"Here goes," I said. "Reed came to see my mom. I wasn't there. She slammed the door in his face. I caught him as he left. I knew immediately that seeing my mom had shaken him. I think he realized he shouldn't have come waltzing into my life without a plan. I don't know what he thought would happen, but seeing my mom really messed him up."

"In what way?" Deacon asked.

"I think they still love each other. My mom has her issues, but she's still a woman. She seems lonely. She's never been interested in finding someone. I think it's because she still loves my dad, even though Aunt Connie has a conniption every time there's ever been any mention of my father. She's a selfish control freak."

Scout touched my hand. "Yes, we know all about Aunt Connie. Tell them about your dad."

"Right. He was rattled when I saw him. He said trying to see my mom was a mistake and that he was leaving for a while."

"He came back in your life only to abandon you again?" Deacon shook his head. "I don't like that. It's not fair."

"Maybe not, but it happened."

"Why did he bother at all?" Deacon persisted. "What was his point for being here?"

"That's where it gets tricky," I said. "Reed Logan was here because he was acting as an Agent for the Destroyer."

"I knew it!" Mary couldn't hide her rage. She looked like all the basic comic book characters did before their veins and muscles bulged and they turned into superhuman creatures with exceptional strength, and started smashing things.

I rushed to get in her face. "Stop it, Mary. This is my story and I'm not finished telling it. I told you to stay calm and think."

She crossed her arms and dug her nails into her own flesh on her biceps. "I'm trying."

"I don't think Reed Logan was always a bad guy," I said. "In fact, I think he was one of the good ones. I think he loved my mother and wanted it to work, but he was a soldier, and my Aunt Connie and my grandma did their best to interfere and keep them apart."

"He was a grown man," she shot back. "Adult Marine soldiers can do what they want."

"I know, but I also think war scrambled his brain. You saw him at the Shack when the wall fell."

"But what did that really tell us? A lot of soldiers have PTSD. Does this story have a point about how he and Gavin almost killed us in the gym?"

"We already know Reed has abilities. I think Shanar got to him when he was in battle. I think he was persuaded to do some things he wouldn't normally do. So, when he came back, he was not the same. Not only that, he'd somehow already sided with Shanar. He made the wrong choice."

"And then he just happened to show up at Stonehaven and cause a fire? He had to know you were there. We've already established he's had eyes on you for years."

"I know. That's the hardest part for me. You said it. *He had to know I was there.* What did he want with me? If I've learned anything it's that we can't hide from our enemies. We might as well have neon signs on our foreheads that tell the other side who we work for. I don't know about you all, but I can pretty much spot someone who works for the Destroyer in any crowd. That's the point of our training, I think."

Deacon shivered and wrapped the towel around his shoulders. "Wait. We've agreed it's all out in the open. We know our people. They know their people. We all know each other... But Reed is your dad. Did he come here to do you harm?"

I shrugged. "Maybe. I don't know. I think Shanar had such control over him that he headed down the road with Gavin to cause trouble."

"You mean to kill me and Jacob," Mary ground out.

"Maybe," I said. "But then I think after that fire, when he realized who I was and who I worked for, his heart changed. I think he wanted to be better. I think he wanted to switch sides."

"And in that hopeful idea," Scout said. "He thought he could get to know Ivy and turn away from the Destroyer."

"But that's not easy," Deacon said. "I've seen Shanar. I know how persuasive he can be."

"Whatever," Mary said. "What's the bottom line here, Ivy?"

"The bottom line is my dad didn't come right out and say it, but I saw it in his thoughts. I saw the struggle. I saw the turbulent history in his eyes, and I saw his allegiance was no longer solely with Shanar. He didn't admit he was in on the Stonehaven Gym Fire with Gavin, but he didn't have to. And then he left because he knew his presence here was a danger to me. The sight of my mom took him by surprise, and I think he's off to settle some things."

Mary raised her hands in the air. "Please! What's he going to settle? He's pure evil. Do you think he's going to find some kind of a New Age healing spa or spiritual sweat lodge and sit around naked with a bunch of other demons and make a better choice?" She leaned close to me with a harsh glare. "Was he in Colorado to kill me and Jacob on that mountain?"

"No."

"And you're sure about that?"

"Yes."

"What do we do with this information?"

Scout pushed off the swing and swiped sweaty hair from his

brow. "I don't think there's anything we can do. He's already been picked up and cleared by the police of any involvement in the Stonehaven Gym Fire, and he didn't do anything in the big fire. He's gone and they'll never find evidence to prove anything now."

"Which means this information has not been helpful at all." Mary sent me a snarky expression. "It's only confirmed what we already knew—Reed Logan is the enemy."

"I think he's trying *not* to be the enemy anymore."

"You think we can just trust that he's gone and isn't coming back?"

I closed my eyes and rested my hand across them. I was so tired of the twists and turns in my own mind, but there was no doubting what I'd seen in Reed Logan's.

"Yes," I said. "He's not coming back. My dad is gone again because he thinks it's the right thing to do to protect me. To protect all of us."

Mary turned to leave.

"Where are you going? We need to discuss this. There are fewer and fewer people in our lives every day we can trust. Isn't it enough for you that my dad is gone?"

She spun back. "He might be gone, but the battle rages on. Gavin is still out there. He's gotten away with numerous crimes with who knows how much of your dad's help."

"I know, but we have to stick together. We can only trust each other. Please stay and let's talk."

"I can't talk any more today."

"Why?"

"My special project just got bigger."

CHAPTER 28

Mary

I drove around the same orange cones and blue barrels Gavin had a few days before, and headed to the top of the parking garage. I figured the worst that could happen was, again, we'd be caught and asked to leave. Darkness eased across the early evening sky in dusty, gray-hued patches of clouds that promised rain. As I waited, a few—but not all—lights flickered on and illuminated the still-growing monstrosity. The pile of concrete parking bumpers had been moved into place. They sat as if anticipating a perfectly parked row of cars.

One was slightly askew.

Headlights bounced off the walls below and then everything went dim as Gavin killed his lights and crept to the top to join me.

I swung my legs from the hood of my grandma's old car and tried to look glad to see him when he rolled to a stop beside me.

He rattled his keys between his fingers and then dropped

them in his pocket as he made a slow approach. "I'm glad you texted. I didn't know if I'd hear from you again."

"I kinda like it up here. Especially when there's a breeze. It was hot today."

He leaned against the closest concrete column. "Did you hear the news about the school?"

"Yes. What are you going to do? Stay and play ball on a smaller scale, or move to the big high school in the district we're zoned to?"

"I don't know. You?"

I didn't want to answer. I slid off the hood with a squeak instead and headed for the edge of the top level. The growing breeze ruffled through the tops of the trees and whipped hair across my face. Far below, lights twinkled as they came on at surrounding businesses, and the untouched natural side of the garage glowed only with small lanterns along the path.

Gavin stayed close. "Do you want to go get something to eat or do something else?"

I leaned against the boundary wall. "No. I wanted to talk to you again."

"About what?"

"Anything... Everything..." In a quick movement, I hoisted myself up and swung a leg over to straddle the ledge.

"Mary!" He rushed toward me as if worried. "What the heck? That's not funny. Get down."

"I'm fine. It's nice. Hop up."

"No thanks."

"You said you weren't afraid of heights."

"I'm not, but I don't want to use that ledge as a tightrope." He stepped closer and held out his hand. "C'mon. Get down. It's windy."

"I don't think a little breeze is going to blow me off the ledge. It feels good."

The alarm in his deep brown eyes turned to flecks of

mischief. Then his gaze morphed to reveal the very snarled roots of his once-sweet nature that had been completely obliterated by Shanar.

I placed my hands in front of me and pushed myself to a standing position on the ledge. Like an acrobat, I planted my feet, one in front of the other, and held my arms out for balance. I didn't look down.

In my periphery, Gavin froze. "What are you doing, Mary?"

"There's more room than you'd think. It's a wide ledge." I held my face against the wind. "It's all about the balance."

"Get down."

"Why? I'm making it easy for you. We have no more secrets, you and I. I know what you did… And what Shanar expects you to do. And here I am."

"After everything we've been through, how can you not know what I really want?"

I stretched my front foot a little farther out in front of me. "What do you mean? You no longer have a choice, right? I mean, I'm always the first one to say a person always has a choice, and I believe they do, but you pretty much sealed your own fate when you drove us off that mountain and killed Jacob. Now all that's left for you to do to satisfy Shanar is kill me. Isn't that right?"

"Please come down, Mary."

"And what about Reed Logan? You two are quite the troublemakers. Where is he now? Did he leave you here to take the blame for everything?"

"I don't know what you are—"

"Stop right there. Ivy means a lot to me and that man has caused her a lot of pain. He won't get away with it. Neither of you will get away with anything. You understand that, right? You both will pay for what you've done. You should probably just tell me where he is."

"Get down so we can talk."

I dropped my hands to my side and looked straight at him. "I'm confused, Gavin. What is there to talk about? Do you intend to tell the police what you did and take responsibility for your actions?"

He dropped his gaze to the ground.

I thought he would have made his move by then. I had no intention of falling off that ledge. I expected him to lunge toward me, or use a pinky finger to try and simply push me to my death.

But he didn't.

I wouldn't have gone over, and he'd have been seriously sorry he tried, but I didn't expect the hesitation.

I spread my arms again. "I see." I attempted a pivot. It seemed like a good idea at the time, and such a basic move. I simply... turned. I turned on the balls of my feet like a gymnast on a balance beam. And it worked. I ended up facing the opposite direction.

"Mary, stop. Get down. *Now!*"

"Why stop now? There is literally nothing left for us but to end this."

"I've been trying to tell you there is another way. Be with me. Work with me. Come back to me."

"You're trying to convert me? To the dark side? And you want to have some great love affair in the name of Shanar and the Destroyer?"

"Don't talk like that."

"Are you serious? How else am I supposed to make that sound?" I was at a loss for more coherent words. "This isn't a movie. We're not negotiating. I... I... I can't even understand those words."

"I can save us both, Mary. There's a way out of this. We were meant to be together. It's not a coincidence we were born and raised together. Shanar wants something from you, but even he understands your value. We can both make it out of this alive."

I knew we couldn't.

We never would.

I turned to face Gavin straight on and let my arms fall to my side.

He still thought there could be an *us*.

He inched his way toward me. I was ready to fight, but he had no fight in him right then. He wrapped his arms around my legs and lifted me from the ledge.

I shook like thunder inside as I slid down his body to my feet. His warm hands touched the flesh on my legs below my shorts. He held on like I was precious to him…fragile.

He pressed against me, his hands at my waist, and his hips crushing too close to mine as he kept me in his tight embrace. "We can do this," he whispered in my ear. "I love you, Mary, and you're all I've ever wanted. Come. Back. To. Me."

Nausea and his suffocating words took my breath. Control slipped away as his wicked presence tried to suck me in.

I would never be swayed.

"I have to go. I'm late, and if I don't go, I won't be able to be out this late again."

I jumped in my car and sped to the bottom of the garage and found the nearest exit to any street.

A mile later, I pulled off on a side road. I puked in the nearest clump of bushes and then swallowed a quart of water from the jug I carried in my trunk.

I'd played the game.

I'd confirmed my opponent's weakness.

Nobody died.

Yet.

CHAPTER 29

Ivy

I picked up the dish rag and wrung it out.

My mom always just pulled the plug out of the sink and let the rag sit in the bottom as the water swirled away.

Drove me nuts.

No one wanted to pick up a wet, cold, and bacteria-infested dish rag the next morning at breakfast.

But my mom was healthy, taking her meds, working... And washing dishes.

I sat with her at the small round table with my computer and prepared to catch up on school modules—and to ask the hard questions.

She tugged on the teabag in her cup. "What's on your mind, baby girl? Did you and Scout have a fight?"

"No. I need to talk to you."

She patted my hand. "What's up?"

I'd purposely waited until Aunt Connie was out of town, and

I'd put my mom's phone on the charger in her room. She had to talk to me.

"I don't want to upset you, but I need to know about my dad. It's time, Mom. You and Aunt Connie have spent years avoiding the discussion, but it's time. I need to know."

Her lack of an immediate response surprised, alarmed, and encouraged me. Part of me still felt like I was dealing with a loaded gun. There'd been times I didn't know what I was going to get from her.

Right then, it was silence.

She wound her teabag around her spoon and flicked it into the trash can that was an arm's length from the table in our small apartment. "I'm guessing this has come up because he's made contact?"

"Made contact? You make it sound like he's some alien that landed a spaceship on the roof to *establish communication*."

Her lips curved into a small and unexpected smile. "He's different. Some would say odd, weird, or even special, but not from another planet. That I know of." She took another sip. "And you have met him, right? Otherwise we wouldn't be having this conversation."

"Yes."

"And you know he was here."

"Yes." I twisted in my chair. "I don't understand what's happening right now, Mom. I don't know if I thought you'd be crying hysterically or throwing pots and pans around the kitchen, but I didn't expect you to be so calm about this. Grandma and Aunt Connie always—"

"Grandma and Aunt Connie were always first-class pains in my—well, you know."

"I know. And I'm not three-years-old and I don't think that's even a curse word so, say what you gotta say."

"Don't get me wrong. They thought they were doing the right thing, and they probably were at the time. I wasn't well, and your dad was being called away. Mental illness, postpartum depression, medication, breastfeeding, sleep deprivation, stress and worry about deployment... All those things don't exactly go together. There are entire months I don't remember, Ivy. Those two meddlers kept you alive and happy, but they also did irreparable harm to any chance I had with your father."

"I don't know about that." I closed my computer. There would be no schoolwork. "Why haven't you talked to me about this before?"

"I should have. You have a right to know everything, but in case you've forgotten, I have stumbled over the years and your Aunt Connie picks up the slack. We're where we are because of her. You're going to finish high school and go to college."

"We're also where we are because you fought to stay well. Aunt Connie can't and shouldn't take that away from you."

"I appreciate that, baby girl, but we all know her money and her pushiness has kept us out of some jams. I am not, nor will I ever be, a candidate for Mother of the Year."

I had to agree, but not in a mean and ugly way. She was simply a textbook example of all her diagnoses. Part of that meant she sometimes decided if or when to take her meds. There'd been many conversations over the years about how she was convinced she didn't need them because she was in control —and how they made her feel funny, so she just stopped.

That's when we got into trouble.

"Forget all that," I said. "I happen to think you could be Mother of the Year. You are making it work and we are still a family."

"Thank you for that, but let's get down to it. What do you already know, and what do you want to know? I agree. It's time, and Aunt Connie can butt out."

I still couldn't believe spoons and spatulas weren't being tossed out of drawers or that she hadn't turned into a sobbing, rocking heap in the corner. I hadn't given her enough credit. Clearly, the woman had been more aware than Aunt Connie ever acknowledged, and my mom had played the game for my sake. Yes, there'd been times of mental health crises. And yes, there'd been many days I knew she simply could not cope and needed a break in a psych ward to get regulated. And no, I didn't believe for one minute we were so out of the woods that I could stop checking her weekly medication organizer. Did I ever think we could get out from under Aunt Connie's heavy hand?

I started to believe that day we could.

"Did you love Reed Logan?"

"Yes."

"Did you think there was a future with him?"

"I did. You were a surprise, but we could have made it. It did get bad, though, and he had to leave, and in came the meddlers."

"How did he leave? Was there an agreement? Did you talk?"

"I don't think so... I don't remember."

"What does that mean?" I leaned forward and rested my arms on the table. "How do you not remember a conversation when someone goes off to war and there's a newborn involved?"

"It was one of the bad spells, Ivy. I was a mess and your dad had to concentrate on doing his job and staying alive. I always thought he planned to return or that I'd hear from him. Neither of those things really happened."

"I think they did happen, and Grandma and Aunt Connie made sure you didn't know."

"That's probably true." She took her cup to the sink and turned to lean on the counter. "How did you meet him?"

Oh boy.

I imagined a Warrior-Creator-Shanar-Destroyer conversation with my mom, and my head almost exploded right there in the kitchen.

I took another path with no intention of letting her know too much.

"He approached me one day. Outside. Not too weird or anything, and just told me who he was."

"You talk to every strange man who approaches you now?"

"No. Stop. He kept his distance. We talked. A few times."

She crossed her arms tight across her middle.

Time to back off.

"Anyway," I said and went to the fridge for a Dr Pepper. "Scout knew and kept an eye on me and advised Reed should talk to you and see about, I don't know, getting together. Or something."

"Or something."

"Right." I ran my finger around the cold rim of the can before I snapped it open. "I was hoping that would happen."

"Well, you should know he came, and I slammed the door in his face."

"And, to be honest, you should know I was downstairs with Buster that day. Remember? I waved when you texted me to be careful? I talked to Reed. He was beside himself."

"He wasn't the only one."

"Should we take a break and pick this back up later?"

"No." She waved for me to keep talking. "Let's get it done."

We both ended up back at the table with a bag of cookies, and she'd poured a fresh cup of tea.

"He referred to you as Maddie," I said.

Her gaze softened, and every tight line around her eyes and on her forehead seemed to open up her face in a happier place. "Yeah," she mused. "It was quite a shock to see him and hear that after all this time. He hasn't changed much, you know?"

"I wouldn't know. That's part of the problem. I don't even have a picture. I shamelessly snooped through Aunt Connie's things hoping to find something. I didn't."

"I've got some things for you, baby girl."

I found that astonishing after the many years of snooping I'd already done in my mother's things too. The fact she still had hidden photos or documents during all her ups and downs and all our moves... She was full of surprises."

"Did he ever try to come back for us?"

"I honestly can't say for sure. I'm sorry. That's on me."

More like it was on my grandma and Aunt Connie—and on Reed, the shell-shocked Marine making questionable decisions about who he should serve in the universe.

"Don't take all the responsibility for this, Mom. There's a whole cast of characters here who could have helped the situation."

She turned the cup in her hands. "Did you like him? I know you don't know him, but did you a least like him when you met?"

"Yes."

"You two are very similar. He had this keen sense about people, and I've watched you do the same thing in your head when you meet someone. Like you're trying to puzzle out whether you can trust them or not. Your dad did that. One night we were driving along, and some guy looked like he was having car trouble on an old road near Katy where his parents had a house. He chose to stop instantly and help out and it turned into this big thing where they got to be friends..."

"And?"

"And then, not two weeks later, on the same road, there was an old lady and a beat-up Buick with a flat at dusk. I thought for sure he'd stop and get out immediately. It was so hot and the mosquitoes were swarming and there was no one in sight and your dad drove right by. I got aggravated, and I was like *it's an old lady...we need to help her.* And he kept driving. When we stopped later, he looked me right in the eye and said, *you have to trust me on some things. That was not someone I was supposed to help.*" She flicked her second teabag in the trash. "You and he are alike in so many ways. That same intuition. That same confused look in your eyes like you're hearing voices." Panic washed across her face. "No! Don't get me wrong. Your brain isn't twisty like mine is."

Twisty. It was so hard not to laugh out loud. She had no idea.

"OK Mom, I got that. And I also know Reed didn't come back from serving without problems. He has...issues." I pushed my can around the table as I thought. "Where does this leave us? Why did you slam the door in his face?"

"Fear. Shock. I don't know. He was there, and I didn't know exactly where you were, and I had no idea what to say. I was scared."

At first, I thought I was angry she'd sent him away. Then I was angry he'd been there at all because of who and what he was. How dare he infiltrate my life and upset my mother? Then, I was only confused. I was glad he took his evil tendencies and hit the road, but what was I supposed to do with the wounds he'd opened in us?

"I don't think he's coming back, Mom."

Her lips twitched and then she pulled her mouth into a thin, hard line as if she were trying to remain neutral. "Well, he left once, and it's not like I put out a welcome mat when he tried to come back so…"

"But my intuition tells me he loves us. Both of us. He was clearly shaken by seeing you again, and it's interesting neither of you ever moved on. I think he needs to be away and get better."

Ha! Get better. More like take responsibility for the Stonehaven Gym Fire, get help for his PTSD, and ditch his alliance with the masters of all vile and evil things.

My mom's gaze darted from object to object, and she pulled on her fingers like she did when she was starting to lose ground.

I was completely and pleasantly surprised by our conversation, but I had to do what I always did.

I intervened. I comforted. I made it all right.

I slid my chair close to hers and wrapped her in a hug.

"I'm sorry, baby girl. I'll get you that box of stuff I told you about."

"Yeah, I know you will."

"And I'll stand up to Connie more," she said, even as we settled into the slow, familiar rocking motion that always calmed her down. "If Reed ever comes back, we'll talk. If you know how to reach him, you should. I'll see him."

It would have been a great offer if the option of my mother being in the same room with one of the Destroyer's best soldiers was ever a real thing.

My mind reeled with all I'd learned, but I kept hugging my mom.

And she took all I had to offer.

CHAPTER 30

Mary

It was all I could do to get in Gavin's car.

It'd been a week since our last meeting on the top level of the parking garage, but he'd started to question my renewed commitment to our... I couldn't call it a friendship or a relationship. On my end it was a plan to obtain a confession and justice—and maybe some painful payback. On his it was a renewed romance where we rode off together and proved my worth to Shanar so I could live.

It was so insane, I wanted to laugh like a maniacal clown head in a horror movie.

I knew I wasn't thinking clearly. I didn't care. I just couldn't make anything feel better no matter how hard I tried. All control was slipping right through my fingers.

"I brought food," he said.

I didn't notice any Styrofoam cups in the holder, or any

paper bags with grease seeping through the bottom. "Something smells good, but where is it?"

"Fancy container in the trunk. It's real food. From that Italian place you like."

"Oh. Classy." I put on my seatbelt. "What's the occasion?"

"Last time at the parking garage. It opens next week, so I'm sure all the cameras and lights are near completion. Won't be able to sneak in there anymore unless we really mean to park."

"Right."

There was little to no conversation as we made our way to the usual place. Gavin didn't park his car in any designated spot. With us alone up there, he didn't need to. He just stopped it as an afterthought, pointing toward the boundary wall, and in view of the slowly disappearing multi-hued sunset.

Garlic and marinara smells wafted out of the back.

I glanced around at the complete hardened structure. "I don't see a comfortable place for a picnic."

"I got this." He pulled out two yoga mats and a blanket. "See? Not so bad."

And it wouldn't have been so bad if I hadn't been there with Gavin. What had I been thinking?

I should have run then, when I still had the chance.

From silver plastic utensils to store-brand sparkling Italian water bottles, he'd planned a romantic and above-average spread—for a fake and useless attempt to win me back.

"C'mon." He tossed his keys on the quilt and tried to get comfortable as he opened a steaming foil tray of manicotti and a decorated cardboard box of the restaurant's famous rolls. "There's salad in here too, but I'm not sure about trying to eat that up here."

"Doesn't sound easy," I admitted, and found a spot near him. "I already can't eat a salad without dripping dressing down the front of my shirt. You should fridge that for your lunch tomorrow."

I poked at gooey cheese with my fork and tried to avoid eye contact.

Gavin scooted closer and dipped his head in an effort to make me look up so he could catch my wandering attention. "Are you going to the thing tomorrow?"

My return glance to his question couldn't have held a bit of recollection of what he was talking about because I had no idea.

"The crawfish festival, carnival, and vendor fair thing at the county fairgrounds. Out where they have the rodeo—"

"I remember." I'd totally forgot. "Yes, I'm going. There's going to be an area for Stonehaven Academy people in the vendor building. Fundraising and stuff…"

"I thought maybe we could go together." He placed his hand on mine. I was repulsed by his touch, but didn't want to pull away too quickly.

I scrambled for an answer. There was no way I would show up to a public event with Gavin. My Warrior team would never understand. I could barely stomach the thought of it myself.

I slipped my hand out from under his and set my food aside. "I have people to meet there. I'm manning a booth for a while."

Frustration simmered in his gaze. "Look, Mary, I'm doing all I can here. You need to make a commitment soon and stick with it. Stick with me. We're running out of time."

"Time for what?"

"Don't make me say it all out loud. I've tried to explain the only way we both make it out of this alive is if we stick together—"

"And work for Shanar."

"Yes."

"And just forget everything else and move on?"

"Yes. We get out of school, we get out of this town, we move on to college, and see what happens next."

Pure rage and utter sadness overtook me. I remembered my time with Jacob. Snowflakes, warm-but-frosty kisses, a wool blanket and his arms around me. I thought of the next day at the fair. Jacob wouldn't be there, but I'd be holding a purple Saints football t-shirt with his name and number in memoriam on the sleeve. I'd be dying inside, but Gavin would be there smiling and assuming I'd be under his possessive thumb again and that somehow we were going to outrun my grief and his sin, and in some sick way it would all be OK.

He was out of his freakin' mind.

But before I could process how lost I really was in my mixed-up plan for some kind of revenge, Gavin's lips were on mine.

He pressed his body onto me until my back almost reached the soft pallet he'd made on the hard concrete.

I couldn't breathe, and I could barely think.

His lips were on my cheek and at my neck.

When my hand fell away to try and push off the ground from beneath him, I felt his keys.

I held them tight in my fist as he used both hands to grab my waist in an attempt to pin me down. His head landed on my chest, and then one hand crept up to tug on my shirt and grab my breast.

That was it.

I bucked him off my body and scrambled to stand. Blood oozed from a nasty, burning scrape where my leg had met scratchy cement somewhere in the struggle.

"No." I held out my hand. "Don't come toward me. I'm warning you. You do not want to do this."

"Do what, Mary?" He righted his clothes and smoothed his hair. "Seems to me I can do what I want where you're concerned. You keep saying you're so mad and that I'm going to pay, but yet, here we are. When are you going to get that we are destined to be and work together?"

"No, we're not."

"Yes, we are. Shanar isn't the sharpest tool in the shed. In fact, he's just a bully for the Destroyer. He even let Reed Logan walk away. He doesn't have the power to hold on to anyone. The whole reason for this mess with you is because he couldn't finish the job when you were three. Your whole miserable existence has hinged on the fact he failed a job he had to do years ago."

"He failed because I defeated him."

"Is that what you really think? That you're so special the Destroyer has wasted years messing with you? That you have such power you can defeat someone like me?"

"I can defeat you and your kind."

"Can you though? You're only even in this fight because Shanar messed it up the first time." He laughed. "I think you're more than he bargained for, but his only objective is to finish the job he started."

"He can't kill me."

"Really? Who has the power in this situation, Mary? Who has the car and the game and the plan? Who has the future?"

"It isn't you, Gavin."

He snarled. "Who had the power on the mountain?"

My blue eye twitched until I felt it would explode in my head.

Realization flooded my brain, but it was far outweighed by anger. I could kill him, right? Would anyone in the universe not understand that? Did he not deserve to die for what he did?

"Look at you struggle, Mary. You want to come at me but you're afraid."

"I'm not afraid of you, Gavin."

I *was* afraid, but not of him. It wasn't strength I lacked, it was confidence. I'd never been without confidence. I'd never let my own personal anger or need for revenge override my true calling. I'd never had to. Everything until then had been simple.

Everything until Jacob.

I had to get out, but I wasn't afraid of Gavin or Shanar or the Destroyer...

I was afraid of myself.

In one quick move, I jumped in his car and locked the door.

He pounded on the window. "What are you doing?"

"I'm going home. You can get your car later."

"Get out! You don't have the keys."

I tossed them on the seat and pushed the ignition button. "Sure I do."

"I'm warning you, Mary..."

I put the car in drive. "Warning me?" Anger ruled my foot as I hit the gas and I slammed the front of his precious car into the wall.

Dust rose as concrete cracked.

He yanked on the handle.

I backed up and did it again. "Get out of my way!" I screamed.

That time I'd made it through to rebar.

"I'm calling the police."

"The police? I figured you'd call your buddy Shanar." I nodded toward his phone in its fancy nest in the cup holder. "But OK. Let me know how that goes for you."

I backed up farther and slammed into the wall again.

The amount of damage to both the vehicle and the wall warned me I'd probably gone as far as I could without going over. I doubted by then I could even drive it away.

I took a deep breath. "Enough," I yelled. "Get away from the car. I'm putting it in park and I'm walking away."

"Not a chance."

Fine.

I cracked the door. His hand slipped in within a heartbeat and grabbed a handful of my hair. He smashed my face into the window. "You'll pay for this."

Blood from my lip smeared on the glass. "Like Jacob paid for being my Protector?"

"Yeah. Like Jacob paid."

It was the closest I would get to a confession that day.

It was enough.

I stomped on the accelerator and twisted out of the car as it flew off the top. We tumbled to the ground amidst the crackling of tree limbs and crumbling concrete.

I hurried to my feet to run. Gavin grabbed my ankle and I hit the ground hard. Every injury, every broken bone, every hour of physical therapy came back to me in a fresh rush of pain.

I kicked myself loose and tried again.

I turned to see his pathetic, defeated body on the ground.

He didn't look up. "There's no coming back from this, Mary. This was your last chance."

"Wow." I wiped blood from my face. "And here I thought it was yours." I turned to leave and then spun back. "By the way, I lied about putting the car in park."

He rolled onto his back in a fit of laughter. "You have no idea what you've done…what's about to happen now."

"I think I do." I pulled long strands of hair off my shirt and let them float away in the breeze. I touched my tender scalp. He'd actually pulled my hair out by the roots. "You should know something too."

He didn't bother to answer.

"The only reason you weren't in your car when it went over is because I'm a better person than you."

CHAPTER 31

Mary

I darted down the stairwell and started the long walk home. Sirens blared close by. I prayed no one had been anywhere near the back side of that garage when the car went over. It didn't seem likely anyone would be around, but at that point, I would have grieved a disturbed bird's nest or a flattened squirrel if it died because of my anger.

The scent of frankincense wafted across the path I took through the closest subdivision, hoping to find the quickest way home. The little walking-guy icon on my phone told me I had a long way to go, but I knew I was about to be slowed down by a conversation with an Enforcer I'd been avoiding.

The sidewalk opened up to a well-lit main intersection near a Starbucks in a strip center. The source of the frankincense became clear when I spotted Sebastian in his human form at a patio table with a cup in front of him.

It was only the second time I'd seen him in a physical body. I knew I was in trouble.

I approached with caution and paused at his table. "Can everyone see you?" I whispered under my breath.

"Yes."

"Good to know. I didn't want to be the person who looked to be sitting here talking to myself."

He raised his cup to me. "I'm here. Have a seat."

"I need an iced something and a bottle of water. Be right back."

Yeah. Probably wasn't a good idea to leave my supernatural being waiting, but what else could I do? I also had to pee.

I returned to the table and sat. "Sorry."

He shrugged. "Busted lip, bloody leg scrapes, near bald spot..."

I absently reached for my head. "I didn't think it was that bad. And I tried to clean myself up."

"You missed some spots."

"Well. You look... Exactly the same. Same wrinkles, long, messy dark hair, big dark eyes. And I'm pretty sure you're too big for that cheap, metal-looking bistro chair."

"Is there any end to your sass, Warrior?"

"Probably not. It's been a long night. Sorry. How did I score the honor of your physical presence?"

"We need to talk, as in a full conversation. I thought it would be easier for you like this."

"And you just happen to show up after my dinner with Gavin?"

"That was *dinner*? I'd have gone more with demolition derby. But what do I know?"

I sat back, stuck a straw in my mouth, and tried to talk around it. "I messed up, I guess. I let him get to me. I lost control of the situation, but at least I didn't kill him."

"Did you intend to kill him? With malice in your heart?"

"At some point I did. And then I thought maybe justice in the courts would be enough, and now I realize it would be a miracle to find enough evidence to make it stick. He'd have to confess, and I don't think that'll happen." Iced coffee slid down my throat and was so cold it burned my chest. "He doesn't even care. He has no respect for life. The Gavin I knew is gone."

"And what about your respect for life, Warrior?"

"Having been dead at least once, I can tell you I have never been disrespectful of life."

"But you actively hated and wanted to kill Gavin."

"I get it, OK? I had to get through all that. Maybe this was part of it. I could have killed him at any time using my own human power or my supernatural strength. But I didn't now, did I? Because I know right from wrong and I know I serve the Creator and my team of Warriors, and I have to get better. I know that."

He nodded.

"What? What am I missing? Yes, I know I made a mess tonight. I know Gavin is coming for me, but he was always coming for me, wasn't he? I've never been completely safe. Gavin is just a puppet of Shanar's. Shanar wants me dead. If Gavin doesn't succeed, he'll send someone else. Unless the Warriors can completely defeat Shanar."

"But the Destroyer is over Shanar. Even if you defeat him, the Destroyer still rules much of Earth. Have you ever wondered why it's Shanar you fight with? Why it's Shanar that kept you up at night?"

"I know why. I'm a personal battle to him. He lost me. He wants to settle the score and mark me as a win and not a loss on the Destroyer's great whiteboard of death."

"Well, then. If Shanar is somehow banished from your realm, then it's no longer personal, and the only real battles you have are with your assignments as they come up. Shanar is just a middle man in your bigger picture."

"And he can be completely defeated. As in destroyed."

Sebastian cocked his head with a questioning gaze.

"Shanar can be completely defeated!" I repeated. "He's only been here for us to learn from him. To see how it's done. And once he's gone—"

"Settle down, Warrior. Back to the matter at hand."

"Which is?"

"Your anger, wrath, and rage."

"That's all the same thing."

"In your case it's so big it looks like three things."

I made a face at him. "I'm getting better."

"Yes, you're doing so well there's a car upended beside a parking garage. You know there are cameras everywhere."

I knew and couldn't help but to laugh a little inside. That would teach him for putting his hands on me again.

"Gavin could press charges," I said. "He won't want to admit I got the best of him, but he'd want even less to say he lost control and did that himself. There are damages to pay for... His insurance company is gonna love that call." I tried to fluff my hair around my new bald spot. "What do I do?"

"I can give it a shot," Sebastian said. "But there's only so much I can do to intervene in human affairs. Maybe the cameras aren't online yet, maybe Gavin will make something up to distance himself from the scandal of it happening with you. I don't know. No guarantees."

"I know you'll do what you can. If not, I guess I'll see what happens. Natural consequences and all that." I popped the lid on my drink and scooped a pile of whipped topping in my mouth. "Gavin mentioned Reed Logan. What's that about—besides the fact he's an Agent for the Destroyer and could harm Ivy and her mother, or any of us for that matter?"

"Things are not always what they seem."

"I'd like to trust you on that one there, Seb, but you and I were both at the Stonehaven Gym Fire, and now Reed is gone and has broken his daughter's heart. It's pretty clear."

"Seb?"

"Never mind. Earth thing. Nicknames."

"I'm glad to see you are taking your work for the Creator so seriously. Is there any point in this conversation where we will actually make progress?"

I let out a heavy sigh. "I assume you came a long way to see me, and that it was a difficult journey like you said it was last time because of the protective barriers you provide for me and the other Warriors' safety." An involuntary snort escaped my mouth before I knew it was coming. Then I laughed. "I'm sorry, but Gavin's car..." I made a whistling sound and mimicked with my hands the way it made a slight arc and then went tree-surfing over the edge. "Gavin was groping me. He had his hands on me again and he... He..."

Sebastian leaned in. "I know you've been hurt and abused by Gavin, and that is not OK and will not be without consequence, but I don't think you realize the severity of the current situation."

"I think I do. That's why I need these moments of hysteria to get from place to place." I leaned in too, to meet him halfway across the rickety small table. "Jacob is dead. He's dead because of Gavin. And me. And you couldn't help us."

"And someday you will have to forgive me and yourself for that."

"Someday."

"Listen, Warrior. Tough times are coming as you get to the next part of your journey. There is closure for some things, and in other ways, you'll just be learning how to work in the fullness of your calling. You need to focus now more than ever and you need to pull together with your team and be ready. Do you understand?"

"Yes. I'm trying."

"Try harder. Find your peace and concentration, and stop playing games with creatures like Gavin. That is not what you were chosen for."

"Message received." I gathered my bottle of water and checked my car-service app. Suddenly, home seemed too far away. "Are you going to do that thing now where you walk into the bushes and sprout wings and disappear?"

He stood. His full height and extra-wide chest caused others to take a second look. "No. I'm going to do that thing now where I get more coffee and try to clean up your car mess."

CHAPTER 32

Deacon

I had no idea I was going to a crawfish festival.

Claire Cannon had to explain it to me on the way in the car. I knew crawfish season was big in Texas, but I hadn't remembered the festival was supposed to be in March, and got rained out in one of our three-day floods. It'd been rescheduled for the bitter end of the crawfish season, and I was still signed up to help.

I didn't even eat crawfish.

I didn't eat anything that could look me in the eyes—dead or alive—right before it went in my mouth.

But the unprecedented day was just getting started.

I knew it when I stepped out of Claire's mother's car on the fairground parking lot.

Something wasn't right, but by the time I found the others at the Stonehaven Academy vendor booths doing everything from selling Saints t-shirts to pasting temporary Saints tattoos on kids' cheeks, the feeling had faded. Mostly because no one else seemed the least bit concerned.

I motioned for Scout, Ivy, and Mary, while trying to keep Claire from hearing anything Warrior related.

"Hey!" I half-shouted over the crowd. "I need you guys."

No one looked the least bit alarmed.

I waved like a maniac.

What? Scout mouthed back.

I gave him the same look my mom gave me when she expected me to either move or get booted into the middle of the next week. It worked. He passed his wad of dollar bills and the roll of raffle tickets to someone else and grabbed the others to meet me outside the vendor tent.

I wasn't proud of sending Claire to the ticket booth with a twenty-dollar bill to get food and game tickets, but I did.

My mother would have been so disappointed.

Ivy approached with a large purple butterfly on one side of her face. Its glittery wings distracted me in the bright sun. "What's going on? I'm in the middle of a dragon back there. That six-year-old isn't going to sit still forever."

"Something is not right here," I told her as the others arrived.

She looked around. "I feel nothing. I see nothing. Did your hands heat up?"

"No. It was only a weird feeling."

Scout took a long drink from his bottle of water. "I don't usually know until we're right in the middle of it so... Yeah. I got nothing."

I turned to Mary. "Anything?"

"No. Sorry. I think we're good, but I had a weird night so you may not be able to count on me."

"Seriously? The one time I know something's up and no one else feels it?"

Mary looked at the ground. "Um... I saw Sebastian last night because of a thing we had. I think he would have told me if there was something up here today."

Scout's expression turned to utter disappointment. "You *saw* him? In human form?"

"Yes."

"Aww, man, I wanted to see him. Wait. What did you do? What kind of thing did you have?"

She shifted her gaze away from us. "I screwed up."

When everyone opened their mouths to answer, she stopped us. "Yes, I know I've been doing that a lot lately. Save your breath. I'm trying to do better, but have you all heard anything?"

"Like what?"

"Like anything about, you know, anything last night? Have you seen Gavin?"

"No," I said, but I think I passed his stupid-expensive car in the lot out there. He's here somewhere."

She shook her head and continued to avoid eye contact. "I don't think it was Gavin's car you saw."

Scout's squinted at her. "What happened, Mary?"

"Gavin's fine, all right? Leave it alone." Her agitation grew. "Is that all? At least there's a fan on us in the vender shelter and we're out of the sun."

"That reminds me," Scout said. "My grandparents have closed on the lake house. First weekend in June is all ours. Yes, we'll be helping my grandparents move boxes, but you know they're good about leaving us alone. We can stay all weekend."

"Thanks," Mary said. "We need some time away."

"Yep. And if my grandpa hasn't hit a stump and sunk his boat by then, there should be water activities. And you know how excited I am about that."

Ivy snaked her arm around him. "You're doin' great with all that, Scout. It'll be fun."

I glanced over my shoulder for Claire. "And no one thinks anything is wrong today?"

Mary shrugged. "Not really. We'll keep our eyes and ears open. Like always."

"What are we looking for?"

The male voice startled us. I jumped and turned to see Mr. Parrington with a tub of popcorn in his hands and a pair of sunglasses that seemed too small for his round face.

"Geez, Mr. P. Where'd you come from?"

"I've been right here. I saw you four huddled together and that could mean anything. Had to check it out. Have you had your mudbugs yet?"

"Ewww. No."

"Aren't you originally from Louisiana? That's embarrassing, son." He adjusted his baseball cap. "Don't know what you're missing. Anything else going on?"

"I was about to ask you the same thing," I said. "I think something is up, but no one else is feelin' it. How does it work for you, Mr. P? Being a Guardian and all. Do you get feelings or thoughts or what?"

"I keep my ear to the ground." He glanced around for passersby. "I get the word on the *big picture* stuff. Don't always know the details, but sense when there's discord. There was a disturbance last night in the realm. Somebody ticked somebody off." He grabbed a handful of popcorn. "Anybody know anything about that?"

We all looked directly at Mary.

"*What?* I told you it's fine. I worked it out with Seb—my Enforcer, and it won't happen again."

"Stay aware," Mr. P said. "I've got to judge a pie contest and then I'm taking my kids to the rides. You guys coming to that side?"

"Of course," Ivy said. "The carnival is where the cotton candy and caramel apples are."

"Yeah," Mary added. "We're about to finish our shifts. Maybe we'll see you over there."

He practically skipped off like he was going to a party.

Oh, wait! He *was* going to a party. A party to celebrate some seafood someone caught in a swamp—or somewhere—and boiled alive. And all I could think about was how fast something could go bad and how to keep my girlfriend safe and from knowing too much Warrior business. I couldn't keep sending her off on stupid tasks I should have been responsible for myself on a date.

That was no way to treat a lady.

And why didn't my fellow Warriors know anything about the impending threat I felt deep in my bones and that sat in my stomach like a spicy crustacean trying to escape?

"I have to get Claire," I said. "Then I'll see you in the tent. We have to give away Saints rubber bracelets and sell those coupon card things for an hour or so."

We dispersed, and I'd never felt so alone as a Warrior. Maybe we'd been right. Maybe our training was all about learning to act on our own. Maybe I had an assignment that day and no one else did.

I wasn't ready to work alone.

Scout laughed so hard he doubled over and snorted. "You're kidding, right?"

Claire frowned as we pooled our tickets together to see how many we had left for rides. "What's wrong with that one? He was fine on the Ferris wheel and that other spinny thing."

Scout pointed. "Look at it."

"Stop talking about me," I said. "I'm right here."

The hot afternoon morphed slowly into early evening. Vendors packed up booths as the crowd moved on from crawfish and crafts to the carnival and the concert hall where a local band would play a barely tolerable set of country covers. Beer flowed as the lines at the portable bathrooms got longer, and every pack of teenagers was separating and pairing off to make out and drink contraband alcohol in whatever dark corners they could find.

Except for us. We weren't having that kind of fun.

Scout and Ivy had at least two fights over who would win a prize at a game that cost them way too much money to still be losers, and Mary was staying too quiet about whatever happened the night before.

All Claire Cannon wanted to do was kiss and cuddle on rides and take selfies, but I couldn't relax and lose the stone in the pit of my stomach that said something wasn't right.

"What are you all rambling about?" I paused as we got in a new line and looked ahead. "Oh. Yeah. I don't think I want to go on that one."

The large black structure called the *Spider* loomed in front of me with six—not eight—arachnid-looking arms and spun in a circle, and cycled through a series of heights and levels. Two black pods were attached to each arm where laughing passengers swirled inside in an alternating pattern. One arm up, another down... Bright lights flashed in varying colors along the creature's arms, and the large, red mark from the Black Widow's belly decorated every shiny black surface. The whole thing looked like a black and white horror movie I'd seen once as a kid, and then slept with the light on for months about it.

Scout laughed and Mr. Parrington fell into line behind us. "See? I told you he wouldn't ride this one."

Claire pouted and stuck her lip out at me. "Why not? You've ridden everything else."

"I hate spiders."

"I know, but it's not a spider, Deacon. It's a ride."

"Looks like a spider. Looks like a whole spider's nest. A whole spider's nest with eggs and stuff all over it. And I'll be trapped in there. And what if a spider is in that seat thingy with me. I'll have no place to run because I'll be twenty feet in the air in a spider's nest."

Claire wrapped her arms around my neck. "I'll protect you."

Mr. P's boys laughed behind me. I shot them the meanest pretend glare I could muster. "I don't like spiders."

"I don't either," the oldest kid said. "But I'm gettin' on that ride."

"Are you riding, Mr. P?"

"Nope."

Mary stepped over to us and strained to see the spinning buckets. "Looks like the three of us would fit," she told the boys. "We can get in the one on the same arm as Deacon and Claire and make fun of him. We'll take pictures of him crying. And post them on the internet."

The younger boy laughed. "Or put a video on YouTube."

"I knew we were going to be great friends," Mary said.

When it was our turn, Scout and Ivy raced to a pod and strapped themselves in. Mary and the boys ended up across from them, and claimed the pod beside them for me and Claire.

I pulled the bar tight against us. "No matter what stupid thing I will probably say or do later, Claire, remember I rode a spider for you today. And I hate spiders."

She attempted a laugh that was stolen by the sudden bump of the ride. She fanned her face. "I'd say kiss for luck, but I already can't breathe."

Mr. P's boys attempted trash talk from nearby, but failed to gather enough momentum to spin our way when the ride took off slow.

Within seconds, our arm was high in the air, and I was eye level with the giant lighted spider that topped the cylinder in the middle and held the whole works together. It was a long way away, but still... The menacing thing did nothing to help me find spiders endearing.

Claire's hair flew in my face as she attempted to take a

picture, and all we managed to do was slide into each other across the metal seat and pin each other in the corners on every turn. Loud laughter came from Mary's pod, and there was no way she was getting any pictures either.

Our buckets dipped together, as Scout and Ivy's flew upward on the other side. A sudden jolt startled me. It was out of rhythm with the rest of the arms and pods.

My hands heated up.

Crap!

I tried to look at everything while spinning and nothing caught my eye, but it was clear our arm was no longer moving like the rest.

"Claire! Did you feel that?"

Another jolt bounced us straight up. "I felt that! What's happening?"

"I don't know."

"We're going up," she yelled. "But not as fast as we were."

I caught a glimpse of the long, steel, braided wire that secured the arms to the center pole to, I assumed, keep everything balanced.

It had started to fray.

I wanted to tell Claire to hold on, but for what? Power, hot hands, or not, I could not fly. I couldn't teleport us out of the bucket, I couldn't send telepathic thoughts to the operator to cut the power and get us on the ground.

I screamed for Mary, but got no response as our bucket gained height and our tether continued to fail.

"The wire's just an added precaution," I mumbled. "The arm is what does the work..."

Sebastian! Are you here?

I got no response from him either.

The wire snapped and flopped around as it recoiled, and danced like drops of water on a sizzling pan.

I shielded Claire from what I thought might be a whip of its debris, but felt nothing.

"Stop the ride!" I screamed. "Stop!"

But nothing happened, and no one heard, and everything kept spinning.

Until our arm cracked and our buckets fell straight down to the ground.

CHAPTER 33

Mary

I knew nothing.
   I heard nothing.
   I felt nothing.
   I had no idea what was about to happen until it was happening, and my hair was whooshing around my face and standing up on my head in a straight-down drop.
   There were two intense and frightening thuds. One was when our bucket hit the ground, and one when what I imagined was Claire and Deacon's bucket hit ours—and sent us skidding across the grass.
   Alarm bells rattled in my ears, and I had no idea if the clanging was real or if it was all in my own brain and I was about to die from a head injury. Dirt sprayed our faces, and elbows and knees banged together until there was total darkness.
   The boys screamed.

And I screamed both inside and out. "Deacon!"
Sebastian!
There was no answer.

Grinding metal sounds came to a slow, sickening stop as the bells kept ringing.

From what I could tell, we hung face down because we'd flipped completely over. At least we hadn't been hit again by an oncoming pod, and though that could easily crush us, we were somewhat momentarily shielded by lesser hits by our own hard-shelled prison.

But what did I know, and what about the others?

"Shhh... Shhh...," I said to the boys. "Stop screaming so we can see how we are and how to get out of here, OK?"

We could see nothing. I had no idea if either of them was even still conscious once we took the second hit and they stopped yelling.

Heavy and gasping breaths came from my right.

"Someone will be here soon. Try to take slower deep breaths."

"I can't. This bar is on my chest."

Panic swept across me like a tidal wave. It was an unfamiliar feeling. Yes, I'd been in worse situations. Yes, I'd suffered injury, loss, and catastrophic events. Yes, I'd saved people—because I was a Warrior. But no matter how hard I tried to summon my Warrior confidence, power, strength, and help, I felt nothing like a Warrior.

"OK, both of you talk. Say anything. Are you awake?"

Their words didn't stick, but they made sense to my ears which I considered a win.

I struggled in the crowded dark space to reach the cloth strap pinned tight at my waist. I felt for the boys' too in hopes of easing the restrictions. There had to be an emergency release somewhere, but I'd never find it in the dark while pinned in my seat with no way to move.

Without supernatural powers, I was useless.

The younger boy on my left babbled in shock. "I'm OK. My arm hurts. Where's my dad...?"

"I really can't breathe," the boy on the right repeated as he stopped talking and started to wheeze.

I pushed on the bar with all my might. I called for Sebastian. I searched for my strength and found nothing.

A little boy could be dying beside me because his chest was crushed, and I had nothing.

Nothing.

I was no longer a Warrior.

CHAPTER 34

Deacon

Claire's head banged into mine so hard I saw stars.

Then she was gone, as pain ripped through my back.

Her petite body simply bounced from the fallen bucket and flew to a resting place, face down in the dirt nearby. Before I could react and free myself to help her, another pod from a different, still-attached arm, hurdled toward me and knocked my pod into Mary's.

I didn't see where it landed.

You have to stop the machine.

The calm, feminine voice was unmistakable in my ear—and completely unfamiliar.

You have to do it now.

Was I imagining things? Or was I dead?

"How? How do I stop the machine?"

Break free of your seat and stop the arms.

"I can't do that."

Yes, you can. You have amazing gifts of strength. I will help you.

"Where is Sebastian?"

Stop the machine.

The moment I attempted to move I was infused with power. I don't remember leaving the bucket, but it felt effortless to become free of it and move toward Claire as the arms erratically slowed, but continued to move.

Stop the machine.

"I have to check on Claire. And Mary... and Mr. P's boys."

Stop the machine first.

"How am I supposed to do that?"

I turned. The next giant arm headed straight for me at its lowest level. Alarm bells rang in my ears and people screamed all around me.

I braced myself on the ground and pressed my hands onto the arm. I staggered back, and pressed harder and harder still.

It held. Against all odds and all reason, it held. "Somebody shut this thing down," I screamed.

The scent of an electrical fire swirled to my nose, and then with a hiss, all the remaining working arms drifted to their positions near the ground and the lights went dark. With a final spark of crackling power from somewhere in the center pole, the spider died.

Well done.

Claire moved.

"Stay put," I said when I skidded to the ground at her side. "Don't move. We don't know where you're hurt."

"I think I'm OK," she sputtered and spit mud out of her mouth. "Everything seems to be working."

"Still, don't move." I placed my warm hand on her back. If there was anything left of my healing abilities, I begged the Creator to let them work for me. *Please... Claire has to walk away from this...*

Others converged on the scene to help. "We've got her,"

someone said, and I realized the emergency lights had come from the first responders who were on standby at the festival as more sirens blared in the distance.

"Mary," I whispered.

Claire waved me away. "Go. Mr. Parrington's boys. Go. I'm fine."

"And Scout and Ivy!" I stood and looked around. Was it too much to hope their position on the opposite side of the evil spider had kept them safe?

I turned my attention to Mary's bucket. Scores of people had already gathered around it, trying to lift it, but unsure as how to best proceed.

"The fire department will be here soon," someone said. "They have equipment for this."

"But they could be seriously injured under there," someone else yelled.

"And we could be losing valuable time if we wait for help to move it," yet another person argued.

"Stop!" Mr. Parrington yelled. "Listen!"

Clanging from the underside caused a collective sigh of relief to ripple through the crowd.

Mr. Parrington dove to the ground on what appeared to be the back side, looking for any way to see inside the flipped container.

Mary coughed. "Deacon! Are you there?"

"Yes." I hit the ground to hear her better.

"You have to hurry and move this thing. The bar is crushing our chests. One of the boys can't breathe."

"OK. Get ready to work with me. We got this."

"No, we don't," she said. "I have no Warrior strength. Do you understand? It's all you."

"We're Warriors, Mary, this is what we do."

"No time to argue. I have nothing. Hurry."

I stood and didn't even know where to start. Whatever

mechanism held the pod to the arm was twisted beyond recognition. I had no idea if something else would snap and bring down more heavy metal on us all.

Lift the container.

The female commander was back. She hadn't let me down the first time.

"How?"

Lift it. I will help you.

Goosebumps pebbled on my flesh as green flecks of light danced on my arms and hands and spread to the ends of my fingertips. They tickled and soothed my skin like dancing ice chips on my body. They trailed across my neck and moved to cover the entire pod. My hands heated to temperatures I'd never experienced before. Not even when I pushed against the arm.

"Stand back!"

Clumps of mud and grass made the edge I found slippery. I knocked the debris away and lifted. Others rushed to help, but seemed unable to get any closer as long as the green energy grew.

The pod lifted. I changed position to glance underneath and see the best way to proceed.

Mary gasped. "You're doing it, Deac."

Limited light from around us seeped into the dark space. I'd never seen Mary so scared.

"Everyone OK?" I asked. "I don't want to make it worse."

"Try to tilt us up a little more and then get the bar. The bar is the problem."

"Right. None of the mangled release latches are going to work." I tried to survey the big picture. "Hold on. This might hurt."

She held the boys. "Do it. Quickly."

Mr. Parrington rushed forward.

"Stop!" I said. "I've got this. I promise."

He looked me up and down, his gaze surveying me top to bottom. Did he see green?

"Those are my kids, Warrior."

"I know."

"Give him room," he shouted.

I righted the pod amidst the sound of grating steel, and braced for more debris to crack, fall, or otherwise rain down on my head or the others. When none of that happened, I waved for Mr. Parrington.

I tapped the top edge of the opening. "Push against this while I get the bar."

"Got it."

Just as with the wall, firefighters arrived as I pulled it back in a long, agonizing, slow-motion movement.

Help rushed in and crowded me out of the way. I didn't care as long as Mary and the boys were OK.

Scout and Ivy? Check. They'd already made it to our side of the ride and seemed to be walking fine.

Claire Cannon? Check. I caught a glimpse of the top of her head as they loaded her into an ambulance. I rushed her way, but they wouldn't let me close enough.

"Claire! I'm here. I'll call your parents and head to the hospital."

She waved, and jingled the keys to her mother's car at her side on the gurney. Leave it to her to be thinking ahead.

The paramedic tossed them my way.

I disappeared into the crowd.

Well done.

CHAPTER 35

Mary

I cradled the older boy's body in my arms as the bar set us free at Deacon's command.

"He got the worst of the bar to the chest," I said. "He's wheezing."

"We'll get him, but don't move," the EMT said and smiled. "We need to immobilize everyone. There's a good chance of injuries to your spinal cord in a fall like this, but we've got you, OK? It's important you don't move."

Yeah. I knew the drill. Immobilize me. Leave me behind. Let me die. I'd lost my ability to help others, and that made me as good as dead in my Warrior world. I was a sitting duck for Shanar and wouldn't last without my Enforcer, Sebastian—or my Protector, Jacob.

Jacob... What would that day have been like with Jacob?

I shook and wanted to cry as I fought against the cervical collar. Yes, I knew it well, and if I was strong enough to want to get up, I probably didn't need it. I knew more about serious injuries and backboards than most people should.

My friendly EMT waved a light in my eyes. "Take it easy now. What's your name?"

"Mary."

"OK Mary, we're gonna get you checked out."

"The boys... Take care of the boys..."

"We've got it covered."

Then I was alone on a gurney in the midst of chaos. Lights flickered and blurred in my teary eyes as the thunder beats of running people pounded around me.

"Sebastian," I whispered. "You didn't come. You said you'd always come and you didn't.

I tried to reach you, but it's hard to work with you when you fight with your own kind.

"You *are* my own kind. I needed you. I couldn't use my Warrior abilities, and you didn't show up."

I tried, but your aim was not true on your target. You were not in the situation.

More rage prickled in my heart. I wanted to scream at him, but I also didn't want to earn a trip through the psych ward or any more brain scan machines than were necessary. No one checking on me as I awaited my ambulance ride would have understood either side of the supernatural realm conversation I was having.

How was I not in the situation? I snapped back at him in my head. *I couldn't have been any more in the situation. I was the one in the spider pod of death. I was the one holding scared and injured young boys. I was the one screaming for help and you didn't come.*

But where did your thoughts really go? He questioned back without hesitation. *Who was on your mind?*

Gavin, of course! All I could think about was how Gavin was responsible for all of this. If Jacob hadn't died... If Shanar hadn't used him... If I hadn't let my emotions run wild...

I found it impossible to lie still. The hard collar pinched everything and made it difficult to breathe. I was on the edge of panic while strapped to a hard board, and Sebastian's question and my real answer pierced my Warrior skin and bruised my Warrior heart.

He was right. Everyone was right, and Gavin had won the battle I thought I had in the bag—the battle of my mind. I knew he'd never get me physically, and I assumed I had the upper hand in the mental challenge. But I had not been able to rise above the angry and vengeful thoughts I carried for those who wronged me and killed Jacob. I'd been playing a game I could never win, and talking a talk that would never be true. I'd put revenge ahead of dealing with grief and it'd weakened everything I was.

Losing Jacob should have made me a better, stronger, and wiser Warrior.

I hadn't given anything the time or rational processing it deserved.

I'd only let the pain and anger rule my head, and that had stolen my Warrior abilities.

Just as the Destroyer intended.

All they had left to do was take my life.

It would be easy.

CHAPTER 36

Mary

I tried to buck myself off the gurney as the emotional storm came in waves and wouldn't stop.

A warm hand captured mine. "Shhh… Stop. You'll hurt yourself worse," Ivy said.

"You don't know what I've done," I wailed. "I put everyone in danger."

"Step back, miss," someone commanded.

"In a minute," Ivy barked back. "I need to call her parents. And why is she just stuck here anyway?"

There was no answer for that as I continued to panic. "Listen, Ivy, everyone is in danger. I've lost my footing as a Warrior. It's my fault. None of us are safe. You have to warn Deacon and Scout."

"Oh, I think Deacon has everything under control. Right now, you need to rest."

"I can't. I've messed up."

Ivy put a gentle hand on my chest. "Girl, you are holding on to some stuff. And not in a good way. Your insides are about to blow."

"What?"

"Not your physical insides, they're fine. It's your emotional insides."

"Yes, I know, that's what I'm trying to tell you. I'm not a Warrior anymore because I can't focus on anything but Gavin and my pain and destruction. Sebastian tried to warn me, and I didn't listen. You have to tell the others and stay safe."

"No, I don't. You're very much a Warrior—just a distracted one. I know you still have a lot of grief to process, but you have to start letting things go."

"I can't, don't you see? If I start letting it out, I'll never stop crying or screaming or spinning out of control."

Ivy snorted. "How is that any different than the last half hour?"

I tried to smile. "Right?"

Ivy tugged on my own shirt and sleeve to swipe moisture off my face and dab my eyes. "Listen. Your grief is going to take time, but you have to find a way to set aside the anger so you can get back to doing your job. You can't let the Destroyer win."

"It may be too late."

"It's not. And I can help. We need to open the door to let the poison out."

"Believe me, if I could have let the poison out, don't you think I would have done it myself?"

"No, you wouldn't have, because you've enjoyed holding on to it. It's given you something to do instead of suffer the actual loss of Jacob."

"There is nothing about the last several months I've enjoyed."

Ivy sighed. "Except for maybe looking for ways to get revenge on Gavin? Maybe leading him on, spending time with him, and trying to catch him in a lie?"

"When did you get your degree in psychology, and since when have you been following me around?"

"C'mon, it's not like you hid it well."

I hadn't, and I hadn't cared—until the moment I lost it all.

Ivy stood at my side and leaned down.

"What are you doing?"

"I can't hug you and they're going to take you any minute, so I'm trying to make contact with your pain."

"Did you hit your head too? Do you need a gurney?"

"I'm fine. It's a new thing I discovered. It's part of my Warrior job. It will help us all."

"Is that so?"

"Yes. Humor me."

"I have nowhere else to go."

Ivy took both my cold hands in her warm ones and tried to get as close as possible to me without jarring my body or pressing into my torso.

Butterflies circled my stomach when she closed her eyes.

"I felt that," she said.

"Felt what?"

"Something stirred."

"Wait. You felt *my* butterflies in *your*…uh… something?"

"Yes."

"Don't get excited. It's probably an internal injury."

"It's not. It's the poison stirring. It wants out, but you want to keep it."

"No I don't."

"Concentrate, Mary. Let me have some of that anger. I'll take it and get rid of it so you'll feel better."

"Now you're making crap up. If you want to help me, cut the straps on this collar and help me up."

"No. Stay down. Think of one thing. One thing about Gavin or that day… Think about it and let me have it."

I closed my eyes as sweat pooled where the collar strangled

me, and anxiety settled in more when I couldn't move freely. I imagined Gavin on the slope, sliding by me in the spray of snow that started the whole domino of events that led to Jacob's death. The way he arrogantly carried his body with the skilled moves of his poles when I hadn't realized he could even ski. I hated the deception, I hated my oversight, I hated the outcome. I despised the moment I realized it was all about to go badly and I was caught off guard.

I knew the moment Ivy tugged at the thread I offered her. Of all the things that flooded my mind—and there was a deluge of horrifying memories—that was the first one I could pinpoint and grasp, that first turn onto the slope toward death.

I let her pull it out of the bundle that was tangled in knots inside me.

The memory would never go, but the anger would ease.

I felt it, I knew it, and it was enough at the time.

Our eyes opened and we caught each other's gaze in surprise.

Ivy smiled. "See what I mean?"

I was too stunned to speak. Maybe I could do it. Maybe I could get better.

Two first responders grabbed the gurney. "Sorry you had to wait, darlin', but it's your turn to fly."

I squeezed Ivy's hand.

I felt a tiny bit lighter.

CHAPTER 37

Deacon

I had to park Claire's mother's car about a mile from the emergency room entrance.

When it looked like there were about a hundred people milling around the door because of the accident and the usual ER patients, I headed around toward the ambulance bay. It was too busy to slip by the rig that was parked at the large entrance. There was a side door that required a key card—and a cop right in front of it.

When he spotted me, I did what my parents had always said to do. I stood with my arms and hands still at my sides.

"There's no public entrance back here. You'll have to go around."

"Yes, sir."

"Wait. You're that kid," he said.

"Sir?"

"You're the kid everyone's talking about. You stopped the ride and picked up the bucket."

Picked up the bucket? I remembered lifting it, but I hardly picked it up. As I thought about it, I didn't remember much about the exact order, timing, and way I did things, just that things had happened.

And there was a new voice in my head that was neither Shanar or Sebastian's. So, there was that. Some other female supernatural being was now speaking to me and I didn't know where to begin with that.

Scout and Ivy rounded the corner.

"See, I told you it was him," Scout said.

"Hey, guys."

"We'll go in the front of the hospital," I said. "Thank you."

"Stop."

Ivy took over with a smile. "What's up, officer?"

"I recognize all of you."

She pursed her lips and considered the night sky. "We've never been arrested. How do you know us?"

"I interviewed all four of you after the Stonehaven Gym Fire. You three and the other girl who saved that football player. I was on duty that day."

"Oh. Well, uh… Thank you for your service?"

He hooked his thumbs at his belt. "All right. What is it you all need? I mean, who am I to question our local superheroes?"

I shook my head. "Nah. No such thing as superheroes."

"There have been too many incidents and you have too many fans out there who beg to differ. A lot of times in police work, the answer is right in front of us. If it looks like a duck and quacks like a duck…"

"Yeah," I said. "It's a duck. But I'm no superhero. I don't know what happened back there."

"Whatever it was, it wasn't humanly possible. Now, what can I do for you?"

"My girl and our friends are in there. They were in the pods that fell."

"Yes. I know. The one who flew out and the blond one. I saw the video."

"And we're very concerned about Mr. Parrington's two boys," Scout said. "They were with Mary."

He held up his phone. "Yep. Video. Do your parents know where you are?"

"Yes, sir," we answered in chorus.

Scout scrolled through his own screen. "This is worse than all the other times. The only difference is all the heat's on Deacon this round." He stepped my way. "Maybe we should just get you out of here. There will be chaos if you walk in those front doors."

"I have Claire's mother's car and I can't leave. I brought her to the festival. I need to talk to her parents."

"This way," the officer said. "If I let you in this door, you'll be in the ER. You can find your friends and then get back out. Stay out of the way and don't get in anyone's business. There are sick people in there and it's no time for peeking behind curtains and disturbing patients. Lay low, get it done, and get out. I'll help you get away." He flicked a card into Deacon's hand as we passed. "I'm here on extra-duty work. If you find yourselves in need of hiring personal security, I'm your man."

We slipped inside the door.

Scout laughed. "Did that cop just ask you for a job? Like to be your bodyguard?"

"That's ironic," Ivy said. "Superheroes shouldn't need bodyguards."

"Whatever," I said. "I'm not a superhero."

Ivy grabbed my arm. "You should wait till you see the video. People have reason to be going wild about this. The cop isn't kidding. You might need help to get safely home."

"My parents are coming to get me since I have Claire's

mother's car. Believe me, as soon as I know everyone is OK, I'm outta here."

"We should find Claire," Ivy said. "She came in first."

My heart caught on one of my ribs as it tried to beat out of my chest. "That's because she flew out of that pod thing like a rocket. She talked to me, but I have no idea how bad it is."

Scout read the monitor above our head. "I'm guessing room two or four."

"Why?" I asked. "Why would you guess that out of all these rooms and the beds parked in the hallway?"

"From the tests ordered and the location of the trauma rooms. Go."

My knees buckled as I searched for the numbers while trying to stay out of sight.

"Here," I said. "You two stay here."

They pinned themselves against the wall as I made a knock-knock sound on the too-cheerful white and blue striped curtain. Claire was almost sitting up, but resting.

Her dad came straight for me. "How did this happen at a crawfish festival?"

"I'm sorry, sir, it was a freak accident. I had no idea—"

"Stop," her mother said. "You couldn't have predicted this, Deacon. We understand. Thanks for helping her. You were quite the hero today."

Claire's eyes fluttered open and she tried to smile. "Everyone else all right? Are you OK?"

I moved closer and took her hand. "I'm good. Where are you hurt?"

"They don't think it's anything major, but they're making sure. I don't remember much."

I glanced at her mom.

"The x-rays were clear so far, but she's headed up to CT to confirm no internal injuries. She's stable, but she'll be sore a while."

"How are the others?" Claire asked.

"Trying to find out. Came to find you first."

"You can go now," her dad said. "And expect to have to make some formal statements to the police and our lawyers, but for your own protection, you should keep your mouth shut and talk to your parents before you say a word to anyone."

"Stop badgering him," her mother said.

"No, he's right," I agreed. "We weren't safe on a simple carnival ride. Something went wrong and people got hurt."

"Maybe there's hope for this one yet," her dad grumped.

Claire winced but tried to smile. "Come back by later, please. I'll know more and I need to tell you something."

"Sure. I just need to check on the others."

I handed her dad the keys. "I brought the car. It's in lot F."

I wanted to comfort her, but I couldn't get out of there fast enough.

Ivy looked disgusted. "We heard. He's going to make a big deal out of this and we're all going to be tied up in a lawsuit for years."

"Maybe we should be," Scout said. "And it won't be years. They'll want to settle." He shook his head. "We could have died on that ride."

"And we could die crossing the street tomorrow," Ivy said. "And we're Warriors. Anything could happen. Do you know how much time and energy a lawsuit is going to take? My mom will have to act on my behalf. Can you imagine the stress of that?"

"Hey, not that this is the time," Scout continued. "But that wild ride on a poorly maintained machine could pay for your college if the company is proven to be negligent in its care of the equipment. I hate frivolous lawsuits, but I also hate reckless disregard for public safety."

"You continue to amaze me," she said. "I really thought you

should be a doctor and cure cancer or something. Now I wonder if you should fix the legal system."

I looked at the same monitor Scout did. "Or maybe he should use his powers to find Mary and Mr. P, and then keep Claire's dad from killing me. Wouldn't that be a better use of our time right now?"

Scout pointed. "Mr. Parrington is right there."

I don't know what I expected when I rushed toward him, but what I got was a big dad bear hug. "Are you OK?" he asked.

"I'm fine, but who cares? How are the boys?"

"What do you mean *who cares*? I care! You saved my kids' lives."

"I don't think I did that…"

"Deacon." Mr. P put his hands on my arms and squeezed. "Do you know what happened back there?"

"Not really."

He looked around and lowered his voice. "Do you remember the colors?"

I would never forget that green-hued light show that started on my arms and spread around my whole immediate area. "Yes."

Ivy stepped forward. "It was amazing, Deacon. It was an even bigger display than at the Smoothie Shack. You've definitely picked up additional abilities."

"Did everyone see it? Is that why they're talking about a video?"

"I didn't," Scout said.

"No," Ivy said. "Not everyone."

Mr. P shrugged. "I think I only saw it because I was close and it involved my kids."

I struggled to understand the whole color thing and the new voice in my head. "Forget all that. How are the boys?"

"They're stable, but upstairs for tests with my wife. There is some concern about the chest injuries, but they'll be fine.

They're calm and resting, and all they can talk about is what you did."

What I did. Apparently, I only knew half of what I did.

"We need to find Mary."

"She's right here," he said and pointed his head next door. "I'm waiting for her parents. They let her out of the collar and there's some concern because of her injuries in December, so they'll have to do some tests, but they're not worried."

"OK... Hey, Mr. P, you have to tell me... No one died, right?"

"No, son..." He paused and dropped to a bench and patted the spot beside him. "No, Deacon, no one died. Probably because of you. You literally stopped the oncoming arms that hadn't broken. That caused the whole thing to shut down. If those arms had kept coming, those buckets would have kept crashing into each other until they were powered down and had a chance to slow. I don't know much right now, but the operator wasn't even at the controls. I've already heard people say he'd stepped away to get a drink or something. I don't have all the facts, and I've never had the pleasure of seeing Warrior energy like I saw today, but you were it. You saved everyone."

"I need to get to Mary."

"Of course."

"I don't know if I can get back," I said. "We promised the cop we'd get out of here." I stood on wobbly legs.

Mr. P hugged me again. "I can't ever thank you enough."

"No problem. And watch out for Claire Cannon's dad. He's already talking lawsuit and probably has his team of lawyers on their way."

CHAPTER 38

Mary

My parents texted from the road.

Turning into the hospital. About to try to park in this madhouse. Be there ASAP.

I pulled the warm blanket over my chest and adjusted at least three ice packs. Of all the things that hurt, it was my wrists and hands that were the worst. I'd pounded them over and over again on the stuck bar, and tugged and squirmed until my nails bled and the bones in my hands screamed for mercy.

I'd been trapped with two kids in a small, dark space, and I'd never been so alone. Ivy could talk all day about healing and anger and letting things go—and she was right—but I'd messed up so bad with the Creator that I didn't know if I'd ever be useful again.

The curtain flew up as Deacon rushed to my side with Ivy and Scout.

"I'm sorry, Deac. I couldn't help." The words rushed out

before they could talk. "I've been a mess for months and you all have been so patient with me, but you were right when you all knew I wasn't myself. You tried to tell me I was too distracted and too angry and I didn't listen. I should have known better after I couldn't help at the Smoothie Shack, but I didn't get it."

"It's fine," he said. "We knew it would take time."

"But I've put everyone in danger. I literally gift-wrapped the upper hand and gave it to Gavin when I pulled that stunt last night." I paused and glanced at their questioning faces. "Yes, I know I haven't told you about it, but you're going to be so freakin' proud of my antics. You know it was bad if Sebastian had to show up and fix it, and now I'm not even sure I can be a Warrior."

Ivy rubbed my leg. "It's fine, Mary. It's all going to get better from here. You're going to get better, and we'll all get stronger."

"I completely failed you today. I wasn't there for the fight. I was useless. Same as at the Shack only worse."

Scout rested his knee on the only chair in the small room and leaned across the back. "You had to work through it."

"Yeah, everyone keeps saying that, yet here I am. A useless ex-Warrior."

Deacon leaned down. "Listen to me. You will never *not* be a Warrior. This is temporary, and we'll be back on the same page in no time."

"But if we're not..." I lifted my phone from beneath the covers. "You've got it all under control."

He pushed it away. "I'm not ready to look at that."

"Deac, you were everything a Warrior is supposed to be. Everything I wasn't."

"I don't care. I tried to disappear into the crowd, and instead I'm right in the middle of it again. And you don't get to quit because of Jacob, Mary. Pull it together. We can't do this without you."

"I'm trying!"

Mr. Parrington slipped into the room. "Hey, what's going on here?"

"I'm sorry, Mr. Parrington," I cried. "I shouldn't have been on that ride with your boys. I just pushed my way in there. I should have left them alone because I couldn't help when they needed me."

"Yes. That would have been very helpful because they would have been totally alone when the accident happened. C'mon, Warrior, your mere presence kept them from being more scared than they already were."

"We're not getting anywhere here, people, and this is exactly what the Destroyer wants," Scout said. "I keep trying to tell you we cannot be divided. We have to stick together."

Mr. Parrington nudged Scout away from the chair and sat. "He's right. Now listen to me because my boys will be back soon. Enough of this. You have a tremendous call on your lives, but you're still kids. Kids who are preparing to graduate early and make college plans, but still kids. You go to festivals and eat nachos and get on rides and try to have fun. Mary, there's no crime in offering to go on that ride with my boys and teasing Deacon. None of this was anybody's fault. Deacon, you stepped up when you got the call. Ivy, Scout, I'm just glad you weren't more in the middle of it and got hurt." He paused to breathe. "It's a hard job you have, but you won't be teenagers forever. Things will even out and you'll learn all the boundaries and how to deal with everything. You still have to have time for fun."

I pressed an ice pack into my hand to slow a sudden throbbing pain. "But I messed up. I let the Destroyer get ahead of us, and I had no power today."

"Mary, you can't mess up so big that the Creator can't still fix it. It's kinda the point. So whether you believe this was an attack of the Destroyer or just poor maintenance on aging metal, help showed up. You have to cut yourself some slack. You're as much a Warrior now as you've ever been. When you need to show up you will. Everyone you help is someone's kid, or mother, or brother... They are important to someone. You have to stay out of your own way, Mary. Maybe today wasn't about you. Maybe it was about showing Deacon how he's supposed to work and respond. Trust me. He did it in the biggest way I've ever seen."

Joy surged through my otherwise black mood. "The colors were back, weren't they?"

"I didn't see them," Scout said. "Then again, I have no idea why I'm here..."

Ivy elbowed him. "Stop that. Yes, Mary, it was amazing."

Mr. Parrington laughed. "It was. I've never gotten to see that."

"I wasn't able to see them," I said.

"You were otherwise occupied with my boys."

"Yeah, but I got to see it last time."

"This time it was all the colors of green," Ivy said. "It was beautiful and glowing and flowing from him..."

"Was it Sebastian?"

"No." Deacon cleared his throat. "It wasn't Sebastian. I heard another voice. A new voice. It was—"

"Ah, here they are." A nurse nodded to Scout, Ivy, and Deacon.

"What's wrong?" Scout asked.

"An officer is looking for you three."

"Why?"

"Everyone on the ride has to be examined. Somehow you three slipped away. Come with me. Call your parents."

Mr. Parrington stood. "Yeah. *Somehow*. I have to get back. You all behave yourselves."

Deacon stopped at the door and winked back at me.

He was never going to let me forget he won the day.

I was happy for him.

CHAPTER 39

Deacon

My parents crisscrossed their pacing lines at the foot of my bed with their noses in their phones. They were studying every video available.

My dad paused. "How did you do it?"

"I don't know."

"How did you move so fast? It looks like this video was doctored to speed you up, but that can't be. These are phone videos shot not two hours ago. All the people in the background are moving normally."

"I don't know."

They resumed pacing.

Then my mom stopped. "This happens so often now, I don't even know where to start. There's a cop guarding this room because of the hordes of people who want to see you, thank you, touch you, or interview you."

"I'm sorry."

"Don't be sorry, son," my dad said. "Just tell us what's happening so we'll know what to do."

"I would tell you if I could," I said. "Things happen and I seem to be able to help."

"People get to be real heroes maybe once in a lifetime, and that rarely happens. You? You get to regularly save peoples' lives, or be in the vicinity when a tragedy either occurs or nearly occurs, on a regular basis. And sometimes you get hurt. You're scaring us."

"I don't know what to say, Dad. I don't go looking for this."

Then they decided to talk about me like I wasn't there.

"Do you think it's psychological?" my mom asked in a whisper that didn't work.

"What do you mean?"

"Like those people who dress up like Superman and Batman and go out looking for crimes to fight in the street. Do you think he's been sneaking out at night? We should check all his devices for odd behavior or contacts."

"Should we ask for an evaluation?"

"Are you two serious right now? If anyone in this room needs a psych evaluation, it's not me."

"Watch it," my mother said.

"Well, listen to yourselves. You know where I am all the time. I'm usually at the same places with the same few people, or I'm at home. I have no big fantastic life. Claire's my first steady girlfriend. Geez. Would you feel better if I told you I smoked weed behind the school or put vodka in a water bottle?"

My dad's gaze narrowed. "Do you?"

"No!" I dropped my head on the pillow and lowered the bed. "I need to see Claire. Can we go?"

My mom snuggled up beside me in one of the most awkward cuddle sessions we'd ever had. "We're worried, honey, that's all. You've been injured in all these events."

"Not recently."

She waved her phone around. "How are you not hurt?"

"I don't know, do you want me to be hurt?"

"No, of course not, but it's hard to believe nothing is wrong from the way this looks."

"My back had a pain for a moment when the pod fell, but now it doesn't, and the x-rays show nothing."

"We're taking every precaution," Dad said. "We don't want to get you home and find out they missed something."

"They've scanned me from head to toe. I'm not hurt."

"They're admitting everyone who was directly involved. Fall injuries are dangerous, even when it looks like someone got up and walked away. You're not leaving here until we're sure."

Wonderful.

"I need to see Claire," I said again. "I promised her I'd be back to check on her."

My mom left my bed. "She's already up in her room."

"OK. I'll text and find out which one."

My dad scrubbed his hands across his face. "That reminds me. Her dad's out for blood. He's already got lawyers on this."

I repositioned myself to stretch my legs. "I know. He warned me to talk to you before I spoke to the press or anyone else."

"That was nice of him, despite the fact all his blustering about suing everyone is disrupting everyone's rest, not to mention the investigation."

"Who's resting?" I asked. "You want to send me to psychiatric care."

"No, we don't, honey, we only want you well. And we'd kinda like to know how this keeps happening." She froze. "Oh no."

"What?"

"I'm going to have to go through another round of fruit trays, flowers, and muffin baskets, aren't I? There were so many last time, I think even the places I donated to hated to see me coming."

My dad scowled. "That's what you're worried about?"

"No... I'm worried about Deacon. But yes? Kind of?"

Those two went at it for another half hour while I tried to work on a plan to see Claire and then doze off.

The nurse came to move me to my room.

I smiled up at her as she unhooked whatever I was hooked up to and secured me in the bed. "Please tell me I'm on the same floor as Claire Cannon and the others."

The bed in my actual hospital room was much more comfortable than the bed in the ER—if there was such a thing as a comfortable bed in the hospital.

My doctor held up yet another video. "This is why you're here," she said.

She had a shot even my parents hadn't seen. It came from the carnival and fairgrounds surveillance system, and though the picture was grainy, it was a birds-eye view of the whole fiasco from start to finish.

I looked away.

"The thing is," the doctor continued. "This was a hard drop, and everyone else has moderate to serious injuries. We want to make sure you're OK before we send you home. Humor me, please, and I'll get you out of here as soon as possible."

Sure. Whatever.

I was allowed to get up to go to the bathroom, but only if I called for help because they put a yellow *Fall Risk* bracelet on my arm. I wasn't that medicated for the pain, but everyone seemed determined I had an unseen internal injury somewhere, or a broken bone in my back, so they kept running tests. I appreciated the concern. I didn't want my parents to take me home and have a big surprise, but all I wanted was to talk to Claire and go home. I wanted to play video games with my brothers and sort out all that had happened and try to figure out for myself what was with the new woman's voice in my head. And I needed to have a serious talk with Sebastian or someone somewhere about how I could work anonymously. Or not work at all if that wasn't possible.

But I was stuck there and they wouldn't let me eat. That was a huge problem.

My parents headed out to check on my brothers and find food—for them, not me, because they were starving and didn't want to eat in front of me—and my mom was going to come back and embarrassingly sleep on the reclining chair by my bed.

I stayed busy monitoring the wheelchair that occasionally went by my room with or without someone already in it.

In the late-night hours, I waited for it to randomly pass as I sat in the chair in my room.

"Excuse me," I called out. "Can I get a ride down the hall to see my girlfriend? I promised her I'd get back to her."

"She's probably asleep," the guy said and tugged at the top of his scrubs. "You should sleep too."

"C'mon, dude. Can't we check? You got the rolling chair. Who's gonna know? It's late."

He glanced over his shoulder. "One quick trip, and don't bother asking for pudding because all your tests aren't in yet."

"Deal."

Claire's room was dark except for the dim light from the bathroom that spilled across the middle of her bed. "Hey. Claire. You awake?"

"Deacon?"

"Yes. Who else would it be? Can I come in?"

"Sure. How are you feeling?"

The driver stopped me by the bed. "Five minutes, and then you both need to sleep while you can."

"I feel fine," I said. "But they don't believe me. They won't let me go. How are you?"

"They have to do repeat scans tomorrow. They don't think anything is serious, but there was something that looked like it could be bleeding."

"Bleeding? Shouldn't they be operating to fix it?"

"Not yet. They'll see how it looks tomorrow. It was minor and they said it could even be about a torn muscle and nothing major. My mom is spending the night and she'll be back soon."

"I'm sorry about this, Claire." I reached for her hand. "We shouldn't have been on that ride."

"No one could have predicted this, Deacon. You didn't do anything wrong. We were at a carnival. If anything, you were there for me when I was hurt. I felt that thing you did…"

I choked. "What thing?"

"When I was on the ground and you put your hand on my back. I said I was fine and I think I would have been, but my insides felt like a big bowl of mashed potatoes or something. I didn't really know if I was fine, but when you touched me, things got warm inside me… I can't explain it. It's like everything was going back to where it belonged."

"You took a really bad fall, Claire—a flying leap out of a bucket, and you landed hard on the ground—"

"C'mon, Deacon, you know it was more. Whatever's going on with you… I can't…"

"Why do I feel like you're about to say something bad?"

She pulled her hand away. "Because I am, and I'm so sorry. Listen, Deacon, I've had a great time with you and I love spending time with you…"

"But?"

"But I don't understand your life. I don't understand how you can pick up massive walls and save children, and I don't understand how you stopped that arm. I was lying on the ground, but I could see everything. I couldn't believe what I saw and it wasn't anything normal people can do. I know something happened when you touched my back. We've been together twice when tragedy has struck and all the people you care about are in the hospital this time."

"Not every time is bad or even scary."

"No, but I was just lying here thinking about that first night at the barn with Ivy's dad. Something happened that night and you sent me away. And you and your friends are always talking in code… Believe me, I don't want to know, especially after this, but let's face it. I'm not cut out to be the girlfriend of the guy who has over two-hundred-thousand views and counting on Twitter and YouTube right now."

"Your parents are making you break up with me, right?"

"They're not thrilled about any of this and they have their concerns. I'm sorry my dad has gone ballistic with wanting to sue everyone, but this is not them. It's me. I can't do this every time we go to a concert or fireworks or even bowling. I'm sorry, Deacon. I like you. A lot."

"I'm sorry too, Claire. I wish I could explain."

"You don't need to explain. I want what's best for you, and I don't think I can be there for all these things I don't understand."

My mouth turned to cotton. "I get it. I understand." I fumbled with the brake on the wheelchair with no knowledge of how to steer the stupid contraption out of her room. I was too embarrassed to yell for help, and too afraid I'd cry like a baby if I stayed a second longer. Where pain had been absent before, it rushed in like a hurricane as emotion caused every muscle I had to tense up.

"I hope you don't need surgery," I said and tried to turn the wheel and back up. "Tell your dad to talk to my parents and I'll do whatever you need for your lawsuit."

"It'll be your lawsuit too, Deacon. The ride's manufacturer or the carnival's owner should be responsible for these medical bills."

She sounded just like her dad.

I made an awkward charge for the door as help mercifully arrived.

"Thanks," I said as I was tucked into bed. I took my next offered pain pill and prayed for sleep.

One time my mom told me that though a person might feel like it, people didn't usually die from broken hearts.

They only wish they did.

I knew what she meant.

CHAPTER 40

Scout

The longest walk I ever took was that thirty-foot trek down the dock toward the water.

Deacon the Dolphin jumped off the end and splashed in the bluish-brown water, while Mary and Ivy smeared on sunscreen and then effortlessly jumped in with him to head to the swim pad farther out in the mid-sized community lake.

And all seemed right with the world in the perfect little residential area where upscale rustic cottages dotted the shoreline behind the waving branches of old trees. My grandparents sat on their new deck with a well-deserved drink after they'd spent a weary day of pointing at things for us to move. The only burning question I had left was, *why did two old people have so many boxes of dishes and books, and why did they bring them all to the lake?*

Someone nearby was firing up a grill for dinner, as I faced

the blazing late-afternoon sun and looked for Deacon on the flat surface of the quiet lake.

I held out the small brown box. "Hey, Deacon, I got something for you."

"There better be a chili dog in there."

"No." I laughed. "Time to settle a bet."

"You're gonna be like that now? Just when it's time to have fun?"

"C'mon out. This will only take a minute. I wasn't going to do this today, but this little guy was slithering through the grass near the house and I was able to snatch him up."

Deacon sputtered as he pulled himself back onto the dock. "You shouldn't have."

Mary and Ivy hurried back to scurry up the ladder and grab their phones.

"We're ready," Ivy said. "Let the snake-petting begin."

I pulled the harmless common garter snake out of the box.

Deacon smirked. "You're kidding, right? That's not a snake, that's a worm."

"Yes, it is a snake, and this is part of your problem. You spend a lot of time worrying about creatures that are so small and have no interest in you."

"They have no interest in me because I stay away from them."

"No, they have no interest in you because they *have no interest in you.*"

"Fine! Let me have the snake."

"Be gentle. It's thrashing around like crazy, but it won't hurt you. Say some nice things to it, then let it go in the grass at the end of the dock. Not the water end. The dry end."

Deacon twisted his face into the most annoyed expression. "Yes, I know where the grass is."

I passed the snake to Deacon. He held it away from his body, gave it a pat—and then screamed and ran toward land to drop it.

He came back, victorious. "How long did I hold it?"

"I'll show you the video in a sec," Ivy said. "I'm adding music and effects."

"Don't post that," he warned.

"Too late." She patted him on the back. "You were magnificent."

"Yeah, well, Scout better magnificently get his butt in the water."

"I am. I've only been practicing in the pool, but I think I've got this."

Ivy sent me a sly smile and dropped her towel. "I'll meet you out on the swim platform."

If that didn't get me in the water, nothing would.

But it wasn't like I was going to dive in or anything. It would still take some time. I started down the ladder and hoped to get my bearings and take a nice leisurely dog-paddle to the platform. I hadn't yet managed to get my head all the way under water in the pool. I knew I wasn't going to drown. That didn't make anything any easier.

"What was that?" Ivy shouted.

"What?" Deacon headed her way in a kicking splash of spraying water.

I couldn't see them where they'd swam to the other side.

"You're bleeding," Mary said.

"Why am I bleeding?" Ivy asked.

Ivy? Bleeding?

That was the moment my love for Ivy overrode my fear—and it was the simplest thing I'd ever done. I headed straight into the water like an Olympic swimmer coming off the marker. It took a sec to get my arms and legs working properly together, but I was at Ivy's side in record time.

Blood trickled down the side of her face and onto her neck.

"Scout! You're in the water."

"Yes! You're hurt. What happened?"

She wrapped her arms around my neck and kissed me. I grabbed the side of the platform to keep us above water as her body enveloped all of mine. I forgot where I was for a minute.

I had to finally push her away. "Hang on. What happened?"

"Stupid piece of wood or a nail or something. I came up too close and something caught my head."

"Let me see." I peeled wet hair away from a gash above her ear. "It doesn't look too bad, and scalp wounds bleed a lot. I don't think you need stitches, but we have to clean this up quick."

"Now? You're in the water." She messed with my hair. "Your hair is wet."

"Yes, we're in lake water, along with all the bacteria that comes with it. We have to get out."

She swam in a circle away from me and came back. "I can't believe this. We're playing in the water together and we have to get out."

I gazed into her huge and hopeful brown eyes. "Yes. Sorry."

She kissed me again. "Are you sure?"

"That's not going to work."

"It always works."

"Not this time. We need to clean that wound." I paused to pull her tight against me. "I do have a question for you though."

She batted her long, wet lashes. "Yes?"

"Do you remember when you had your last tetanus shot?"

Ivy pouted across from me at the picnic table.

"Look, I'm sorry," I said. "But you can't risk flesh-eating bacteria or something getting into that wound. It's worse than I thought, and you won't let me take you to urgent care, so you'll have to wait until it closes a bit. We have all weekend to swim."

"What are the chances of me getting flesh-eating bacteria?"

"Staggeringly low," I admitted. "But it's not worth the risk."

Deacon grabbed the ketchup bottle and made it squirt as loud as possible onto his paper plate. "Yeah, and you don't want one of those brain-sucking amoeba things to get in there."

"That's not going to happen," I said.

"But you're so sure bacteria can?" Ivy took the mustard from Mary and overdosed her hot dog. "Whatever. I've waited a long time to swim with you."

"And we have a pool and a lake house. I promise there will be more swimming in the future."

Deacon shoved a hot dog in his mouth—and then decided to talk. "Enough of that. Mary? How are you? You haven't said much since we sat down."

"I'm fine. I've just been thinking about everything. I'm sorry I was out of sorts. I'm trying to straighten it all out."

"We had your back," Ivy said. "And we understand you're grieving. We all still are."

"I went too far with Gavin and the whole car thing. That got out of hand fast and could have been so dangerous for us."

"I only wish there was video or something," Deacon said.

"Definitely," I added. "Really wish I could have seen that."

"I was wrong to mess with him," Mary said again. "I put us all in danger."

Ivy scoffed. "We're already in danger. Apparently, we can't even go to carnivals." She crunched a chip between her teeth and glared at me. "Or swim in a lake."

Mary laughed. "Cut Scout some slack. He's trying to take care of you."

She tossed the rest of the chip aside. "I know. Sorry."

"Anyway," Mary continued. "I have to get back in good graces with Sebastian, and I have no idea what Gavin's going to do next. I'm not afraid of him, but his number one goal is to kill me. I'm literally just waiting for the other shoe to drop. We need to be aware."

"We are," Ivy said. "We're watching. Always. I'm not afraid of Gavin, and Deacon has obviously moved to the next level of his abilities in a big way."

"Speaking of that," I said. "Have you heard the woman's voice again?"

"Nope. I don't know who she is or what the colors are all about, but I'm not questioning it. It worked."

We all spontaneously raised our soda cans.

"To the mysterious woman's voice," I said. "May she show up the next time we need her."

Deacon took a long drink and grabbed another hot dog. "Have you heard from Reed, Ivy?"

She dropped her gaze to the table and picked at the edges of the vinyl, red-checked covering my grandma thought we couldn't eat without. "No. He's gone. I still say he loves my mom and she loves him. She and I talked, but he's gone."

Deacon nodded. "Maybe he'll be in touch."

"Maybe... Have you talked to Claire?"

"Nope. But she's fine. She does not want to get back together. Her dad's still on a rampage."

"He's got all our parents on a rampage," Mary said. "That was a major accident. All kinds of agencies, corporations, and insurance companies are involved. I went to see Mr. Parrington's boys. I felt like I needed to, you know? Like we'd been through something together and I needed to take them candy and hug them or something. I don't know..."

"I know," Ivy said. "It's like every time we go through something as Warriors. We have to talk it out in Scout's rec room and eat fruit. It's a thing."

"But we're going to graduate at the end of this year," I

reminded them. "We'll go our separate ways to college. How does this work?"

"I've always said this time together has been about training," Ivy said. "Deacon and Mary have already proven they can work alone, and we've been saying there shouldn't be this much attention when something happens. Somehow, we need to complete assignments and walk away like Char does. Like she was never there."

"You worked with Corey alone," I said. "And I still don't know what I'm doing here—"

"Stop that," she said. "You're a Warrior, Scout. We wouldn't know half of what we know without you."

Grandpa practically tumbled over the hill with two ancient rowboats. "Look what I found in the shed."

"Put 'em back," I said. "Nothing about those things looks watertight."

"I checked them out. They don't look too bad. I even found oars." He clanged two of them together as he headed on over the hill and booted one of the boats into the lake. "Where's your sense of adventure?"

Ivy snorted. "I used mine up with a nail to the head?"

"It'll be dark in a couple of hours, Grandpa."

"Yeah," Mary said. "We'd need flashlights—maybe a lantern—and at least a truckload of bug spray."

"And life jackets," Grandpa said.

"Sadly, Scout has all that," Ivy said.

Deacon laughed. "I'm game."

"Great," Grandpa said. "Go out exploring. There's a little slough I've heard about where the fishing is great. But it's a stump field so be careful."

"Stump field?" Deacon asked. "What the heck's a stump field?"

"And what's a slough?" Ivy added.

"A slough is like a little cove or inlet," Mary said. "I did the whole lake house thing with my grandparents too."

I stood and collected trash. "And a stump field is tree stumps under water. We have to be careful not to get stuck or tip. Not really a problem in a small boat, but you don't want to get tangled up in there with a motor boat or hit a stump going fast."

"I wouldn't want to hit a stump going slow either," Deacon said. "Or tip out of that rickety boat."

"Forget the stumps. We're not doing that. We had a lot of rain the last couple of days, so the water's up anyway."

"Good," Deacon said. "So, the boats are crap, the water is high, and when I fall out, I'll be impaled on a stump."

Grandpa laughed and reached in the boat. "Life vest."

"I'll get lights and bug spray," I said.

I figured the trip would be a quick one once we got a look at how bad a shape the boats were in. Forget circling the lake and looking for sweet fishing spots. We wouldn't likely make it past the dock, and we'd all end up wet and swimming to shore anyway.

Which led me to the most astounding question of my day. How was it I went from being completely unable to handle a simple backyard pool, to getting into a death-trap of a rowboat with my friends, knowing full well it would sink and I'd be under water?

I glanced at Ivy.

Some things were much bigger than my fear.

CHAPTER 41

Mary

I checked the strap on my water sandals and settled into the boat. "Why do we have to take two boats? This one has four benches."

"Easy," Scout said. "When one of them sinks, we'll have another to send for help."

"I think your grandpa is messin' with you, Scout. These aren't that bad. He didn't find these in that old shed. More like he bought them from a neighbor or something for you. Or if he did find them, he's already checked them out." I examined a spot where it'd clearly been cleaned, and noticed a shiny new oarlock. I remembered a few things about my dad and a rowboat from when I was in grade school.

"Maybe," he said. "How we doin' this?"

"Definitely girls' boat and guys' boat." I waved for Ivy to hurry. "We'll see you out there."

"They took off," Deacon shouted behind us. "I can't get my

uncool life thingy on. Do I have to wear it? Never mind, don't answer that."

"Yeah, my grandma won't let you come back if you don't follow the rules. Sorry."

"It could be worse," he said. "At least it's not like those old giant orange ones."

His voice trailed away as Ivy and I glided across the flat, sparkling water. Ripples played tricks with my eyes as dragonflies and other insects kissed the surface and twirled away in the evening sun. Turtles slipped off smooth brown rocks and submerged tree limbs at the shoreline and disappeared with bubbles as we passed.

"This is fun," Ivy said.

I laughed. "That's because you're not rowing yet."

"Well, here. Let me try."

"Once you get in a rhythm and figure out how to make turns, it's not so hard."

Deacon and Scout caught up to us.

"We forgot snacks," Deacon yelled.

"We just had dinner," I yelled back. Our voices echoed across the water. "And why are we yelling?"

"I don't know."

A couple of boats zig-zagged across the lake, one with a skier in tow. When the wake finally reached us, we barely rocked.

"That's what I'm talkin' about," Deacon said. "When do we ski?"

"Grandpa has a small fishing boat. You don't exactly ski from a bass boat. Well, I guess you could, but Grandma didn't let him get anything with a big enough outboard."

More than an hour had passed when we drifted far beyond sight of Scout's place. Dusk crept in, and the whine of boaters faded away as everyone packed it in for the night.

Ivy looked around. "Should we head back?"

"Soon," Scout said. "Layer up on the bug spray."

"Wait," Deacon said. "I think that's the place your grandpa was talking about. There's a place there where you can float into a... It's like a cul-de-sac in the water. Let's check it out."

"Do we have time?" Ivy asked. "It's getting dark."

"I have light," Scout said, and showed both giant flashlights and a lantern.

"Are there snakes?" Deacon asked the obvious.

"Yes," Scout answered.

"Are they poisonous?"

"Venomous," Scout corrected. "And yes, they can be. There are Water Moccasins, and we want no part of that. More likely to see a Texas Diamondback Water Snake. The two are often mistaken for each other."

"Yes. We don't want to have that problem."

The sarcasm in his voice made us laugh.

"But it's about dark," Scout said. "We won't see anything anyway."

"That helps," Deacon said. "It truly does. Thank you for sharing."

"We're fine. No snake wants anything to do with us making all this noise, and it's not like one is going to jump in the boat with us."

"Again, thank you for that insight. It's amazing information. Now shut up."

The low hum of an approaching boat surprised me. It got louder as the sky darkened.

We never saw it coming.

CHAPTER 42

Scout

My worst nightmare returned in exponential proportions.

I heard the speeding boat, I saw its inadequate running lights, I knew the moment it was too close…

I waved my flashlight in a futile attempt to alert the irresponsible captain, but we were charged in what looked like an intentional attempt to swamp us.

Mine and Deacon's boat flew up in the wake and it tossed us sideways. The shift of our weight and the momentum threw us overboard and flipped the boat. A dull thud in the chaos could have been the boat hitting a stump—or even a part of Deacon's body.

I squeezed the flashlight and prepared to be submerged. I glanced at the shore to see what I thought were two moving silhouettes with the other light. Hopefully, that meant Mary and Ivy had been pushed closer to land and were out of the water.

Hopefully.

I kicked against sloshing water and fought against my vest to sweep the bottom and judge the depth. I grabbed something to pull myself up, and met with the jagged, woody, and slippery side of a broken tree limb or the end of a slimy stump.

Muddy liquid left my eyes gritty and blurred when I popped to the surface and tried to look around. "Ivy! Mary!"

"We're here," Ivy yelled and attempted to illuminate the area, without much success.

"Do you see Deacon?" I yelled.

"No." Panic laced Mary's voice.

I pushed to my right, and tried to move the sinking boat through the heavy water. "Deacon!"

No response.

My tactical, waterproof flashlight—an expensive impulse buy at the lowest point of my life—felt like my best friend when Deacon's complaining voice didn't hit my ears.

"Deacon!"

Mary and Ivy clopped across the swampy ground, but the sliver of moonlight and one lone beam did little to help as I drifted farther out and barely heard them.

"I can't see anything!" Mary yelled.

"He was wearing his life vest," Ivy called out. "He has to be right there."

Right there seemed like a million square miles when he could have been bonked on the head and sucking down water. Even if the life jacket kept him up, he was likely face down.

When my search on the surface turned up nothing in the immediate area, I went under—and could see nothing without goggles to protect my eyes. Blackness surrounded me as I begged for help from Sebastian.

Relax and reach out...

The voice in my head was clear amidst all the other muffled sound.

Then I panicked as my memory somersaulted through time

to the flood event that took the lives of my parents and brother. I was in the most useless and painful spot I could be. I couldn't help my family and I couldn't help Deacon—and I was likely to die myself just yards from shore because I could no longer breathe.

I pulled my head out of the water and rested in the buoyancy of my vest.

"I can't do it," I yelled into the darkness.

Yes, you can. Relax and reach out...

We were both out of time. He had to be there.

Ivy and Mary's light bounced off the water as they scrambled to scour the area in what looked like an absolute lost cause.

I couldn't be a part of a lost cause again.

I couldn't be a lost cause.

I was not a lost cause.

Relax and reach out...

I took a breath and forced myself under to comb the bottom and then emerge to look again for Deacon's floating body.

I knew he couldn't be far as I worked my way inland. When under, I closed my eyes and methodically moved foot by foot and touched everything directly in my path. The edge of the boat, the eventual muddy bottom near the shore, the slime-covered stalks of cattails...

The feel of a human leg.

I immediately surfaced and flipped Deacon's body over.

"I'm good," he sputtered. "And it's about time."

"Why didn't you answer us?"

"First, I had to free myself from under the boat, then I got stuck in something disgusting and lost my shoe... I couldn't turn myself..."

I put him in a resting position against me so he could catch his breath, and backed toward the bank.

"...then I panicked and couldn't call out because it was hard to keep my head up. I kept needing to cough, but I couldn't without sucking in more water. Not to mention it's completely black out here and there are snakes everywhere. But I figured you'd rescue me eventually, seeing as you're the Eagle Scout and all."

We hit the shore and crawled to a stop in the mud.

"...and can you believe that for the second time I lost a shoe in one of our escapades? I think this pair belongs to my brother. I am in deep, deep sh—"

"Shoes? That's what you want to talk about when you've nearly drowned?"

Mary shined a light into our faces. "Are you two seriously bickering during your own big water rescue moment?"

Ivy dove to the ground and kissed me square on the lips. I pushed her away. "Sorry, Ivy, and believe me, you'll never hear this again, but please don't kiss me. I literally have a mouth full of lake mud."

"I don't care."

"Gross," Deacon said.

We struggled to sit up.

"That was intense," Ivy said.

I thought of Sebastian's voice in my head and how my fear could have paralyzed me. I didn't ever want to feel that way again. "I'm just glad Deacon's all right."

"Thanks, brother. You saved my life."

"Not really, you were holding your own. You were practically at the shore when I found you."

"Dude, the only reason I knew where I was and what to do was because of you. All the smart things you say, all you've taught me about water safety and first aid..." He paused to put his arm around me as we struggled out of our vests. "And I would have panicked more and may not have been able to stay calm and breathe if I didn't know you were coming for me."

"But why would you think I was coming? You're the one who has the mad hero skills."

"I just knew. I knew you had it. I knew you would come. And you did. And now I can breathe. Plus, I heard you looking for me."

I considered his words. It had never occurred to me not to look for Deacon and find him.

Had Deacon been...?

We stood and assessed the damage in the darkness.

Ivy snuggled up to my wet and stinking body. "You know what this means, right Scout?"

"What?"

"You had your first solo assignment and you nailed it."

"I was at the right place at the right time. We were out there together."

"Do you hear yourself right now?" She turned my body and shined the light across the water. "I know it's dark, but look. Mary and I were all the way over here, already in the cove. We were able to jump ship quickly and get on shore. But you and Deacon were still a ways out when that boat came." She pointed first one direction and then the other. "You were dumped out there, and Deacon landed with the boat way over there. Then you did all you had to do, fighting against that life vest—which did its job, by the way, but isn't suitable for going under and looking around—and you managed to find Deacon when he was really beginning to struggle."

Mary stepped forward. "She's right. You have no idea how much area you covered so fast and so efficiently. You completed your first solo assignment."

"In the water. In the dark," Deacon added. "You know what that means?"

"What?"

Ivy smacked my arm. "C'mon. You're the brilliant one in the group. Do you not see what's happening? One of your abilities involves dealing with water. Don't you get it? You've been petrified of the water and now we know why. It's not *because* it caused you great loss, it's *in spite* of the great loss it caused."

"She's right," Mary said. "The Destroyer would like nothing more than to keep us from using our gifts. You can't be used by the Creator in the water if you're afraid of it. Now that you know that truth, you've conquered your fears. The Destroyer can't use that fear against you anymore."

"Wow."

"Yeah, wow," Ivy said and almost kissed me again.

"I'm the water guy," I said. "The water guy. And I've been completely unable to use that because of my fear."

"You're also the essential oil guy," Deacon quipped. "But we won't talk about that."

The low whine of an engine sounded in the distance. It could have been anything.

We knew it wasn't.

"I hate to be a downer right now, but we have a problem," Mary said. "What happened was not an accident."

We stood there wet, muddy, devoured by insects, and smelling like rotten fish.

And we knew she was completely right.

"I know what I have to do," she said.

"My phone is gone," I said.

"Mine too," Deacon added.

Ivy pulled her old phone out of her pocket. "Y'all know this old thing has crapped out because it got a bit wet."

"I have no bars," Mary said. "Where are we, Scout?"

It was hard to tell. I tried to map the area in my brain. "What do you hear?"

"I hear that boat that tried to kill us," Ivy said. "It's far away, but I hear it."

"What else?"

"Water," Deacon said. "Like rushing water."

"Right," I said. "That's the dam. We need to go there."

"You're crazy. Why would we need more water after this?"

"It's not the big manned dam from the big lake. It's a smaller detention reservoir with an uncontrolled spillway. There's lots of water because we've had lots of rain, but it's also a popular hangout on weekends. There are probably people there partying and we can at least borrow a phone and let my grandpa know to come get us. There is nothing if we walk the other way, and who knows how long it will be before we run into someone or pop out at a public place."

"So, we walk through the woods like we are, and maybe we'll run into a tweaker at the spillway party and find a phone to borrow?"

"Do you have a better idea? We can't just swim back across the lake. It's too far and too dangerous. We can't see anything."

"No, I don't have a better idea, but I did lose a shoe again so this is going to be loads of fun."

"Well, the lantern went down with the boat, but we have our flashlights. Did you at least save your sock? We'll help you watch the ground."

Mary sagged against a tree and held the light up to create a cone. "You guys should stay here. I'll go and send help back."

"No," Deacon said. "Why would you say that?"

"Because we're saying everything but what's really happening here."

Ivy swatted bugs away from her legs. "What do you think is really happening here?"

"This is it. This is the battle. Shanar always said there would be one, and after my last stupid stunt, Gavin said he was coming for me. It's time."

"But Gavin's been after you for a while now, and we've always known who our enemy is. We'll handle it."

"This is different."

I think everyone was still in a bit of shock, but she was right. We knew the minute that boat swamped us that it was intentional. It was taking time to come around to asking how and why, but it seemed our enemy had tired of playing and was ready to settle the score.

I knocked a chunk of dirt and wet leaves off of Mary's sleeve. "How is it different? Who was in the boat?"

"Gavin."

Ivy scoffed. "That's a bit out there, don't ya think? No one knows exactly where we are. How did he magically get a speed boat and know where to come? Can he even drive a speed boat?"

"I didn't think he'd ever hit me or try to sexually assault me either. I didn't know he could ski..."

Her last words trailed off, thick with emotion.

"The point is..." she continued. "The point is, it doesn't matter whether it was Gavin or another Agent of the Destroyer. Their resources are unlimited. We posted that video of Deacon, and a million human Agents knew where to find us. And even if it wasn't social media, we're not dealing with mere mortals. I'm not living like this anymore. I've been in a haze of anger and pain. Now I just need to take care of business with a clear head. Shanar wants my life, and he's using Gavin to get it. But they can't have me."

She turned and stomped away. "Stay here."

Deacon laughed and hopped after her. "Oh, no no no no... You are not doing this alone."

"I have to. I started this alone when I was a toddler in that pool, and I will end it alone. It's my fault you're all in this. Let me take care of it."

"That's not true," Ivy said. "You didn't bring us into this. We're here because the Creator called us. It just happens to be your crew he called us to. We're a team, Mary. You're not going anywhere alone. It will take us all to annihilate Shanar."

"You know she's right," I said. "If you go, we go."

"And what if it's bad? What if he really gets the best of me?"

"He won't."

"What if he does?"

Ivy chewed her lip. "Then we all go down together."

"But we won't," Deacon said. "We can't. It's the whole point."

Mary shined the light in his face. "Look. You guys can defeat Shanar. You can combine your authority and power and banish him from our realm, never to be seen again. You can do that. But I have to handle Gavin. He's coming for me, and I have to break him. Maybe I can still help him."

"Let's go," I said. "If Gavin's here, he'll find us soon enough. We're wet and disgusting easy prey as we are."

Mary took the lead with one light, and I brought up the rear with the other to shine it for Ivy and Deacon to watch the ground.

Mary paused and turned. "If I don't get to tell you later, thank you. Thank you for sticking with me, even when I wasn't doing well."

"Not a problem," Ivy said. "It's what we do."

"I'd like to say everything is fine tonight and we'll be back at the lake house eating snacks by midnight, but I don't think it'll be like that. There's something strong banging around in our realm. Shanar himself could be behind that next tree."

Deacon shrugged. "Mary. We've been at this a while. The scent of frankincense is all over these woods, and my hands have been pulsing heat for a half hour."

"My intuition for danger is off the charts," Ivy said.

I flicked the flashlight. "They're right, Mary. Keep moving."

"All right. Just wanted to make sure you knew what we were getting in to."

"We're Warriors, Mary. We already know."

CHAPTER 43

Mary

I hated that I ditched my friends.

It had to be done.

I knew we were a team, and I knew they wanted to help. I expected them to show up, but I had to confront Gavin alone first. So, when I touched the flashlight and it dimmed in my hand, I knew all I had to do was turn it off long enough to race in the direction of the sound of rushing water. I knew Gavin would want to use the most theatrical setting to make his move.

I wouldn't disappoint him.

It was pitch black, but I knew the rest of my Warriors would get there under Scout's direction—eventually.

"C'mon, Sebastian." I darted and swerved and caught low-lying brush against my scratched-up ankles. "I know you're here. Help me get out of this and keep everyone safe."

A single light bulb on a rickety pole barely lit the way at the edge of the dam. At one time there may have been more light, but kids with rocks and lack of maintenance had left the sloped concrete spillway in near darkness.

I edged up the steep side and stood to hear rushing water tumble over and hit the hard bottom before rushing off across the flat surface and racing to join the flow of the river nearby. Recent heavy rains kept the lake draining at a swift clip, and I was glad I couldn't see all that was churning over the side.

I headed across the paved trail over the spillway. A thin, wooden rail and a patch of grass marked the place where, on dry days, fishermen could drop a line in the reservoir, or parents could walk with children to observe deer munch on grass at twilight.

But after a heavy rain, the dam was no place to be.

Straight ahead, there was no light from partying and pot-smoking teens as Scout had hoped, and no phone screens or shadows from cars with sweaty couples inside. I glanced at my phone and whacked the light against my hand to rattle the fading batteries. I had no bars and very little illumination.

What I did have was the overwhelming pressure of Shanar's presence in my space. His usual suffocating tactics lingered in the air like thick clouds as the sound of water thundered in my ears. It would be like he and Gavin to make a grand gesture to kill me in that dark and dramatic place where my body might never be found.

But I wasn't going to die that night.

Within seconds, the familiar and musky-sweet scent of Gavin's cologne reached my nose.

I had yet to see him clearly, but I knew he was there with slightly sweaty hair from the humid air. There would be dark curls at the collar of his vintage car racing-team polo, and he was likely as damp as I was from his turn in the boat that could have killed us all in the cove. I knew him so well it sickened me to know what he'd become.

I also knew what I had to do.

"I knew you'd get here sooner or later," he said.

I sensed he stepped forward, but still didn't have a clear view of him. "Hello, Gavin."

"Those eyes of yours… Even in this darkness they practically glow. Especially that new blue one."

"I have something to tell you," I said. "I'm sorry about your car. I let my anger get the best of me. I shouldn't have done that. I wasn't myself."

His silence told me my confession caught him off guard.

"Your apology means nothing," he finally said. "I gave you chance after chance to come back to me and work by my side to save your life. You refused. You knew how much I loved you and you refused."

"Love is not what you had for me, Gavin. You wanted to own me, possess me, and control me, but that's not love. You're so lost in the Destroyer's lies that you don't know what love is."

Shanar's dark form grew behind him. It swirled in the foggy air and circled Gavin like a friendly cat who rubbed up against its owner's legs. Hairs prickled on my neck and my blue eye twitched as my own supernatural cells bubbled inside me and grew until my body seemed unable to contain them all. I'd never been so close to another natural death, not in the fire, and not even on the mountain. I was closer to my last breath than I'd ever been, and everything in my body was on guard to fight.

Wafts of frankincense drifted through my realm as Sebastian hovered nearby in full battle mode. Shanar shrank for a moment when I sensed my angelic particles coming together for the good versus evil confrontation.

Flecks of white brightness skittered along my arms and cast a dim glow where I stood. I had become my own light source and didn't even realize it. I tossed the flashlight aside as Gavin came a step closer. I could see him then, wrapped in a darkness so inherently evil I couldn't look at it. I tried to meet his blackened gaze, but it was not possible.

What are you waiting for, boy? Finish her and be done with it.

Shanar's familiar voice jarred my concentration for a second as Gavin presented a dagger and waved it near my face. I steeled myself against the fear and didn't flinch.

"What are you going to do with that?"

"I'm going to plunge it into your chest," Gavin said. "That's my job. And then Shanar is going to reach inside the open wound as you lay dying, and he's going to pull out your heart to present to the Destroyer. Then we'll all be even. We'll all have paid our debt to the master we serve."

"Is that so?"

"I will toss your body over the side. The water will carry you through the concrete blocks that direct the water and tell it where to go. You will come apart and be scattered at their command and float in a million scraps of flesh from the lake, to the river, to the sea."

I shook my head. "No. I don't think that's it."

He lunged for me, but the dagger was an easy grab from his quick hands.

He seemed surprised when I tossed it away.

"Did you really come to this fight with only a blade?"

He came at me full force and knocked me to the ground. His hands found my neck until his darkness clouded my light. I was no match for his human strength as he rested on my chest and bore down with all his weight at my throat.

I summoned all my supernatural strength and used my feet to gain leverage and raise my body while flailing at him with my arms. In a moment of his weakness, his grip loosened and I pushed out from under him.

I struggled to get far enough away to gain control, and while I knew Sebastian was there, he didn't seem to be fully engaged in the fight.

Shanar came upon me and covered me with his form. I

refused to expose my chest to him, and kept twisting out of his grasp as I'd done so many times before in our battles.

"Sebastian? Some help here, please?"

You have taken a great deal of my supernatural power, Warrior. Use it.

"You choose this moment to make a thing out of what happened on the mountain?"

I called on the particles in my body to come to my aid. The bright white flecks appeared again—but that only alerted Gavin to my exact location with Shanar as I scrambled away in the darkness. He tackled me again, and I had to turn on him to fight back.

For a brief and surprising second, my body shifted. I intended to pull away and move backward. The movement propelled me upward instead. I landed on the ground several feet away from Gavin's grasp.

Wait. Had I just flown?

Shanar was fast to catch up as pressure intensified on my chest. I focused. I drew on my determination and my strength, but I couldn't defeat their immense power as it became harder and harder to breathe and I was once again on my back.

Sebastian! Has it really come down to this? Are you going to let Shanar rip my heart from my chest?

A dark green haze filled my field of vision. "No. No, he is not."

"Deacon!"

CHAPTER 44

Deacon

Ivy stumbled and stepped on my bare foot.

"Seriously?" I asked. "We have all these woods to stumble around in, and you choose the one place to stomp on that is already occupied by my bare foot?"

"Sorry! But if we don't stay shoulder to shoulder, we'll never find the dam."

"Shhh," Scout said. "Look. I think we found it."

"Good," Ivy said. "And if we all live through this, I'm going to kill Mary for leaving us."

"She was trying to protect us," I said.

"Whatever."

"That way, and it looks like the battle's already underway," Scout said.

Heat pulsed in my whole body as I spotted the tiny light in the distance and saw a possible hazy, white, and moving glow from the same area. I could barely contain the green pattern that tried to appear in random dots on my skin. It was like trying to contain feathers in a windstorm. Power and green energy was popping out faster than I could hold it in, but then I realized if it was trying so hard to get out, I must need it in the worst way.

I took off running with the others close behind.

"Be careful," I yelled. "I can barely see."

"No doubt," Scout shouted back. "But Mary's obviously in trouble. It looks like some sort of demented laser show over there."

Ivy zoomed ahead. "Hurry!"

We reached the dam with no clue as to where the sides began or ended. We stumbled blindly into what could only be Shanar's mass of evil. I'd only experienced a bit of it before, but I knew it when I felt it. Shanar was all over the area, and he had Mary clearly pinned down.

Gavin appeared from the billowing presence of Shanar. I headed straight for him, only to find he'd lost Mary and was trying to find her as well. Our only clue as to where her human body existed was the faint glow of white light.

I thought she could handle Gavin in basic human form. I also thought she could handle Shanar after years of practice. But could she handle them both if they'd started to get the better of her?

Apparently not. She gasped for breath on the ground as Shanar completely covered her.

I unleashed all the green energy that'd been bursting to get out. I called on the Creator to help me.

Defeat Shanar. The feminine voice had come back.

"Are you the Creator?"

No, I am your Enforcer.

"I thought Sebastian was our Enforcer."

He was your Enforcer, but now I have been assigned to you only. Defeat Shanar. You are running out of time.

"How? How do I save Mary?"

Mary can save herself. Defeat Shanar.

"How?"

Use your abilities. The Creator's weapons will always be stronger than the Destroyer's.

"Scout! Ivy! You have to help me draw Shanar away from Mary. We have to destroy him."

"What do we do?" Ivy asked.

"Like the gym doors. I've got this, but join forces with me."

I pulled all the heat and pulsing green whatever-it-was from inside me. The large mass of energy was nothing more than pure supernatural and possibly angelic help. I tossed it toward Shanar and sent him reeling back. It devoured part of his form and hovered nearby.

"Wow," Scout said. "Does that come in other colors?"

"What?"

"Can you do it again?"

"I don't know."

Mary coughed on the ground and tried to stand. As Shanar regrouped and the original charge of green dissipated, he tried to approach again.

"C'mon, Mary, we need your help!" I yelled.

She didn't answer or come.

Instead, when I glanced her way, she and her glowing white light was gone.

Scout tried to shine our only flashlight where we'd found her. All we saw was her dangling legs as Gavin dragged her to the edge of the dam.

Then Shanar overtook us.

CHAPTER 45

Mary

Gavin once again had a hold of my hair. The thought of it alone enraged me, not to mention the pain of having it come out in clumps in such a brutal way. I fought to free myself as he dragged me through the dirt and across the rough cement to the side of the spillway below.

Water roared louder as thousands of gallons of it per minute crashed across the barrier. A fine mist rose and dotted the air and my skin. I reached as far as I could and grabbed for his ankles as he walked. Each pull and thrust of my arm and wad of hair sent spikes of shock through my body.

Sebastian! I called out again in my mind. *Help me!*

Mary, you can do this, and you have to do it on your own. You have to settle your heart with Gavin. You have to make it right.

Considering I was the one in the dirt and about to be tossed to my death, I wasn't sure how I was supposed to make it right.

I once again summoned all the angelic particles in my body

to line up and work with me to overpower Gavin. Warmth tingled in my muscles as the shimmering white glow started to reignite. I twisted on the ground until my legs came around to get tangled with Gavin's. A large chunk of hair came loose and my shoulder popped first one way, then back, but I succeeded in tripping him, and he fell to the ground.

At the edge of the concrete, I managed to straddle him and get the upper hand.

"Stop it, Gavin. I've had enough of this."

He turned his face away.

I pinched it until he was forced to look at me. "I know you can see me, Gavin, and I can see you. The guy I know does not want to murder me."

"The guy you *knew* does not exist. The guy I am now is going to push you off this dam to your death and never look back. You should have let me love you, Mary. All of this could have been avoided."

"I did love you, Gavin, but like you said, the Gavin I loved does not exist anymore."

He growled and flipped me from on top of him until I barely clung to the edge on my side. I couldn't get away before he turned. With one shove of his big hands, the rest of my body slipped until I hung over the edge.

I grasped for the post from the rail, a crack in the concrete… anything that would hold me against the slippery wall. My best hope was to swing one of my legs up to catch myself before he completed the task of watching me fall.

He stood over me as I struggled, and then knelt to peel my fingers, one by one, from my tenuous hold.

But while he did that… I swung my leg up and grabbed his shirt with my other hand. He braced to not fall. That allowed me time to rest one leg on the top, and wedge the other in the vee of the structure. Had I been one inch the other way, I would have missed that opportunity in the black of night.

In the split second it took for Gavin to lose his balance and fall forward, I rested in my abilities. I focused. I concentrated. I used the part of my being that defied space and gravity to lift myself upward, even as Gavin came down. The balance of our opposing forces, the strength between us...

I grabbed him as he fell.

CHAPTER 46

Deacon

Shanar swirled in front of us like a whirlwind.

We clung to the ground with all our might as he unleashed a massive surge of his anger, hatred, and frustration into a tornadic force against us.

Ivy dropped to the ground and shielded her face against flying debris. "What do we do?"

"I don't know," I answered.

Defeat Shanar.

Right, lady, I snapped back in my mind. *How?*

Use the power I have given you.

I was going to try, but I could summon green masses all day, and that didn't mean Shanar was going to roll over and disappear forever. I wanted him gone for good. Not just for that day.

"Let's try again," I shouted at Scout and Ivy. "Stick with me. We'll push forward with more of whatever I have that's working."

The energy flowed from my body. Most of it was the dark, rich green I'd seen before, but some came out as green stripes with golden borders. Other hues floated into the mix as we moved forward.

"This is what happened that first day at the wall, remember? There were other colors!" Ivy said. "It's working!"

The wind slowed as we moved against it.

As I grew weary and wondered if I could take a breath, another image crept to my mind from the right.

"Snakes!" I yelled. "Snakes are coming over the dam."

I saw them. Lots of them. Brown ones, black ones, striped ones I could only see because of my light. My concentration broke as the forward motion stalled and Shanar's retreat stopped.

"What snakes?" Scout asked.

"*Those* snakes!" I yelled back. "They're coming over the dam. The water is carrying them up as it rises."

"No!" Scout said. "I don't see them. They're not real, Deacon. He's messing with you so you can't work. Don't you see? He's using your fear to stop you. You're not afraid of snakes anymore. You petted one today, and you know very few of them can actually hurt you. You recognize that now so he can't use them to harm you. They don't exist."

The snakes vanished as quickly as they'd appeared.

"Wait," Ivy said. "They're gone. So why are we fighting?"

"What do you mean why are we fighting?"

"I mean, why are we fighting? This enemy can never beat us. The Creator is always more powerful than the Destroyer. This is not a fight. It's mental gymnastics."

Scout peered at the large dark mass before us. "She's right again. It has no real power. Even Mary told us that. It can only harm us if we let it—if we acknowledge our fear of it."

"Or if maybe there's a human component to help it," I said.

"Because we're only human and we're susceptible to being hurt by other humans."

"Which is why Mary is in actual danger with Gavin," Ivy said.

"Yes," I admitted. "But I've been assured Mary can take care of herself with Gavin, and this is our part of the job."

Scout pointed my way. "Alrighty then. Fire up some color and let's banish this thing back to hell or wherever it came from, never to be seen by us again."

I turned and spotted something. "Wait. There's another person right there with Shanar."

"*What?* Where? I can barely see."

"Right there," I said. "He just appeared."

Scout reached for Ivy's hand.

Terror filled her gaze. "It's Reed Logan."

CHAPTER 47

❦

I vy

My dad was back, but he couldn't have shown up at a worse time or place.

"Reed? What are you doing here?"

He didn't answer. He twitched a bit and didn't seem to see me. The distance between us, the darkness, and Shanar's interference made it hard to make eye contact.

He was there, but he wasn't there.

Awww... Aren't family reunions the best? Shanar's voice echoed in all our heads.

I tore away from Scout's grasp and ran toward him. "Reed! Talk to me."

"Ivy, come back." Scout was one step behind. "It's not safe."

I turned on him. "Isn't it? I thought we decided this bully is just that. A bully with no real power."

"Fine. But this could still be a trap. Whatever or whoever this is can't seem to see or speak to you."

I assure you he's listening to every word I say. And this is what I say, Reed Logan. Kill them.

I stumbled back. "My dad is not going to kill me."

Isn't he?

Reed's stupid blank face enraged me. I yanked him by the arm and dragged him away from the massive brute Shanar was pretending to be.

"You've got a lot of nerve, soldier. You leave me not once, but twice. My mother loves you, you know. And I know you love her, and you're too much of a coward to just say the words. You just ran away." I dropped our flashlight on the ground nearby. "And when you ran away, you said you were running toward the fight. Is this the fight? Is it against me?"

Anger consumed me further when he didn't respond. I shoved at him and intended to knock him down. He didn't fall. I settled for pounding on the solid wall of his chest. "And you have been a sucky father and a terrible person. You show up here playing for the other side. Why did you come at all? Where's your backbone, Marine? Are you going to let this bully of a demon run your life forever? You still have a choice!"

He grabbed at my wrists and startled me. The vacant look in his eyes started to disappear.

"Stop it, Ivy. I left to protect you and your mother."

"And yet, here you are. And you think you're going to kill me? Kill *us*?" I yanked my hands away and balled his shirt in my fists. "You can't lie to me, remember? What does this bully have on you?"

"We have a long and complicated history."

"Who doesn't? Look at me and my mom. We have a long and complicated history because of you."

Ivy, stop.

The sound of his voice in my head stopped me in my tracks. I didn't know what was going on between him and Shanar, but I'd always suspected our personal shared abilities allowed private conversations between us the Destroyer could not read or hear—if I permitted Reed to get far enough into my head. I guess I was just desperate enough to hear him.

I relaxed my grip. *What's happening here?*

You have to trust me.

I laughed out loud in my own head. I was surprised at how goofy it sounded. *Ha! There is nothing about you I trust. Where do I start? You're an Agent for the Destroyer, you're responsible for helping Gavin try to toast a gym full of people...*

There's no time for this, Ivy. My first allegiance was not to the Destroyer. I was called by the Creator, just like you, but I didn't understand it and got sidetracked along the way. It's a long story for another day.

Then why are you here at Shanar's command to end us?

Give me some credit because you're right about one thing. I do love your mother and should have never left. But I also love you, and if you think for one minute we can't finish this miserable being off, you're not the strong young Warrior I thought you were.

I glared at him as I reached down. "Here. Hold my flashlight."

CHAPTER 48

Deacon

Reed's demeanor morphed before our eyes.

He went from some zombie-like robot who stood in Shanar's great dark mass, to more of the casual and easy-going guy we got to know as Ivy's long-lost dad.

I still didn't trust the guy as far as I could have thrown him, but his strengthening vibe did seem to send off more of a powerful and united stance with us, rather than that of some mechanical Agent who was going to try and kill us.

More power blossomed between us as Reed glanced my way. "Are you ready for this?"

From the top of my soaked and matted hair, to the way my wet cargo shorts rubbed my legs raw, I was completely ready to be free of Shanar.

And I knew we could beat him. I just didn't know how. "How do we do it?"

"What's one of the first rules of battle?" Reed asked.

"Divide and conquer," Scout chimed in.

"All right. We'll go with that. As a big threatening blob, he seems scary and smarter than us. He's not. He's just a supernatural apparition of nothing. Get it? As long as we believed he could harm or threaten us, he could. As long as he thought he could make us do things, he could."

"But he can't make us do anything," Ivy said. "We've made our choice to work for the Creator, and he has absolutely no power."

"Exactly. All this time has been about you learning that. It's been your training."

"So why are we still entertaining this being?" I asked. "And why do people like you and Gavin go all in?"

"Because we're human and make mistakes. Because we're promised things. Because we get desperate and confused..."

"Which is just the way the Destroyer wants us all," Scout said.

"Let's get on with it," I said. "Mary is somewhere around here with Gavin."

Reed stood with us, side by side, and faced our enemy.

"Deacon," he said. "You have all the power you need. I'll help you. We're going to make a pile of little rocks out of this big boulder of an enemy."

"How do we do that?"

"Like Scout said. Divide and conquer. Blast him apart with your strength. Then we gather the smaller parts. We contain him and press him into tiny stones to be tossed in all directions, never to find each other and connect again."

"Umm... Sounds good. I guess."

I was tired. I was wet. I was unsure. But I leaned into my strength. I called on my Enforcer—whoever she was—to help me. *Will this work?* I tried to ask her.

Defeat Shanar.

Duh.

Shanar began to stir. *Did you not hear my command, Reed Logan?*

"I heard you," Reed shouted back. "And I choose not to listen. I denounce you, I reject you, and I do not serve you or your master."

That is unfortunate—for you.

"No, it's unfortunate for you. You have tormented and underestimated these Warriors long enough."

Who are you trying to be now, Reed Logan? Father of the Year? There are consequences for the things you have done. Without my protection, you will be exposed. You'll have to answer for your crimes among the humans.

"So be it."

Reed looked my way again and shrugged. "C'mon, kid. Get on with it."

The green color burst from my flaming-hot hands as if it'd just been waiting for me to light the fuse. Reed, Ivy, and Scout stood behind me with their abilities and encouragement as the beams sliced through Shanar's form with laser-like precision and cut him to ribbons.

He countered with his own demonic energy, but it all but fell flat in the face of our faith in the Creator to hold him at bay. His power dwindled before our eyes as he grew smaller and smaller.

Reed rushed forward. "Keep it up, Deacon. Ivy, Scout, come with me."

Ivy and Scout paused—and rightfully so.

Reed turned back. "C'mon!"

"Why?" Ivy asked. "We've been trying to stay away from that thing."

"Trust me. This is the best part."

Scout scrunched his face into a doubtful expression. "Trust you? Best part? You've both been known to try and kill us."

"You're wasting time."

Ivy tugged on his sleeve. "Let's go, Scout."

"Go," I said. "We have to wrap this up and find Mary."

Scout took reluctant steps. "What do we do?"

"Just what I explained," Reed said. "The dark matter can't live when surrounded by someone who works for the Creator. We have to contain all that made up Shanar and crush it into stone."

"Kinda like pressure changes and hardens things over time."

"Yes, but we don't have time. We're going to transform what we can gather immediately under the power from the Creator."

"So Shanar can never regenerate into what he was."

"Exactly."

Scout paused again. "And how do we gather this field of nearly invisible negative energy?"

"Easier than you think," Reed said. "It will be drawn to you because it still wants to fight and defeat you, and all you have to do is crush it in your hands."

Ivy headed into the fray with wild abandon, an angry Warrior determined to finish the job. Tendrils of what was left of Shanar sparked in her realm as if trying to reignite and attack. It would never work since she'd gained the upper hand and understood the mentality to conquer it. She was the first to cup the matter in her fist and produce a small stone—just as Reed had predicted.

"I did it," she said as if it surprised her. "It's a rock."

"And it will be a rock from now on," Reed said. "You've taken control over the Destroyer's work with the power of the Creator. That's how it's done."

"Wait. What do I do with it?"

"Toss it to the bottom of the reservoir. It can't hurt anyone. It's defeated and contained."

Ivy turned it in her hands. "Makes you think about what other things have been defeated and contained and tossed across the earth. I don't think I'll ever pick up another rock. And I like to look at interesting rocks."

My colors dwindled as more and more of Shanar came apart

and lost all the energy, power, and influence he ever held over us.

Well done.

My new Enforcer was again in my ear.

"I still don't understand why you're here," I said to her. "Why do I now have my own Enforcer?"

You have great abilities, Warrior. You are learning to work alone, and I will be there to support you.

"But what about Sebastian?"

He will always be with Mary. They are part of one another.

"What is your name? You didn't tell me. How do I reach you?"

You can call me Emerald.

"I don't think so."

You wish to argue with me about my name?

"It's a little on the nose, don't you think? All the green colors and stuff? There's not a whole lot of imagination in that one. I know from Sebastian you can pick your own name according to where you are in the universe to help. I think we can do better."

Are you always going to be this disagreeable?

"I'm only asking about your name. I think we can tweak that."

As for now, Warrior, you should know that when I say 'well done' it usually means we are finished for the time. Again, well done.

I'd never been dismissed by a guardian angel before. I didn't know what to think of it.

Reed, Deacon, and Ivy continued to dispose of Shanar.

I had to find Mary.

CHAPTER 49

Mary

"Please, Gavin. Enough. Let me help you up and we'll talk."

I hooked my foot around the closest rail post. It dug in my skin as Gavin's weight stretched my arm until muscles and tendons threatened to snap.

"Hold on, Gavin… I can pull you up. Help me."

He anchored one hand on the edge. "If you help me up, it will only go badly for you."

"You can't kill me, Gavin. You can't. But what you can do is make a decision to leave the Destroyer. Admit what happened on the mountain. Find some peace and hope for yourself."

"There is no peace or hope for me."

"There's always a chance for peace and hope."

For the first time in a long time, his true gaze met mine. The funny and honest playful one. The one that held affection for me and took me to the homecoming dance. *That's* the boy I once loved. *That's* the boy I wanted to save.

My heart softened. "Help me," I begged. "I can't hold on to you much longer."

"Then let go."

"No. You are worth saving. You can be better."

His gaze turned dark again. "No. I can't. And you should know I enjoyed our time on the mountain. Sending Jacob to his snowy death was the most fun I've ever had as an Agent, and I'd do it again if I could."

He'd hit his intended target. Everything in me wilted, and my strength and determination melted away. All my muscles went limp.

All except the ones keeping him from tons of crushing water.

I understood it all, then. Everything Sebastian meant, and everything I'd done wrong because I was an angry and hurting human.

"I won't make it easy for you, Gavin. I won't let go. No matter what you've done, I'll still help you save yourself. And I'll do it because I have to forgive you, so that I don't *become* you."

Jagged pain ripped through my wrist as he struggled. I didn't hear the snap over the rush of water, but I felt it the second it broke.

Gavin was gone.

CHAPTER 50

Mary

I rolled on my back, screamed into the night, and pulled my mangled wrist across my chest. I'd experienced a lot of pain over the last couple years, but few injuries compared to the agony of knowing my own hand had nearly been twisted off my arm.

I tried to stand. The others needed me...didn't they?

As all the supernatural activity in my body settled, I was left in total blackness. I inched my way along the narrow path, listening for water, and being careful to not drift too far to one side or the other.

Shock hovered on the edge of my consciousness. That familiar numbness was about to overtake me at any moment. I was injured, and Gavin had surely died. Someone had to call the police.

Someone had to tell his parents.

I choked back the bile rising in my throat. If he hadn't died, I likely would have. How was I going to explain it all? Who would believe me?

I wanted to save him. I tried to save him.

The warmth of Sebastian's presence, closed in on me. The musky scent of frankincense hovered at my nose and calmed my stomach. I rested in his peaceful arms.

You did it, Warrior.

"I accomplished nothing. Gavin is dead."

You offered him help and tried to lead him to redemption. It is not your fault he didn't follow.

"That's easy for you to say. You don't have to walk in my shoes and explain all that happened here tonight without disclosing the supernatural activity involved in all of it."

But I will be with you, and there are others the Creator will put in place to guide you through this difficult time.

"Two young men have died on my watch. Why would the Creator waste any more time on me? I am obviously a failure at this work."

There's a lot of world left to save, Mary. A lot of people only you can help.

"Then I am sad for the world because my help seems to come at too great a cost."

It won't always be like this. I will always be with you, if you will permit me to help and can let go of your anger toward me. Can you do that? Can we find a place of understanding between us about what has happened as we've worked together in our realm?

"I am only a human. I will continue to try."

You are beyond human now, Mary. You are a hybrid angel and a powerful Warrior. Much is expected of you.

I kept moving. "I need to find the others."

Yes. They have had great victory while you've been at war.

"Mary!"

Ivy's voiced bounced through the night with what was left of our light.

"Here," I called out.

Deacon reached me first and steadied me. "Injury report?"

"You're gonna have to rig me up some kind of sling, Scout. The wrist and arm are bad. Pretty sure it will require pins, screws, and whatever else they can put in there."

"Got it." He ripped his t-shirt into a midriff on the spot and attempted to secure my arm to my body so it wouldn't move.

"Where's Gavin?" Ivy asked.

"Gone."

"Gone as in he left? Or…?"

"Gone as in it came down to me or him." I winced with pain as Scout worked, and struggled with the next words. "And I wanted to live. I tried to save him, but that's how my wrist got destroyed."

Reed Logan stepped into the light. "It was self-defense, Mary. He always intended to do you harm."

"What are you doing here, Reed? I thought you abandoned Ivy again."

"I came back to help."

"I don't believe you. More like you came back on Shanar's orders to make sure Gavin got the job done."

"No, that is not what brought me back."

"Why should I believe you? You work for Shanar, and you've done nothing but hurt and confuse my friend and lie to us. There are no coincidences in Warrior work. You knew we were here."

"Yes, I did, but it's not what you think."

"Then what is it?"

"I did know you all were here because of Shanar, but I didn't come to carry out his orders. I had to play along to find you, but I really came to help you all."

"He did," Deacon said. "We wouldn't have known what to do if he hadn't told us."

"Shanar's gone for good," Scout added. "We did it. He's gone."

Ivy nodded. "My dad made the right choice that Gavin could not."

"Well, forgive me if at this point I believe none of what I hear from most people and only half of what I see. Too many people have died or been injured."

Ivy tried to touch me, but seemed unsure of a place that wouldn't hurt. She dropped her arms to her side. "I'm sorry, Mary, but we'll be with you through everything."

"Yes, once again we have to go for medical attention and an interrogation that will likely be all over the news. Gavin is dead..." I tried to stop a body-rocking shudder. "His parents... How do I prove I tried to save him?"

Ivy still tried to comfort me. "I don't know, but Shanar is gone, and I can't help but think that means things will become clearer for us."

"I should have listened to you, Ivy. A long time ago. You looked right at me and told me *Gavin Bagliano can't be trusted*. Do you remember that? I should have listened."

"You couldn't have known. I didn't even know. I was going on intuition, and I didn't know my intuition was such a big deal back then. We all had to learn."

"We need to go," Reed said. "We need to report this and get help. I don't think there's much hope for Gavin if he went over the spillway, but we need to be sure. They need to look for him."

We attempted to move forward with little to no guidance.

Ivy slowed. "But Reed... The police are going to wonder what you have to do with all this. You'll have to admit I'm your daughter and tell them what you know. That means—"

"I know what it means. I intend to tell them everything about the Stonehaven Gym Fire and Gavin. I plan to go to jail, but it's OK. Maybe something I say can help prove what Gavin did to Jacob."

"It doesn't matter now," I said. "A dead guy can't go to jail and pay for his crimes."

"But it might bring his family closure. They may want to file a civil suit or something. All I know is I have to take responsibility for my actions."

"But how does that help the rest of us who are trying to work under the radar? And how does that help Ivy? Your sacrifice looks like another narcissist move to abandon her. You'll even go to jail to make it about you and fail her at the same time. I don't get it."

"He's going to take all the heat to draw it away from us," Scout said.

"But it's us that will have to retell all the stories and revisit every painful event that didn't come with a happy ending."

"It's going to be fine," Deacon said. "I understand it. We're at a turning point in our journey. Reed's confessions will close down the speculation and set us free to move on."

"Where are we going?" I asked. "And where does that leave Ivy?"

"It's fine," Ivy said. "I get it too. It's not exactly the way I hoped it would work out for me and my mom, but I don't know what else I thought would happen, and maybe something will still happen someday. He's right. He has to deal with the natural consequences of his actions."

"And," Reed said. "You all have to move on to the next phase of your lives and your work. Shanar is gone. Your training together here has come to an end."

I still couldn't wrap my head around his part in the whole thing. "How do you know what the Creator has in store for us and about our new lives? You've been working against us the whole time."

"Mary, everybody in the realm knows about you and your Warriors. You're the one who got away from the Destroyer. How many times now? I've lost count. You four are real and powerful and significant. Your group and my daughter and her mother are the only reasons I was able to get it straight in my head and try to get back to my original calling. You can hate me all you want, but it doesn't change anything. I'll pay for what I've done wrong, and you four need to take what you've learned during your crash course in becoming Warriors and get on with it. The universe is waiting." He stomped off. "Be careful," he called back over his shoulder. "I'm going to try and find some signal or flag somebody down."

We walked shoulder to shoulder in the rapidly dimming light of our last flashlight.

"I'm sorry about Gavin," Ivy said. "I know how long you've known each other and how heavy your heart must be over his parents."

"It hasn't even sunk all the way in." I adjusted my arm and tried not to cry out in pain. "How did you all defeat Shanar?"

"Great story," Scout said.

"Yeah. One we will save for a couple of days until we get back to Scout's rec room with food and Dr Pepper," Deacon added. "You won't believe it."

"I find it hard to believe any of what we've been through, but here we are."

Ivy gingerly touched my arm. "What's next, do you think?"

"You mean after Reed Logan blows up the Stonehaven Gym Fire case?" Deacon asked. "That reminds me. As soon as I can get to a phone, I need to call Mr. Parrington. He'll stick with us through this."

"Good idea," Scout said.

"As much as I hate to admit it," I said. "Reed is probably right. This night has been as bad as it could be, but I already feel more at peace about the future. I know the Destroyer is still out there, but we've survived two beings trying to take us all out. Now we just have to complete our assignments."

Sirens wailed in the distance.

"Reed must have gotten through," Ivy said. "Anything else

before we're swarmed again with police and first responders, Mary?"

"You know my advice. Always tell the truth, and remember who you are. We're Warriors. That's what we are."

"I have a question," Deacon said.

"Yes?"

"On a scale of one to ten, about how mad do you think Scout's grandpa is going to be about those rowboats we lost?"

EPILOGUE

Mary
Many months later...

I lifted my duffle onto the bed and dropped the last of my limited makeup and a fresh new journal from Ivy into the side pocket.

My mom stood at my bedroom door like a surrendered kitten at the shelter. Her *why are you leaving me?* expression wasn't completely accurate—I knew that. She would miss me and was appropriately concerned, but she also couldn't be prouder I was headed to college.

My equally distressed-slash-happy father re-wrapped the cord around my desk lamp and slipped it into a box. He sighed as he heaved it into the small truck he gave me. It had been his. My mom said it was an excuse for him to get the new pickup he wanted. It didn't matter to me, but I knew by the way he checked the air pressure in its new tires that all they wanted was for me to be safe.

"I don't like this," my dad said. "We should be taking you in a month like every other parent. Rite of passage and all that. We drop you off, your mom cries and helps you make your bed..."

My mother stepped forward. "Then we spend another wad of cash at the local Wal-Mart on things we forgot... You know. The usual stuff. Like you got all the way to your dorm without your favorite shampoo and wonder how you did that, and then we're at a stupid chain restaurant six hours from our house and can't believe we drove all that way to eat the same food and buy the same shampoo we had at home..."

"OK, Mom. Stop." I hugged her. "I get it, but we talked all this through a hundred times. Deacon and I need to do this."

She pulled away and crossed her arms and dropped her gaze to the ground. "I know. We understand, and I know I sound ridiculous, but I've never done this before and it's hard."

My dad tucked her under his strong arm. "Do you have your debit card, your gas cards, the emergency credit card, your insurance cards—"

"Dad, you went through my wallet yourself last night. You took pictures of everything—for the second time." I held up my phone. "And every account and phone number is in here. We share all the apps I could ever need for any situation."

"Yeah, well, don't look at that phone while you're driving my truck." He paused and looked like he'd lost his voice for a second. "In our defense, you've been in some incredibly hard, dangerous, and unexplainable situations in recent memory."

"Which is exactly why I can't stay here a minute longer. I can't work here. I don't want to go to my own church here. I can't. You know how hard it was for me to even finish high school. One day I'm a blessing and one day I'm a curse. It depends on who I see or who's talking."

"Things have settled down," my mom said. "The truth came out and people have short memories. They're on to something else."

I know she really believed that, and some of it might have

been true. But I had to try and sleep every night in the same room where I'd fought Shanar, healed from physical injuries, and mourned Jacob and Gavin.

Shadows lurked around every corner of my childhood master-planned suburban community, and Gavin's parents were a constant reminder of an avalanche of pain.

I had to move, change, adapt…maybe even run a while before I could settle again. I hated that it hurt my parents and that they didn't understand, not really, but leaving my home was like busting out of a sealed coffin. I hadn't taken in a real fresh breath for years, and the months since the dam incident were spent frozen in time.

I had to find the ground under my feet again.

I had to breathe.

I had to remember how to be a Warrior.

"I have to go." I glanced at my phone and read Deacon's excited text. "Deacon found the supplies he wanted to secure his bike in the bed of the truck. His parents are waiting to see us off."

My dad squeezed me hard. "Don't forget to check your route every day for construction delays."

"And don't stop at rest areas at night," my mother warned.

"We're going to be fine," I said. "We're going to take our time, and we can't wait to visit Char. We haven't seen her since Colorado. We need to spend some time with her. She has some things planned for us with her friends."

My mom nodded furiously. "I know you need closure there. It'll be good for you and Deacon. Just check in. I won't say check in every day, 'cause then if you don't, I'll worry, and I know you have things to do—"

"Mom. Stop. You'll always be able to see what I'm up to. Just stalk me on social media like every other mother does."

She laughed through a shimmer of tears. "Get out of here. I know we're making you nuts."

I hugged her again. "I'll be fine."

"I know."

"And just because Deacon's campus is less than a hundred miles away from yours, don't go running back and forth," my dad said. "I don't want you driving that much when you're tired or have to study. That's what his bike is for."

"His bike is for getting around his campus because he doesn't have a car."

"Whatever. You know what I mean."

"I do, Daddy."

As much as I hated slamming that door on my parents and putting the truck in drive, it was a freedom I'll never forget.

Deacon's house was much the same story, only with a lot more people. His brothers came by to both tease and encourage him, and none of them were happy he had a brand-new bike and they were left fighting over Combo and the car they had to share.

"No worries," he told them. "When we settle with the carnival people, I'm buying bikes for everyone. And *I'll* be getting myself a car."

"Don't you mean you'll be paying your tuition?" his dad asked.

"Yeah. That too."

In the quiet of the cab, we drove a short distance and I had to pull over.

Deacon looked around. "What's wrong?"

"This isn't our home anymore, Deacon. I know we'll have to make a command performance at Thanksgiving and Christmas and that's OK, but do people like us ever stop moving? Do we ever settle down? Is it ever safe to spend too much time around the people we love?"

"I don't know, Mary, but I can't stay here either. It's like I have to change my view of the world from the crowded place we came from. Nothing here is the same. We don't belong here."

He adjusted the air vent. "What do you think about Scout and Ivy?"

"I think I'm glad we said our goodbyes last night. I almost couldn't bear it. When do you think they'll leave?"

"Who knows? Between Ivy's mom and dad and all the legal stuff, she doesn't want to go. Scout shouldn't stay, but he will until she's ready."

"They'll get it together," I assured myself. "They always do, and Ivy knows she can't let Scout waste his brain and scholarship money."

"We're doing the right thing, Mary. We have to take this long drive and chill and check in with Char and spend some quiet time, I don't know…talking with our Enforcers? Let's climb a mountain in Arkansas and meditate or something. We have to find peace and direction. Are we even capable of getting through college?"

"We are. We're human. But you're right. We need this time."

He nodded ahead. I hadn't even realized I'd pulled into the strip center near the Smoothie Shack.

"Pull up," he said and wrestled money from his pocket. "One more for the road?"

I shrugged. "One more for the road."

ABOUT THE AUTHOR

Carla Thorne has been writing YA fiction since 2013. She is a multi-published, award-winning author as well as an editor, cancer survivor, life-long musician, speaker, and writing teacher.

For sweet contemporary romance and inspirational romance, visit carlarossi.com

Thank you for your interest in Carla Thorne books. Don't miss future releases in the Warrior Saints series. Sign up for Carla Thorne's newsletter for the latest news, giveaways, and special offers.

Connect with Carla at
www.carlathorne.com

Made in United States
Troutdale, OR
06/10/2025